G. LEE TIPPIN

PROPHET OF TERROR

BART
NEW YORK

Reprinted by arrangement with Daring Books

ISBN: 1-55785-011-9

First Bart Books edition: 1988

Bart Books
155 E. 34th Street
New York, New York 10016

Manufactured in the United States of America

FOREWORD

I. THE MAD DOG OF THE MIDDLE EAST.

He believes he has been chosen by Allah to destroy Zionism. He believes he is the first Islam Prophet since Mohammed. He believes that it is his destiny to lead the Pan-Arabic Armies to Islamic world domination. He patterns himself after the mystic warriors of the eleventh and twelfth centuries, the Middle Eastern fanatics who organized the Society of Assassins to eliminate all opposition to their religious cult. He screams, rants, raves, threatens and taunts like a deranged child, strutting through his desert kingdom like a peacock or an animal on the prowl. He rides a white horse and dresses in a myriad of gaudy, bemedaled uniforms and costumes. He described the murder of the Israeli athletes at the Munich Olympics as a "glorious act," called the dead Arab terrorists "martyr heroes," and buried them in Libya with full military honors.

The late President of Egypt, Anwar Sadat, said: "He is a vicious animal, 100 percent sick and possessed of the demon." Sadat was assassinated a few months later and many intelligence experts believe that HE was behind it.

President Ronald Reagan, on April 10, 1986, described him as "This Mad Dog of the Middle East."

If it is true that a mad dog is dangerous, unpredictable, foams at the mouth, bites and kills--then Muammar Khadafy fits the description.

Who is this man who took control of his country in a swift, bloodless coup at the age of 27, who has caused so much fear and outrage in the international political scene and who has made terrorism his creed, practicing it with deadly consistency? A man who has spent billions of dollars supporting terrorists throughout the world. A man whose messianic vision and ruthless fanaticism threaten world stability.

After taking over Libya in 1969, Khadafy--or Brother Colonel, as he likes to be called--set into motion his Popular Revolution, wrote and published his famous "Green Book," declared to the world that he was going to destroy Israel and that the United States was his ultimate enemy, and went shopping for "Nuclear Bombs for Allah." It would be terrifying to visualize a world with Khadafy's errant and unpredictable finger on the trigger of nuclear weapons. There is one thing certain about Khadafy: He believes that anything is justifiable in the pursuit of Pan-Islamic world dominance.

II. KHADAFY AND INTERNATIONAL TERRORISM.

When a group of terrorists from one country joins a group from another and commits crimes in either country or a third country, this is labeled International Terrorism.

The terrible spectre of international terrorism has been increasingly visible since the early 1970s. According to Amnesty International, an organization which investigates and reports human rights violations worldwide, since 1970 more than 500,000 people have died due to terrorist activities.

The collaboration between Marxist and Muslim radicals is not accidental. Modern terrorism has its roots in two movements: Communist totalitarianism and Islamic radicalism. These forces have given terrorism its ideological impetus and much of its material support. Both legitimize unbridled violence in the name of a higher cause, both are hostile to democracy, and both have found terrorism an ideal weapon for waging war against democracy.

International terrorism is an extension of warfare sustained and supported by the states built on the foundations of Marxism and radical Islam. Russia, Cuba, North Korea and Middle Eastern states such as Libya, Iran, Syria and South

Yemen have given terrorists weapons, training and money. They have also provided sanctuary, safe passage and even their embassies to the terrorists. What amounts to a form of low-intensity warfare is being waged by various nation-states to erode the influence and strategic position of the United States and Western democracies in general, and to enhance the power of the Soviet Union, its clients and allies, in particular. Since the early 1980s there has been a "Radical Entente" of nation-states--including Libya, Syria, Iran, Cuba and North Korea--which is coordinating a worldwide strategy designed to expel US Military, Political and Economic presence from key areas of the world. The hostile strategy of this Radical Entente is directed primarily against the US because of its leadership position in the Western world, the ideals and culture of which the Radical Entente considers to be inimical to Muslim and Communist values. The radical Arab states of the Entente also direct hostility toward the United States because of its long-standing support for Israel.

The first major international terrorist act was committed in May 1972, at Lod Airport in Israel, when a group of Japanese Red Terrorists fired into a crowd, killing 26 people and wounding 76. The raid was planned and coordinated by the Popular Front for the Liberation of Palestine.

In April 1973, the first International Terrorist Conference was held in Lebanon, and 15 terrorist groups from Central America, Europe, and the Middle East sent representatives. They agreed to work together whenever possible. From this meeting, a world network of professional terrorists emerged who seek to weaken and demoralize democratic societies by attacking their citizens, their leaders, and their institutions, thereby disrupting their way of life and weakening their political resolve.

Khadafy's support for international terrorism began shortly after he took power. He sent $300,000 to the Black Panthers in the U.S. He later cut off funds to them when he realized their loyalty to Islam was questionable. He spoke out in favor of and sent money to the Irish Republican Army. He began to send arms and money to support the Muslim rebels in Ethiopia and the Phillipines. Little by little he started supporting nationalist, Muslim and anti-imperialist movements all over the world. He set up training camps in Libya for discontented and militant Palestinians. This included members of the militant Black September Group who had broken away from Arafat and the PLO. Before long, hundreds of Middle-Eastern fanatics and zealots were flocking to the bloody banner being waved by Brother Colonel.

The new Libyan-based organization was called National Arab Youth for the Liberation of Palestine or NAYLP. The Black September Group, as part of the NAYLP, with funds supplied by Libya for a staging area, conducted the terrorist attack on the Israeli athletes in Munich.

Khadafy, who never met a terrorist he did not like, continued to set up additional training camps within Libya; and soon terrorists from all over the world were learning their bloody trade: IRA gunmen, Italian Red-Brigade Terrorists, West German Anarchists, Japanese radicals, and Central American revolutionaries. In the last three years, Libya has emerged as a major supporter of international terrorism; and Libya's strong-man, Colonel Muammar Khadafy, has become the *de facto* leader of International Terrorism. Brother Colonel, the Mad Dog of the Middle East, the Prophet of Terror is the Chairman of the Board.

III. MAJOR TERRORIST ACTIONS:
APRIL 1983 TO AUGUST 1985.

1983:

April 18. The U.S. Embassy in West Beirut was devastated by a car bomb. Sixty-three people were killed, including 17 Americans, and 150 were injured.

October 23. U.S. Marine Headquarters near Beirut International Airport and a French military barracks were attacked by suicide truck bombers. Two hundred forty-seven U.S. servicemen and 58 French paratroopers were killed and hundreds were wounded.

November 4. Israeli Headquarters in Tyre was destroyed by a car bomb. Twenty-nine Israelis and 32 Arab detainees were killed.

December 12. The U.S. and French Embassies in Kuwait were bombed, killing six people. Shiite terrorists linked to Lebanon and Libya are blamed.

1984:

January 1. The French Cultural Center in the Lebanese port city of Tripoli was destroyed by a bomb.

January 16. A bomb ripped through a first-class carriage on a Marseilles-to-Paris passenger train killing three and injuring 12. Sixteen minutes later and 120 miles south in the Marseilles-St. Charles railway station, another explosion rocked the luggage office leaving two dead and 34 wounded. The Armed Arab Struggle, whose headquarters is in Libya, claimed responsibility.

January 18. Malcolm Kerr, the President of the American University of Beirut, aged 52, was assassinated outside his office.

January 20. Saudi Arabian General Consul, Hussein Farrarh, was abducted in Beirut by seven gunmen. The Holy Islamic Jihad, which is linked to Libya and Iran, claimed responsibility. They left a note saying: "The diplomat would be tried according to Islamic Law, executed, and his body thrown out."

February 25. Leamon R. Hunt, Director General of the Multi-National Force and Observers in the Sinai, was shot and killed in Rome by three assassins. The Leftist Italian

Red Brigade claimed responsibility.

March 19. An Arab grenade exploded on a crowded bus, in the Israeli port of Ashdod, killing three and wounding ten others.

April 3. A 200 pound IRA terrorist bomb exploded outside a hotel in Belfast, injuring 36 people. It was the third attack this week against Protestant businesses in the troubled city.

May 7. British Policewoman Constance Fletcher was killed by a Libyan gunman firing from the Libyan Embassy at a crowd of anti-Khadafy demonstrators. Eleven of the Libyan dissidents were also wounded by the burst of fire. The British government responded by breaking relations with Libya and ordering the embassy vacated. Khadafy hinted that any action by the British government could have a detrimental effect on the more than 8,000 British in Libya.

May 21. Three Libyan dissidents were executed in Paris by a Libyan hit squad.

June 10. A bomb exploded outside a U.S. Air Force Officers' Club today wounding four persons. This was the second attack this month against American military personnel in Germany.

August 13. An Air France 747, flying to Paris from Frankfort with 61 passengers, was hijacked by Muslim terrorists. The plane was flown to a desert strip in North Africa, where it was blown up. One passenger was killed during the ordeal.

October 1. AGAIN THE NIGHTMARE! The U.S. Embassy Annex in Beirut was devastated by a truck bomb. Thirteen people were killed and 46 wounded. The Holy Islamic Jihad, which has ties to Iran and Libya, claimed credit.

October 22. IRA terrorists attempted to kill Prime Minister Margaret Thatcher by detonating a powerful bomb at Brightons Grand Hotel. Four people were killed and 34 injured. Mrs. Thatcher was unhurt.

December 10. A Libyan hit team unsuccessfully tried to assassinate former Libyan Prime Minister Abdel Hamid Bakkush in Cairo. The would-be assassins were captured and revealed details of a "Khadafy Hit List." On it were such leaders as Mitterand of France, West Germany's Helmut Kohl, Saudi Arabia's King Fahd, Britain's Margaret Thatcher and President Ronald Reagan.

December 17. HORROR ABOARD FLIGHT 221! A Kuwait airliner with 161 people aboard was hijacked by Arab terrorists. Before the ordeal was over, four passengers, including two Americans, were executed.

1985:

January 25. General Rene Audran, French Minister of Defense, was gunned down outside his home in Paris.

January 26. Ernst Zimmerman, 55, Chief Executive of MTU, a major defense contractor in West Germany was shot and killed by two members of the Red Army Faction.

March 11. IRA terrorists fired nine 50-pound shells into a police station in Northern Ireland, killing nine people and wounding 37.

March 12. A car bomb exploded near a crowded mosque in Beirut, killing 75 and injuring 250 others.

March 13. William Buckley, 56, a political officer assigned to the U.S. Embassy, was kidnapped as he left his apartment in Beirut. (A year later he was killed by torture in Teheran, Iran.)

May 15. A boat carrying 28 PLO guerrillas was intercepted by the Israeli Navy. Their alleged mission was to bomb the Israeli Defense Ministry in Tel Aviv.

May 22. The ruling Emir, Sheik Jabor al Ahmed al Sabah, of Kuwait narrowly missed death when a car bomb exploded in his motorcade. The Islamic Jihad claimed responsibility.

June 1. A car filled with explosives was intercepted and disarmed outside the U.S. Embassy in Cairo.

June 3. A car bomb exploded in the Christian sector of Beirut, killing 55 people and wounding 176 (including ten children who were trapped in a burning bus).

June 24. Muslim terrorists hijacked TWA Flight 847. U.S. Navy diver Robert Stetham was beaten and murdered in front of the other hostages.

July 1. An overstuffed gray travel bag left unnoticed beside a trash can in the International Airport in Frankfort exploded, killing three and injuring 42.

Ship me somewhere east of Suez,
  Where the best is like the worst.
Where there aren't no ten commandments,
  And a man can raise a thirst.
For the temple bells are callin',
  And it's there that I would be:
By the old moulmein pagoda,
  Lookin' lazy at the sea.

Rudyard Kipling

PROLOGUE

NORTH VIETNAM, OCTOBER 1966

The black, unmarked C-123 crossed the border between North and South Vietnam at 0100 hours, flying on a magnetic azimuth of 357 degrees. Precisely at 0118 hours, the aircraft changed its heading to 47 degrees. The humid air rising from the jungle below caused the airplane to buck and roll, and the pilot fought the controls to keep it steady and on course. A series of beeps came across his headset from a faraway radio station, and the pilot reached over to his flight panel and flicked on a switch.

Back in the darkened belly of the plane a red light near the port door blinked several times, signaling five minutes to drop time. The passengers, a five-man Special Forces Team, began making a last minute check of their equipment.

They were wearing camouflaged jungle fatigues sans insignia or badges of rank, and they were well-armed. Their faces were smudged with black camouflaged paint, making them look like coal miners coming off a shift. Each of the grim-faced warriors had a rubber-coated cyanide tablet taped beneath his left armpit. One bite through the rubber coating brought instantaneous death. Death was supposedly preferable to capture and torture. A debatable subject--the final decision was left up to each man, if and when the time came.

Death was not new to these professional soldiers. They were highly trained "merchants of death," and the spectre of death hovered over their shoulders as their constant companion.

An air-crew member opened the port hatch, and the warm

tropic air wafted into the plane, mixing with the smell of sweat, gun-oil and fear. The leader of the team, burdened by his heavy gear, shuffled awkwardly to the door and looked out. The night below was a solid wall of black. He reached up and hooked his static-line to the steel cable that ran the length of the aircraft. The other members of his team followed suit. They were now hooked to the cable that would open their parachutes after they jumped and reached the end of their 15 foot static lines. There was no need for the usual jump commands; these veterans knew exactly what to do.

Even his bulky equipment and blackened face could not hide the youth of the leader. He was young, for a Captain-- only twenty-four years--but war tends to age men fast. This young warrior already had spent nearly two years in constant combat. Young in age but old in experience, his daring accomplishments in Laos were already a legend among his fellow Green Berets. He was tall, lean, and whipcord strong. The young captain glanced over his shoulder at his men; they were ready. Their facial muscles were taut and their eyes were set deep with the anticipation and fear of parachuting behind enemy lines.

Just eight days ago, the Captain had kissed his new bride goodby, and he and his team moved into isolation to prepare for their mission. When they moved into the isolation phase at a secret Forward Operating Base, they cut themselves off from the outside world and concentrated on preparing for their operation. They pored over maps and photographs; they memorized intelligence reports; they rehearsed their plans over and over again; they checked and double-checked their weapons and equipment; they fine-tuned their physical and mental conditioning. They lived, breathed, and thought of only one thing--THE MISSION.

By now his wife would be safely in America, at Fort Bragg, waiting for him. The young leader felt a warm sensation as he remembered their last night together. It was a wonderful night! They made furious and exhausting love, trying to store up enough tender memories to last them until they were together again. It wouldn't be long, because this was his last mission for this tour. He was going to return to Bragg as an instructor in the Special Forces School.

He never intended to fall in love, let alone get married, yet it had happened. Nuyen was an extraordinary woman-- one of South Vietnam's top female intelligence agents. When the young Green Beret Captain and the beautiful Vietnamese girl met, the sky opened up and the sun shown through. It was Kismet; they were unable to control their feelings. The romance was short and beautiful. He finally persuaded her to marry him, quit the spy business, and go on ahead to America to wait. They were young, healthy, and in love. In a short while, they were going to live the great American Dream. All he had to do was complete this mission.

The red light blinked again. Two minutes to go! The leader turned to his men and gave the thumbs-up sign. Then he stepped into the door and assumed the jump position--left foot forward, arms spread, hands grasping the outside of the door, and knees slightly bent. His heart beat rapidly. Cold sweat trickled down his forehead making his eyes burn.

The drop zone was small, a jungle clearing no larger than a softball field, and there was no one on the ground to guide the aircraft in. They were using a new technique, the same one used by the Air Force for precision bombing. Two radio stations in South Vietnam were sending radio waves which vectored at the preselected jump point. The aircraft speed, direction, altitude, wind direction and velocity were all calculated. At the pre-designated time, the jumpers would exit the aircraft. If the calculations were perfect, if God was willing, and Murphy's law was absent, they would land on the selected Drop Zone. If not, they would land somewhere in the trees, as they usually did.

Their mission was one that they were well-trained for, one that this group of professionals specialized in. They were to "Infiltrate by air into Phoumi Province, North Vietnam,

17

and terminate with extreme prejudice General Vang Phu Kao." Intelligence reports indicated that the North Vietnamese general was vacationing on his farm near the city of Van. General Vang Kao was operational commander of all North Vietnamese forces in South Vietnam. After the hit, the team was to evade on foot to a point on the coast and be picked up by a U.S. submarine.

Suddenly the light turned green, and one-by-one the team jumped into the black hole of the night. The young leader counted to himself: "One thousand, two thousand, three thousand, four thousand!" He was jerked upward sharply as the parachute deployed. He looked up and breathed a sigh of relief--the damn thing had opened! It always amazed him. He lived with the gnawing fear that someday it would fail and he would be smashed into oblivion. By instinct, he reached down and undid the tiedowns to his rucksack, which fell away from him and dangled on the 12-foot bunji cord. He knew the ground must be coming up fast. He reached up and grabbed his risers, put his feet together, and bent his knees slightly--assuming what he considered a good parachute landing fall position. The black pit of the ground rushed up to meet him, and he hit the mud of the rice paddy with a slurping sound. He rolled to his right; with his left hand he slapped the Capewell Quick Release and the chute floated free; with his right hand he released the tiedowns on his weapon. He rolled on over and sprang to a low crouch, holding his Kalishnikov AK-47 Assault Rifle at the ready. The drop had been precision-perfect. Within minutes his team had gathered and rolled up their parachutes. Covered with mud, they headed toward the black wall to the east which was the jungle at the edge of the clearing.

Suddenly, without warning, the quiet night erupted into blinding day as burning searchlights slapped them in the face. Instinctively, the Americans dropped their parachutes, opened fire, and charged toward the lights in front of them. It was standard battle drill procedure. There was no time to think, plan, or issue orders. They all knew they had walked into an ambush, and their only chance was to attack straight ahead. The jungle night was shattered with the rising crescendo of small arms fire. Tracers began winging back and forth across the clearing, dancing up into the air like angry fireflies. The screams of wounded, dying, and fear-crazed men echoed through the night. Explosions began to rock the ground as the North Vietnamese tossed concussion grenades at the onrushing Americans in an attempt to take them alive.

The young Captain stumbled and fell into the mud. He rolled to his right and jumped up firing his weapon. Something hit him on the left leg, knocking him down. He tried to get up, but the searing pain forced him back down into the mud. There was a deafening explosion near his head--then total blackness.

Slowly, the young officer regained partial consciousness. He found himself lying face-down on the floorboard of a jostling truck. Evidently the shocks had long-ago ceased to be an effective part of the vehicle because each rut seemed to toss him six inches in the air; and each bounce brought a fiery pain to his leg. His head throbbed from the effects of the concussion grenade. His hands were bound tightly behind his back-- they were numb from lack of circulation.

He was startled by a familiar voice: "Are you all right Captain?"

With difficulty he turned his head to his right. Sergeant Braxton was lying beside him. "Yeah Dave, I think so. How about you?"

"Got knocked out by one of them damn concussion grenades," returned the black giant, "Otherwise I'm OK."

"What about the rest of the team?"

"They bought the farm sir--you and I are the only ones left!"

A terrible feeling of hopelessness swept over the young captain. He tried to understand what had happened--but couldn't.

"SHUT UP! NO TALK!" screamed a voice behind them, accompanied by a vicious kick to the captain's wounded leg.

Pain shot the whole length of his body--and he slipped back into the blackness of the mind.

When he came to again, he found himself in a bamboo cage about four-feet square and four-feet high. He was scrunched in the bottom in a cramped fetal position. His cage was located in the center of a small village hacked out of the triple-canopy jungle. Around the clearing were 8 or 10 thatched-roof huts. Braxton was nowhere in sight. Had they killed him? Was Braxton right when he said the other men were dead? He felt very alone.

The action had been too fast; he had not had time to reach for the cyanide pill under his arm. The truth was he probably would not have used it anyway. When he failed to take the deadly tablet, he broke rule number one. If you break rule number one, then you move on to rule number two:

1. Don't let yourself be taken alive.
2. If you do become a prisoner, do not divulge anything for 48 hours. This will give headquarters a chance to take measures to safeguard the information you possess.

The awful realization that he was a prisoner sent a numbing fear through him. He knew information about U.S. covert operations in Laos and North Vietnam that would be infinitely valuable to the communists. His only hope lay in their not being able to identify him. If they did, he could only imagine to what lengths they would go to make him talk. An almost uncontrollable panic swept over him.

His thoughts were interrupted by the turning of a key in the padlock that secured the chain around his cage. A North Vietnamese soldier peered in. The medic, or so the American assumed, examined his leg wound and wrapped a crude bandage around it. The prisoner was then left alone with his fearful thoughts. He lay there in his cramped position fearing and anticipating the worst. Finally, overcome with total exhaustion, he fell asleep.

He awakened the next morning to a cock crowing and his stomach growling with hunger; his lips were parched and he needed water. He lay there, listening to the sounds of the camp coming to life. Cooking fires were lit and he could smell the boiling rice. It was a small village with thatched-roof huts. In one corner was a single wooden building. He tried to move in his small cage but found it difficult because of his injured leg, which had not awakened with the rest of his body. A feeling of loneliness rolled over him. His future looked bleak. There would not be any cavalry riding to his rescue.

His thoughts were interrupted by two soldiers who walked up and peered into his small cage. One of them made a comment and they both giggled like two young children. One took a key from his pocket and unlocked the cage; the other reached in and dragged him out. The prisoner sprawled on the ground and moaned as fire engulfed his wounded leg.

"UP! GET UP!" screamed a guard, in English.

The prisoner tried to obey and finally struggled to his hands and knees. The guards reached down and jerked him to his feet. He stumbled forward, with the guards using their rifle barrels as prods. Somehow he reached the wooden house at the far end of the camp, and, as he entered the door, his leg gave out, and he crumpled to the dirt floor.

"UP! UP!" screamed the guards, kicking him in the ribs.

Somehow, through sheer will power he stood up and he found himself looking at a North Vietnamese officer seated behind a field table. The officer took a deep drag on his cigarette and smiled up at the prisoner.

"Good morning, Captain." The officer stood up and walked around the desk. "I am Major Vo Yun Phoung of the People's Army of Vietnam. I am very pleased to meet you, Captain Stevens."

The prisoner's greatest fears were realized; they knew who

21

he was. A hard knot of terror gripped his stomach and suddenly he needed to urinate.

"Your reputation as a murderer and war criminal is well-known. I hope you enjoyed the little reception we planned for you?" The Major was tall for a Vietnamese, and he wore a pencil-thin mustache. He spoke almost perfect English.

Major Phoung glared up at him. "And now, Captain, down to business. All you have to do is answer a few questions, and we will take care of your wounds and give you food." He paused and casually ran his fingertip over his mustache. "What was your mission in North Vietnam?"

The prisoner remained silent, staring at the Major. It took all of his will to keep from showing fear. He gritted his teeth. A quick blow to his stomach from Phoung doubled him up, and he gasped for air.

The Major spat a series of questions at him: "What are the names of your local contacts? What is the radio frequency of your control base? What are the locations of your safe villages in Laos?" He waved a paper in the prisoner's face. "Here," he screamed. "Here are the questions you must answer!"

The young Green Beret tried to muster his courage. He was afraid to speak--afraid his voice would give away his fear. He clenched his teeth and shook his head, and he steeled himself for the expected blow to the stomach. It did not come.

The Major calmed down, marched back around his desk, and stared at the prisoner. He spoke quietly. A slight smile played around his mouth. "I was hoping that you would be smart enough to cooperate, Captain, but it looks as if you are going to be stubborn." He picked up another paper from his desk and laid it down for the prisoner to see. "I also want you to sign this document. If you don't, I will have to persuade you. How much pain can you stand, Captain?"

The prisoner's eyes glanced at the document, but he remained silent. A twinge of cold fear gripped his heart as he tried to imagine what they would do to him. He wondered how long he could hold out.

The Major nodded, and one of the guards untied the prisoner's hands. Pain shot up his arms as the blood rushed back into the swollen hands. He rubbed them, trying to get the circulation started.

Phoung waved the document in front of the prisoner's face. "This is your confession, Captain. Three months ago you led a gang of mercenaries into Laos and captured the village of Plei Ho Bo. Acting upon orders from your headquarters in Nha Trang, you lined up the entire village--men, women, and children--and killed them all. Before you murdered them, you allowed your men to use the women. It was a brutal and disgusting act of violence. Over 200 innocent, peace-loving people were slaughtered by you and your men!"

The prisoner finally broke his silence. "That's a damned lie and you know it!" he raged.

The Major smiled. "Come now, Captain, watch your language. All the facts are written here. All you have to do is sign it."

"I'll never sign that paper," spat the prisoner. "You can take it and shove it up your ass."

"Oh, I think you will sign it," Phoung said confidentially. "Sooner or later you will sign."

Phoung spoke to the guards in Vietnamese. They pushed the prisoner ahead of them, out of the building and into the small clearing in the center of the village. The NVA Major grinned up at him. "You will stand here for a while. Maybe you will change your mind." He turned and walked back into his quarters.

The guards ripped off the remnants of his torn jungle fatigues. One of them slammed his rifle barrel into his midsection, and the American crumpled to the ground.

"UP! Stand attention son-bitch!" screamed the guard.

The prisoner struggled to his feet, trying to regain his breath. He knew the routine:

Step One in the Breaking of a Prisoner: degradation. Strip off his clothes. This makes the prisoner feel like he has lost his first line of defense. Combine with physical violence.

Step Two: Increase the physical and mental torture.

The two guards relaxed in the shade as the sun began to bear down on the naked prisoner standing in the middle of the jungle clearing.

After two hours in the scorching sun, the Captain's lips were parched, cracked and bleeding. Beads of sweat streamed down his face and trickled in small rivulets down his naked body. The hot sun began to turn his pale skin a burning red. His leg throbbed, and he tried to keep his weight on his right foot. After five hours, he was dizzy and he had stopped sweating. He realized he was dehydrating and on the verge of sunstroke.

Finally, the sun was masked by the tall trees and was replaced by hordes of mosquitoes who went to their bloody work with a relentless vengeance. His guards dabbed themselves with American-made mosquito repellent and put nets over their heads. Two hours later, the exhausted prisoner did not have enough strength left to slap at his buzzing tormentors. They crawled into his ears and nose; and he just stood there, half conscious, as they sucked the blood from his body. He wondered how long it would take for them to drain it all.

Just after dark, a wave of dizziness swept over him and he fell to the ground. The guards were on him immediately, beating him with their rifle butts and yelling: "UP! UP! SON-BITCH! UP! UP!"

The prisoner tried to practice what little he had been taught about mental relaxation. He recited every poem he knew: he made up new poems; he prayed; he talked to himself; he cursed the guards; and somehow he made it through the long night. Several times he either passed out or fell asleep--there really was not much difference anymore--because he had passed into a mental zone of semi-conscious unreality, where pain was not even real any longer. Each time he fell to the ground the guards beat him until he struggled to his feet. Finally he fell asleep standing up.

"Good morning, Captain." The sing-song voice was pleasant. "I trust you had a good night's sleep?"

The prisoner tried to focus his eyes and mind on the voice. Everything was blurred. Gradually his eyes cleared as his senses returned. The Major was carrying a thin leather rod. It appeared to be a cleaning rod wrapped in leather. He placed the tip beneath the prisoner's chin and forced his head back.

"Are you ready to cooperate, Captain?"

The prisoner shook his head, and through his parched lips he managed to form a weak, "Fuck you!" His attempt at bravado surprised him.

"You are a dumb shit, Captain," yelled Phoung, and he swung the whip across the prisoner's face in a vicious slash.

The prisoner felt a fiery streak of pain along his cheekbone. The pain and tears blinded him. Blood spurted from his face, and instinctively he stepped forward and swung at the North Vietnamese Major. Phoung danced back, laughing, as the prisoner stumbled and fell to the ground.

The guards grabbed the Green Beret's arms and jerked him to his feet. They dragged him across the clearing to a large tree where they stretched him tightly with his face and chest against the tree.

The first blow from Phoung's slender steel whip felt as if a band of fire had seared across his back. His body jerked as each slash landed. His back was being cut to shreds. He was acutely aware of the warm, sticky blood running freely down his back and legs. Finally, he couldn't help himself, and he screamed with agony and frustration. Then he passed into a hazy red blackness.

Slowly he struggled through the pain and blackness to return to consciousness. He gulped the welcome water as a guard held a canteen to his cracked lips. He was lying on a wooden bench in Phoung's office. His back felt as if someone was holding a blow torch on it. He knew it must look like hamburger.

Phoung walked over and glared down at him. "It is stupid for you to put yourself through so much pain, Captain. We'll just see how tough you are. Any time you are ready to cooperate, just let me know." He nodded to the two guards.

The guards advanced slowly toward the bench, each carrying a rubber truncheon. They started on the bottom of his feet and worked upward. The prisoner tried vainly to protect his naked body. The blows were not hard enough to break bones, but the pain was excruciating. Finally the American was beyond feeling pain, and he passed into the anesthesia of unconsciousness.

When he awakened it was night. He was lying on the hard floor of his bamboo cage. There was a rough hunk of bread and a canteen of water lying next to him. He wolfed down the bread, dirt and all, and washed it down with water. The basic instinct to survive was still within him. He lapsed back into a pain-shrouded coma.

The next day his guards half-carried him back to the Major's office. They sat him in a chair, but he fell to the floor. His strength was almost gone, and his will to resist was fading. They had to tie a rope around his chest to keep him in the chair.

Major Phoung entered and seated himself at his desk. "Well, Captain, I hope you got plenty of rest because we are going to have a busy day."

One of the guards grabbed his hair and pulled his head back; the other placed a wet towel over his nose and mouth. Then he started pouring water onto the towel from an aluminum canteen. The prisoner held his breath as long as he could. Then his lungs, starving for air, reacted automatically, sucking the water into his nose and mouth and down into his lungs. He was drowning! Panic--uncontrolled panic! He was choking to death! The water

26

began to fill his lungs. He fought feebly with his tormentors, gasping for air with lungs that wouldn't function. Then there was total blackness.

He came to, choking and trying desperately to draw air into his starving lungs. His chest felt as if an iron band was drawn tightly around him. Thousands of tiny red-hot knives stabbed his lungs!

"Well, Captain," spoke Phoung calmly, "I'm afraid we overdid it a little that time. You almost drowned, although I have seen men partake in the little drowning death ten times before their lungs burst. Now, are you ready to cooperate?"

The prisoner looked at the Major. He realized that only the relief of death would stop his agony. He made up his mind to die. He shook his head.

"O.K., Captain. Have it your way. Just remember I can keep this up all day. Can you?"

The guards repeated the process. The prisoner opened his mouth and gulped in the water, trying to force it into his lungs. There was pain, then total darkness. He stopped breathing. The pain left him. He felt himself float out away from his body toward the ceiling of the room. Looking down he saw the Major jump up and start pushing against his chest. His body was on the floor now, and they were working on him, trying to pump life back into him. He felt good--he had beaten them! Then suddenly he felt himself returning to his body. The pain returned, with life, then blackness.

That night the Vietnamese Major sat late at his desk, thinking. He only had three more days to make the American talk; then the Colonel would arrive and take over. He had to be careful. They had almost killed the American today, and that would be bad; but it would be a feather in his cap if he could be the one to break the prisoner.

The Green Beret slipped in and out of consciousness during the night. His desire to live was gone, and all he wanted now was to sleep in peace. If he'd had the strength, he would have killed himself. As it was, he could only lie there and

27

dread what would come with the morning sun.

The next day they had to carry him to the Major's office. Phoung didn't even bother to ask if he was ready to cooperate. They tied him into the chair and attached steel alligator clamps to his testicles and chest muscles. Wires ran from the clamps across the room to a metal box. One of the guards doused the prisoner with a bucket of water.

Without speaking, Phoung reached over and pushed a button on the metal box. Fire flamed through the prisoner's belly. He felt his bladder evacuate as a millon units of pain tore through him. The cords bulged on his neck, and sweat erupted from every pore of his body. A scream tore from his mouth.

The Major turned off the current, and the prisoner sagged in his chair. His leg and arm muscles jerked involuntarily, and there was a loud ringing in his ears. Every nerve, every fiber of his body vibrated with pain. Blood ran from his mouth where he had involuntarily bitten his tongue.

Phoung silently stared at his prisoner for several minutes. Finally he said: "Well, Captain, have you changed your mind yet?"

Without looking up, the prisoner slowly shook his head from side to side. He tried to nerve himself for the agony he knew was coming.

A million fiery spots of pain returned and ripped through him. He felt as if his body was going to explode as it involuntarily arched away from the chair. He smelled the sweet burning of his own flesh. Then blackness crept into the edges of his vision and he passed out.

When he came to, he was hanging from a tree. And there was such pain! His arms felt like they were being pulled from their sockets. A short, fat, acne-faced lieutenant came over and glared at him.

"Are you ready to talk?" Acne-Face asked.

The prisoner remained silent. Acne-Face took a bamboo pole and began beating his legs and back. This produced

28

a double-headed pain: first from the blows, and secondly, from the involuntary jerking of his body which caused unbearable pressure on his shoulder blades. They already were stretched almost to the point of dislocation. Acne-Face kept up the beating until the prisoner passed through excruciating pain into numbed unconsciousness.

This procedure was followed for two days. At first, every time the Lieutenant approached him, his body trembled uncontrollably in dreaded anticipation of the pain that was to come. But finally, he passed from pain and agony into despair.

Pain may be defined as a distressing sensation in a particular part of the body, resulting from an undesirable stimulus to the central nervous system. Agony implies an extreme, continuous, excruciating, scarcely endurable pain, and also, a feeling of despair.

Hanging unconscious from the tree limb, his arms stretched tightly above his head, the man long since had passed from pain and agony into despair. A series of white blisters surrounded by angry red welts covered his chest and stomach, indicating where his captors had played tic-tac-toe with the fiery tips of their cigarettes. Deep, bloody furrows crisscrossed his lean back; the bottoms of his feet were black and swollen; there were ugly black bruises on his legs, ribs, and arms from the rubber truncheons. A deep lesion just above his left knee, left unstitched, oozed blood through a dirty bandage. The prisoner hung, suspended, like a carcass of beef in a slaughter house waiting for the skinner's knife. The pain gradually disappeared as his body numbed. He knew he had them beaten now. All he had to do was await the respite of death. There was nothing they could do now to break him. He felt a sense of triumph. But, unknown to him, his real torment was yet to come.

That evening they cut him down and dragged him back to his own personal House of Horror. But he was ready--he had them beaten! They tied him to the center pole in the room. Phoung entered, accompanied by a heavy-set Colonel.

"Good evening, Captain," said Phoung. "This is Colonel Quang."

The Colonel smiled evenly. "Major Phoung tells me that you have been very stubborn. I admire your courage, Captain, but I'm afraid it was to no avail. Tonight you will answer all of our questions and be eager to sign the confession."

The prisoner looked at the Colonel with a sullen glare. "Fuck you!" he spat out. "I've gone this far, and I can go the rest of the way."

Colonel Quang's smile froze. "We shall see, Captain." He barked a command in Vietnamese.

Two soldiers dragged a struggling woman into the room. Through the hazy mist of his pain-clouded mind, the prisoner tried to focus his eyes on the straining figure. Despair bordering on hopelessness tore through him! The woman was his wife!--but how? She was in America. No--it was his wife! Somehow, the Communists had captured her. Her face was mottled and puffed; dark circles hid her once beautiful eyes.

She looked at the prisoner. "Oh, Frank! Frank, what . . . ?" She broke off with a sobbing gasp as Major Phoung slapped her across the mouth, cutting her lips and sending a bright spatter of blood across her cheek.

Before the prisoner could speak, a rag was stuffed into his mouth. He struggled helplessly in his bonds until the blood from his torn wrists ran freely down his hands.

The Colonel gave another command, and the guards tore off the woman's clothes. She stood nude in the presence of her captors and her helpless husband. Her slender body was covered with dark bruises, and her small breasts were spotted with ugly welts. She tried to cover her nakedness, but the guards grabbed her arms and held her upright. Her big eyes looked pleadingly at the Captain. She noted his bruises and battered body, and tears filled her eyes. For a moment their eyes locked. The prisoner sobbed and his body shook uncontrollably.

Colonel Quang lighted a cigarette and inhaled deeply. He removed it from his mouth and ground the fiery tip against the girl's breast. She screamed, and her body jerked in agony.

The prisoner struggled against his bonds, and panic rose in him like a rushing hot tide.

"Now, Captain," the Colonel said triumphantly. "Don't you think it is time you told us what we want to know?"

The young Captain was beaten! He sagged against his bonds and nodded his head affirmatively.

His wife was dragged from the building. The guards removed the gag from the Captain's mouth.

"I'll do anything you say, only don't hurt her any more," he pleaded.

"Don't worry, Captain," promised the Colonel. "Everything is going to be fine. You and your wife will be treated as prisoners of war."

The prisoner talked; he answered all of their questions, and he signed the confession. They gave him food and water, and finally the guards escorted him back to his cage and tied him securely to one of the bamboo slats.

Several minutes later, Major Phoung walked up.

"Where's my wife?" asked the prisoner.

"Your wife is a traitor of the people, therefore she must pay for her crimes. She will die tonight!"

The prisoner fought his bonds. "You son of a bitch, I'll kill you!" he screamed.

The Major smiled, a thin, cruel smile. "I told you I was going to break you, Captain. By morning you will be a raving maniac. When I leave here, I'm going to go and be with your wife. Then I'm going to turn her over to my men. Just keep your ears open and listen." He turned and walked away.

It started a few minutes later with a piercing, heart-stopping scream that wrenched his soul. He listened helplessly as her screams echoed through the hellish night. Only in the abysmal black pit of his tortured mind could he

31

imagine what they were doing to her. Twice during the night, in her anguish, she called out for him.

Finally her screams subsided to moans and whimpers-- then there was nothing but cruel silence. Nothing!

Deep in his soul, he felt the pains of Hell! The Captain began to scream, a scream that came from the very pit of him--and he screamed, and he screamed!

1

TRIPOLI, LIBYA   AUGUST 15, 1985.

Colonel Muammar al Khadafy, ordained enemy of Zionism, avowed antagonist of the United States, self-proclaimed prophet of Islam, ally and surrogate of the Soviet Union, Chairman of the Board and chief financial backer of international terrorism, and leader of Libya--a nation exporting over two billion dollars worth of oil each year--pushed back his chair and rose to speak to the men seated around the conference table in his office. Brother Colonel looked resplendent in his summer white uniform and six rows of medals. If one did not know better, they would think he was the hero of many battles. His distinctive, black curly hair made him look much younger than his 43 years.

Seventeen years earlier, at the ripe old age of 27, the handsome Bedouin Army Colonel overthrew the monarchy and took over the Libyan government in a swift, bloodless coup. Since coming to power, Khadafy had turned Libya into an austere, spartan, desert civilization based upon his own interpretation of the Koran. The Libyan leader believes that he has been chosen by Allah and that he is a true prophet of Islam--the first since Muhammed. "Why else," he said, "would a poor desert Bedouin rise to the leadership of such a rich nation? And, were not all of the other prophets before him, shepherds too, just as he was? Abraham, Moses, Jesus, and

33

the greatest: Muhammed."

Even as a child tending his father's flocks in the lonely Libyan desert, Khadafy knew he was destined for something greater than being a mere sheepherder. He used to dream of riding a white horse and leading great Arab armies to glory. Shortly after taking power, while meditating in his black tent, deep in the desert wastes of Libya, his destiny was revealed to him: "Allah chose him as Prophet of Islam, and he was born to destroy the unholy scourge of Zionism." He was to organize the Arab nations into a Pan-Arab State and lead their armies in one final Jihad (Holy War) against Israel. And when he entered Jerusalem, on his white horse at the head of his victorious Army, every living thing was to die. Not even the Jewish chickens were to be spared. On top of the rubble of Jerusalem, he would build his temple--his temple to Allah. Then, and only then, Allah's will would be done.

Khadafy sees himself standing alone in the desert, dressed in his traditional Bedouin robes, with the solid green flag of Muhammed flying beside him, a farsighted prophet of Islam and the mighty creator and ruler of the Great Arab Nation, stretching from the Persian Gulf, west across North Africa to the Atlantic Ocean; a nation that would eclipse the West in power and glory and purity. A nation victorious after the complete destruction of Zionist Israel.

However, his messianic vision does not hide his vicious methods and his ruthless fanaticism. To him, the amount of blood that must flow to achieve his lofty goals in the name of Allah is insignificant and necessary. In other words, in a Holy Pursuit, the end justifies the means. Brother Colonel has become the modern-day incarnation of the Society of Assassins, which flourished from the 11th to the 13th Century in the Middle East. The primary tool of his efforts to achieve a Pan-Islamic Empire and the elimination of Israel is terrorism. He believes the West has humiliated the Arab World for centuries and regards himself as the last great hope of Pan-Islam. In his mind this degradation by the West must be avenged, and his number one target has become the United States.

Khadafy was born the son of a Bedouin shepherd. He later entered a military academy and became an ardent student of the Koran and a worshipper of Egypt's leader, Nasser. It was because of his respect for Nasser that he came to dream of a Pan-Arab Empire. After attending school in Britain, he returned to Libya and organized his fellow young officers into secret cells to plan the overthrow of the regime of the aged King Idris, who he regarded as a corrupt tool of Western oil companies.

When Nasser died, Khadafy believed that he was the rightful heir to Nasser's crusade for Arab unity. Shortly after taking power, Khadafy engineered the ousting of British and American military bases and negotiated shrewd deals with the greedy Western oil companies for a greater percentage of the oil revenues. He eliminated all private enterprise and all rental properties and froze bank accounts. He set about to build a one million man Army. He created the People's Committees which were meant to institutionalize the Koran's concept of consultation. Today, the Committees run most aspects of Libyan life and help suppress any opposition to the regime.

In 1978, Khadafy declared that Libya had become the first "famahiriyah," which means a state without a government--or the people's state. He resigned from his official position and took for himself the title of "Leader of the Revolution." In reality, he did not relinquish any power.

Even though Khadafy's writings in his "Green Book" describe the United States and the Soviet Union as equally egregious imperialists, he has made Libya into a Soviet military client. The main reason he has embraced Russia is America's friendship and support of Israel. The Libyan leader is obsessed with wiping Israel off the map, and he believes that only America stands in his way. Khadafy sees the U.S. as the focus of evil in the world and regards America, not Israel, as the ultimate enemy.

Of all the leaders of the world, the Libyan leader has been the most open supplier of money, weapons, and training to terrorist groups around the world. He has broadcast the most inflammatory public appeals for attacks on Americans. He has issued the most insolent taunts and threats of blood and death.

The Libyan leader's persistent bid for nuclear power vividly dramatizes the potential menace of proliferation. For over 16 years, he has been supporting international terrorism and devising schemes to worry the West. If he were to get hold of nuclear weapons, his capacity for trouble-making would greatly increase. In 1981, Khadafy said that the atom bomb was "a means of terrorizing humanity, and we are against the manufacture and acquisition of nuclear weapons." A few days later, he told his top advisors that he planned to channel a substantial amount of money into obtaining a nuclear weapon.

In 1970, he sent a top aide, Abdul Salam Jalloud, to Peking in an attempt to buy an atom bomb. China turned him down. Beginning in 1973, Colonel Khadafy helped bankroll part of Pakistan's bomb-making effort; and even before he was rebuffed several years later by President Mohammed Zia ul-Haq, he had started to make overtures to Pakistan's arch enemy, India. When New Delhi restricted the extent of nuclear cooperation with Khadafy to strictly peaceful uses, Libya stopped shipments of 7.3 million barrels of oil a year to India.

Much to Brother Colonel's sorrow, his fiery brand of religious fanaticism has not yet been accepted by the more moderate Arab leaders who fear his actions might trigger another Middle East War with an inevitable Israeli victory. The young Libyan leader harbors a particularly venemous hatred for Saudi Arabia and its King, because of their closeness to the U.S. The Saudi's moderate approach to world politics is a constant source of irritation to Khadafy. The Libyan strong man is also an anti-monarchist dedicated to deposing any king in a Muslim nation.

Seeing that terrorism was the "New Warfare" and a high-impact method of influencing world politics; and seeing that there were many terrorist groups around the world working in virtual isolation, Khadafy set about to organize an International Terrorist Network with himself as the leader. He had the one thing that all of these groups needed: money!

With that money, the Libyan leader has established terrorist training camps in Libya and paid for others in Lebanon, Syria, and South Yemen. He paid the bill for terrorists from all over the world to attend these "schools of death." He supported any group working against an established democratic government. A massacre in the airport in Vienna; a bomb on a plane in Sri Lanka; a terrorist attack in Germany; and an air-hijacking and murder aboard a plane in Lebanon all have a common denominator: the terrorists were trained, or the weapons and explosives furnished, or the operation paid for and maybe even planned and ordered by Brother Colonel--The Chairman of the Board.

Under Khadafy, terrorism has become a major business in Libya--second only to oil.

The other men around the conference table each had a degree of power in their own right, and all shared a common interest with Khadafy: The destruction of Israel and the formation of a Pan-Arabian Empire.

Ayatollah Aban Ben Sadir was a leading member of the Islamic Revolutionary Council of Iran. An Islamic Judge, he had sentenced hundreds to die since the revolution and the Ayatollah Khomeini had established his own brand of

Islamic Fundamentalism in Iran. Aban Ben Sadir sincerely believed that the Libyan leader was another prophet, and his personal allegiance was to Khadafy rather than Khomeini. The leader of Iran was old and sick and could not live much longer. When he died, there would be a major fight for power. Aban Ben Sadir hoped that with Khadafy's help and financial backing he could take over the leadership of Iran and ally with Khadafy in forming an Islamic Empire.

General Mustapha Rashan was commander of the Egyptian Ninth Infantry Division and secret leader of the fundamentalist religious sect, Al Phatat, which assassinated Anwar Sadat. Mustapha was a student of Nasser, who believed strongly in a Pan-Arabian Confederacy. When the time came, he would rule Egypt and establish a strict fundamental Islamic society.

Abu Nadal was the leader of the Palestinian Liberation Front and the Black September Group, radical splinter groups of the PLO. Both groups broke with Yassir Arafat because they felt he was becoming too moderate. Khadafy's more militant, fanatical and ruthless approach to the Jewish problem was more to their liking. Besides, he had the money to support their activities. Abu Nadal had over 1500 terrorists in training in Libya--preparing for the "War of Terror" that Brother Colonel was about to unleash. He had a promise from Khadafy that the Libyan leader would establish a "New Palestine," after the victory over Israel.

Sherif Ben Rashid was a socialist and Foreign Minister of the Marxist government of South Yemen. He was a bitter enemy of the Saudi Monarchy. Rashid was a direct descendent of Mohammed Ibn Rashid who once ruled most of what is now Saudi Arabia, before the Saudi family took it away. Rashid had established several training camps in South Yemen where several hundred Shiites were preparing to be sent against Saudi Arabia and the other oil-rich Arabian Gulf States. Ben Abn Rashid already had his slice of the Arabian

Empire picked out.

The last man at the table, Major Mustapha Kemal Amak, was Khadafy's Chief of Intelligence and head of the Amoud--Libya's dreaded state police. Amak had helped plan the attack on the Pan Am airliner in Rome in 1973. Amak was the Libyan strong man's right arm for planning, coordinating, and controlling the world-wide terrorist activities. The Major was a sadistic killer who enjoyed his position of power in Khadafy's regime.

Brother Colonel, his dark eyes shining, began to speak slowly and deliberately: "By the grace of most merciful Allah, we will soon be in a position to accomplish our desired objectives: the destruction of Zionist Israel and the formation of a United Arab Confederacy.

"We are well into the first phase. During the last two years we have increased our support of international terrorism. We have trained thousands of men and women from all over the world. We have established new training bases in Nicaragua, Columbia, and Angola. We are now supporting several groups within the United States: A militant faction of the American Indian Movement (AIM); two black separatist movements, The New Afrika Coalition and the Pan Afrikan League; the National Liberation Movement (NLM), a Mexican-American revolutionary group; and the Puerto Rican Armed Forces of National Liberation (FALN). Members of these organizations have received training here in Libya, in Cuba and in Nicaragua. We also have 20 teams of trained Libyans in America, posing as students. More fighters are being trained in Central America and will be infiltrated to the U.S. through Mexico, in the coming months. Next summer, we will turn several hundred trained teams loose on American society.

"America is spiritually weak and morally decadent--The Americans have lost their resolve--And they are stupidly apathetic. They cannot see what is happening to them. They have been paralyzed by the Vietnam War and their own liberal press keeps them in blissful ignorance. The U.S. is kept off-balance by a superb Communist world-wide misinformation program.

"One-by-one, America has deserted her allies, and one-by-one, these former allies are turning against the former Arsenal of Democracy. Many nations are afraid to be America's friend because they are not sure if America will help them--if they try to stand up against the march of World Communism. It is ironic that America pays for her own destruction. Allah gave us the oil, and the greedy Americans buy the oil and give us the money to destroy them!

"Communism is our temporary ally. We need the Soviets in order to get sophisticated weapons and high technology--we need them now. But we must never forget: Communism is only a temporary ally because, in the final analysis, Communism and Islam cannot co-exist! Once the Arab Confederacy is established we will no longer need the Communists. Allah will show us the way!

Khadafy began pacing slowly, his voice rising slowly. "Most of the organizations we support and control do not know our ultimate goal, nor is it necessary that they do. They will play their part by keeping other governments busy. They will, unknowingly, be our vanguard. International Terrorism is the primary instrument in our crusade. By using terrorism, a few individuals can weaken the iron grip and will of nations. Terrorism will keep the western nations off balance while we accomplish great things--while we change the history of the world.

"An important facet of the first phase of our plan was the elimination of Anwar Sadat. Sadat was no longer an Arab--he was a tool of the Americans and Jews, a traitor to the Arab people. He had to die! We know that you cannot make alliances with the Jews--the Jews have to die in order for Islam to survive!"

The Libyan leader paused to catch his breath. The intensity of his dark gaze fell upon the Egyptian General:

"General Rashan has done his job well. We are now rid of the pig Sadat! With him out of the way, there will be no treaty with the Jews, and the Camp David Accord will fade away in the face of growing Arab unity. And, when the time comes, Rashan will be ready to deliver Egypt to our cause."

His dark eyes shining, Khadafy's voice was getting gradually louder. Rubbing the palms of his hands together, he stopped pacing and faced the assembled group: "During the second phase, we will increase our support of International Terrorism. Our Vanguard will strike at the heart of the Western Nations--our main target will be the United States of America. At first, Americans will be afraid to travel in any foreign country--then they will be afraid to venture out of their homes. We will promote and support unrest in the Middle East and Central America. We will especially support our friends in Nicaragua. The Sandinistas are fighting America on its own ground, therefore we will aid them.

"Then when the time is ripe, Allah will show us the way, and we will enter the active combat phase. First we will provoke the Jews to attack Lebanon, Syria, or Egypt. We shouldn't have much trouble getting the blood-crazed, paranoid Jews to attack. Then after a series of Israeli victories, when the Zionists are stretched to their military limits, Libya will intervene and save the Arab world!"

He paused to let his last statement sink home before he dropped his bombshell. He stepped forward and leaned on the table. "Yes, I'll save the Arab world and destroy Israel with my nuclear weapons!"

There was a stir at the table and a low gasp from the Egyptian. Major Amak smiled knowingly.

"Yes, gentlemen," the fiery Libyan leader said triumphantly, banging his clenched fist on the table. "I soon will possess nuclear weapons, and with them I shall destroy the Zionist state! Even now as we are meeting, my scientists and technicians are building these nuclear devices. Allah has given me the means to do his will!"

Khadafy continued, speaking louder and faster. "Then we shall move into the final phase, the formation of the Arab Confederacy, and my nuclear weapons will guarantee our security." He smiled for the first time. "I will be the Savior of Islam and leader of an Arab Empire which will stretch across North Africa and the Middle East to the borders of Iran." He waved his arm around the table. "And you gentlemen, will be by my side. It is Allah's will!"

He stopped to catch his breath, then continued. "In the past, the only thing the Arab nations have been able to agree upon is that they all hate the Jews. We have lacked the key ingredient to unify--that ingredient is power. We possess the economic power in oil, but we can't even agree how to use it as a political tool. With nuclear power to back up the control of oil production, it can be done."

By this time the Libyan dictator was leaning over and pounding the table, yelling at the top of his voice. Even in the air-conditioned room, beads of sweat stood out on his forehead. His eyes glared around the table. The other men in the room were mesmerized by the fiery zeal of the young leader.

Khadafy sat down and took a sip of his tea. He was shaking with excitement; his lips trembled. Finally, he regained his composure. He resumed speaking in a quieter voice. "We have a hidden factory where we are building nuclear weapons. In a few months we will have enough bombs to destroy Israel and a reserve to provide assurance that we will be recognized as a threat to any nation that tries to stop us. I'm not afraid of the Americans. Right now, if it was a choice between Israel and Arab oil, the Americans would choose oil because oil is the breath of life for the United States."

The Libyan leader paused and took another sip of tea. "It is important that we work now to drive a wedge between the United States and Saudi Arabia. Saudi Arabia may be the key to our success. The Saudis are enjoying the fruits

41

of their petroleum stores, and they are willing to pacify the Americans and the Jews. However, American influence is increasing; even now they are training the Saudi Army. We must do everything we can to get the Saudis back into our fold. To accomplish this, we will have to overthrow the Saudi monarchy."

His announcement caused the others to look at each other in surprise. "Also, we must get the Americans to turn against the Jews. Thank Allah, the Jews already are helping us there. The more aggressive the Jews are, the more pressure the United States will have put on them to turn away from their Jewish allies. Without American backing, the Jews can be destroyed easily; and without Arab oil, the United States will become a third rate power."

He stood up again, leaning forward, his hands on the table. "Everything is beginning to turn in our favor, and the time will soon be ripe for us to strike for Allah. The Western nations are puzzled by international terrorism. They don't see a goal for these terrorist groups. Sometimes I don't think most of these groups see one either, but there is one, gentlemen! They are the vanguard of the new Arabian Empire! And, I control the purse strings of this global terrorist army."

Khadafy began pacing again, his hands clasped behind his back in a MacArthur-like pose. "The Iraqi-Iranian war; the disputes between Ethiopia, Sudan, and Somalia; the civil war in Sudan; the struggle in Lebanon; the potential for conflict between Jordan, Syria, South Yemen, and Saudi Arabia; the aggressiveness of Israel--all combine to keep the area in a turmoil. We want to keep it a tinderbox until I both light the fuse and extinguish the fire!"

Khadafy paused and looked around the table: "And now, gentlemen, Major Amak will outline your roles in our future plans." Brother Colonel abruptly stopped speaking and sat down. He took a sip of tea and leaned back in his chair.

Major Amak picked up a pointer and stepped up to his briefing chart.

2

SAUDI ARABIA--THE DESERT KINGDOM.

Several million years ago, when the world was young, ages before man walked the earth, a large, shallow, warm sea covered what is now the Arabian Peninsula. Hundreds of billions of tiny microscopic plants and animals thrived in the murky waters. Eventually they died and piled up in layers in the ocean bed. No one knows for sure why they perished. Perhaps they multiplied to the point where they used up the oxygen in the water, or they ran out of food, or maybe some type of virus killed them off.

As the ages passed they were covered with mud and sand, and eventually they were buried under deep layers of earth. The land areas changed and the seas subsided; diastrophic disturbances caused mountains to fall and spill into the oceans. New mountains and new seas were created. Finally, these billions of decayed plant and animal organisms trapped beneath the surface formed petroleum.

In some places, the petroleum was so close to the surface that it seeped out. As early as 6,000 years ago, the ancient Persians used petroleum, or pitch as it was called, for mortar and glue. Some of these seepages caught fire and became the Eternal Fires of the Persian Fire worshipers. Over 3,000 years ago, in war, the Persians used arrows tipped with the burning pitch.

For centuries, Arabia waited--isolated and untouched by the rest of the world. The interior was considered too remote and too poor for colonization. A loosely associated group of tribes lived along the coasts and a few poor nomadic tribes ventured into the interior, tending their herds of sheep and camels. The vast stores of petroleum lay beneath the sands, waiting.

The two most far-reaching events in Arabia's modern history were the discovery of oil in 1931, and the granting of an oil concession to Standard Oil of California by King Ibn Saud in 1933. Later, three other American Oil Companies (Texaco, Exxon and Mobil) joined to form ARAMCO (The Arabian American Oil Company). The first well began production in 1938; however, large-scale production did not commence until after World War II.

The Bedouin family that originated in the mud huts of an obscure oasis, the House of Saud, found themselves the richest family on the earth, with their backward nation sitting atop oil wealth estimated at between 15 and 19 trillion dollars.

Because of its vast wealth, Saudi Arabia has become the classic prototype of the ultimate welfare state. Each citizen is guaranteed a free education through college, free medical care, interest-free loans, cash grants for those wishing to go into business, and bonuses for marriage and children. Agricultural products and livestock are subsidized by the government.

The Saudis are currently financing a 200 billion dollar modernization program. Entire cities are being built in the desert; new universities, hospitals, highways, office buildings and factories are being constructed at a whirlwind pace. The objective is to transform their backward nation into a modern power within ten years.

The Saudi population is only 7.5 million, so to accomplish

their rapid development plans they must rely on foreign technology and manpower. Working in Saudi Arabia are 60,000 Americans, 90,000 Europeans, 900,000 Koreans, Thais, Pakistanis, Egyptians and Filipinos, plus over one million Yemenis. Ninety percent of the workforce in Saudi Arabia are expatriates, and by the year 2000, ninety percent of the population could be foreigners.

The nation is the Chief Protector of the Faith, birthplace of the Prophet Muhammed, and home of the two Holy Cities of Mecca and Medina. Its Constitution and laws are based entirely upon the Holy Koran. Alcohol, gambling and pornography officially are forbidden. The sexes are strictly segregated. Women must be veiled, cannot drive cars, are forbidden to travel alone, may only work as teachers or nurses, and have no voice in the male-dominated society. A man may have as many as four wives at one time. Since men can divorce almost at will, many Saudi men still marry up to 20 women during their lifetime.

Criminal punishments are dictated by the Holy Koran. Rape, murder, and adultery are punished by beheading. A thief may have his hand chopped off, and flogging is common for lesser offenses. The net result is that Saudi Arabia has the lowest crime rate of any nation in the world.

This desert kingdom exercises a moderate influence over the other Arab countries. Staunchly pro-American and strictly anti-communist, the Saudis earnestly desire a peaceful settlement of Middle East problems, if for no other reason than to enjoy their prosperity. However, there are ill winds blowing over the oil rich sands. Iran and Libya would like to see the Saudi Monarchy replaced by an Islamic Revolutionary Council, and the Marxist government of South Yemen nurses old tribal grudges and territorial disputes.

If trouble comes, it very well may come from within. In 1979, the Saudis were surprised when a group of fanatics took over the Holy Mosque at Mecca and had to be driven out by the Saudi National Guard. The Shiites, who tend toward the religious fanaticism of Ayatollah Khomeini, are potential problems; there are over 175,000 living in the vicinity of the oil fields of eastern Saudi Arabia.

As the country modernizes, its citizens will have rising expectations of more freedom--especially the women. There are signs of trouble within the royal family itself as some of its members, enjoying great financial wealth, are showing signs of becoming disinterested in the governing process.

This thinly populated kingdom--with one foot in the 13th Century and the other in the 20th--which only a few years ago was little more than a desert wasteland inhabited by poor Bedouins, has suddenly emerged as an influential superpower in world politics. Because of its wealth, its new political influence, its religious influence and its strategic location, Saudi Arabia may hold the key to peace in the Middle East.

★　★　★　★　★

KHARAIS MARRIOT HOTEL, RIYADH, SAUDI ARABIA　SEPTEMBER 1985.

His Excellency, Prince Mohamad Al Himoud, Minister of Defense for the Kingdom of Saudi Arabia and seventh in line to the royal throne, sat at the head of the table. The Prince was lean and wiry and appeared much younger than his 55 years. He was wearing the traditional white robe, or thobe as it is called, and a red and white checkered head covering, or shimagh. The color of the shimagh indicated his proud Bedouin heritage.

The first Saudi King, Abdul Aziz Ibn Saud, who ruled from 1932 to 1953, married some 300 wives in order to command the loyalty of the various nomadic tribes that he and his father had conquered. Ibn Saud produced 41 royal sons, four of whom followed him to the throne: Saud from 1953 to 1964; Faisal, 1964-1975; Khalid, 1975-1982; and Fahd, the present King. The exact size of the royal family is unknown,

46

but Ibn Saud's 10 brothers and 41 sons may have produced for the House of Saud as many as 4,500 Princes and an equal number of Princesses. Ibn Saud was truly the "Father of his Country." It also can be said that he physically "screwed his Kingdom together."

Prince Mohamad was in the "inner circle of 12 Princes" which, along with the King who is the first among equals, actually runs the nation. A 1951 graduate of Georgetown University, Mohamad was a staunch friend of the United States and strongly anti-Communist. Although a devout Muslim, he tended toward moderation and was against the radical religious tenets of Khomeini and Khadafy.

To his right sat William R. Emerson, self-made millionaire and owner of the Emerson Corporation--an American firm with varied interests in the Middle East including a multi-million dollar contract to modernize the Saudi Arabian Internal Security Forces. Emerson was a big man, well over six feet tall, with a heavily muscled upper body and a trim waist. His thick, silver-grey hair and neatly trimmed mustache gave him a rugged, distinguished appearance. He looked more like a retired football player than a highly successful multimillionaire businessman. The Californian was a close personal friend of the President and a dedicated Republican.

Sitting at the left of the Prince was James A. Moore, Lieutenant General, U.S. Army, retired. Moore once commanded the Special Forces in Vietnam and later the 82nd Airborne Division at Fort Bragg. His last assignment before retirement was as Deputy Director of Covert Operations for the U.S. Central Intelligence Agency. Moore was recognized as one of America's top experts in the area of Special Operations.

Jim Moore looked the part of a general officer. He was tall, slim, and handsome. His good looks and habitual military bearing made him stand out in any crowd. His wife used to tell him that he was bound to make General because

47

he looked exactly like a general should look. His present job was the Program General Manager of Emerson's Saudi Modernization Project. He and Bill Emerson had been close friends since the Second World War. Everyone at the table was well-aware that General Moore still had close ties with the CIA.

The fourth man at the table, Samuel Bates, was in Saudi Arabia representing the State Department as Assistant Under Secretary of State for Middle Eastern Affairs. Bates was a wolf in sheep's clothing or, in this case, a blue pin-stripe suit because his real position was Deputy Assistant to the Director of the Central Intelligence Agency. His attendance was to ensure that U.S. security interests were protected in the planned venture. Bates was a little on the pudgy side and appeared over-worked and under-exercised.

The Prince placed a cigarette in his mouth and lighted it with his solid gold Dunhill. He spoke perfect English with a slight British accent, acquired while he was Ambassador to Great Britain. "I have studied General Steven's dossier, and I must admit that I am very impressed. Only 42 years old, a General, a Medal of Honor winner, served in South Yemen with the British, trained in Saudi Arabia with his Ranger Battalion--yes, it is very impressive indeed. I think he would have to be my choice."

"The State Department favors Stevens, too," interjected the CIA-man. "He is our most combat experienced officer, and we are confident that he will do a good job."

The Prince looked at Emerson. "And, I understand that your President fully agrees with the circumstances under which this unit would be deployed?"

"Yes, your Excellency," answered Emerson. "I spoke to him just two days ago. His primary concern is the same as ours. He wants a stable government in Saudi Arabia, friendly to the United States. This is in the best interest of both of our countries."

The American administration, fearing that Saudi Arabia

48

might go the way of Iran, had entered into a secret treaty with the Saudi monarchy, promising military assistance in case of outside aggression and cooperation in helping the Saudis build up their forces to prevent internal disorders.

General Moore closed the folder in front of him. "I have known General Stevens for many years, and I can guarantee you gentlemen that we have made the right choice. As soon as I get back to the States, I'll contact him. He probably is bored stiff in his new job, and I think he will jump at the chance to join us."

★　★　★　★　★

FORT IRWIN, CALIFORNIA   0100 HOURS

The man lying naked on the bed was lean and muscular. His body was well-adorned with scars of battle. A long, whitish scar on his left thigh contrasted vividly with his deep California tan. There was a puckered bullet-hole just below his rib cage. Another scar was visible on his left cheek, and his back was a mesh of cross-hatched scar tissue.

The woman with him had long blond hair which cascaded across her face as her hips undulated against him. Her full, round breasts bounced as she moved. The man's hands gently played across her body.

"Honey, that feels too good!" she gasped. She threw her head back and closed her eyes. "Oh God, Honey. Oh, Baby!"

He reached up and placed his hands on her shoulders, pulled her tighter against him, and arched his body upward. Her face contorted as if in pain, and she screamed as she shuddered again and again as spasms of pleasure rocked her body. The man felt a surging moment of ecstacy--then a pleasant release of tension. She gave a final shuddering sigh and slumped forward, covering the soldier's face with kisses.

"Oh, Honey!" she said, trying to catch her breath, "it gets better every time!"

49

Later she lay beside him, spent and sated, her right leg thrown loosely over his, her head resting on his chest, her long blond hair spilling over his arm and shoulders. "I'm so contented," she said softly, "that if I was a cow I'd be chewing my cud." She nuzzled his ear and whispered: "Did anyone ever tell you that you were a fantastic lover, General?"

"No, not in those words," he answered truthfully.

"Are you sure you didn't get all those medals for screwing?" she teased.

"Maybe one or two," he mumbled. Then he lay back and silently studied the ceiling.

The blonde, Joan Baker, was the latest of many women that he had dated since his wife died. All of his life he yearned for the simple things: a wife, a family, and a home. The Uncle who raised him was a good man, but he was a bachelor and his home was devoid of a woman's touch. The General had had an active life of adventure, excitement, and a degree of success in his chosen profession; but, there remained an emptiness, a longing, a desire to love and to be loved.

For a short time he had love--and hope, and aspirations for a home and family. Then that love was taken from him, violently, by the Communists. When they tore her from his heart, they left him with an open, bleeding wound that wouldn't heal. His soul became inflamed, and love was replaced with a hatred and a thirst for revenge. He vowed to make them pay--and pay they did, in blood. In his lust for revenge, he killed and killed, until finally, his pent-up rage to avenge her death was satisfied and replaced with an aloneness and a deep hurt that petrified his soul.

He tried to fill the void with a seemingly never-ending line of women. The physical act of love became an opiate as he charged from one affair to another, unsuccessfully seeking a replacement for his lost love, but none awakened the emotional need in him.

Joan was a beautiful divorcee of 38, who could pass for

25 thanks to a lot of exercise, a good diet, and a little help from a plastic surgeon who gave her a gorgeous pair of breasts. Married to a wealthy rancher, she had spent 13 sexually unfulfilled years. She often said that she never experienced a decent orgasm until she divorced. With the General, as she liked to call him, she lost count. His stamina and virility amazed her. When they made love, his mastery of her body was complete. She had had several lovers since leaving her husband, but none could compare with the inexhaustible General. She once told him that if he could fight like he made love, then he must be one helluva soldier!

Brigadier General Frank Stevens--the most decorated soldier in the Army, hero of Vietnam, veteran of numerous small wars and clandestine operations, paratrooper, Ranger, and Green Beret--was one helluva soldier. He was one of a kind: a perfect fighting machine, a modern professional gladiator, and a legend in his own time.

Joan broke the silence. "What are you thinking about?"

"Nothing in particular," he answered quietly.

She leaned up on one elbow and peered at him. "You're deep, even mysterious. I just can't figure you out. You're the most difficult person to communicate with that I've ever met. You never talk about yourself. Sometimes you're so quiet you frighten me. It's as if your thoughts are a million miles away. I've known you for six months, but I've never heard you laugh. I've tried to make you happy, tried to make you love me, but I just can't seem to get through that hard shell of yours. I love you and want to take care of you, but you don't love me. I think all you want from me is sex."

Stevens heard her, but he couldn't open up to her--and, she was right, he didn't love her. He honestly wished he could, but the feeling just wasn't there. Sex was his only interest in her.

Joan realized that she would never get to him emotionally. She looked at the scars on his body and shook her head. She wondered why men went to war.

He was rescued from the entrapping conversation by the ringing of the phone. The voice at the other end was familiar. General James Moore was the closest thing to a father-figure that Stevens had ever known.

"Hey, Frank. How are you?"

"Just great, General. I tried to call you earlier this evening, but you must have been out. I hope you weren't asleep?"

"No Sir, I wasn't asleep."

Joan reached down and began to caress him.

"Frank, what are you doing now? Anything special?"

"Sir, you wouldn't believe me," Stevens returned, squirming on the bed.

Moore interrupted him, laughing. "I don't mean right this minute. Knowing you, I can guess. I mean what are you doing as far as work is concerned. Can you get away for a couple of days? I would like to have you come to Ventura and meet my boss. We have something in mind that might interest you. How about tomorrow or the next day?"

"Yes Sir, General. I see no problems in getting away. I can drive over day after tomorrow, Friday." Stevens took a pencil and pad from the drawer of his bedside table and wrote down the directions General Moore gave him, as Joan continued to toy with him. "I should get there around 1800 hours, Sir."

"Good. We'll be waiting for you. By the way, tell your bed partner hello for me."

When he hung up the phone, Joan looked up and said in a husky voice: "Just lay back and let me make you feel good."

Stevens lay back and enjoyed her attentions. She was good--very, very good!

General Moore hung up the phone and lay back on his bed.

His wife Mary closed the book she was reading and placed it on her bedside table. She removed her glasses and laid them on top of the book.

Moore turned to his wife and smiled. "Well, my timing

52

was perfect. He was making out with some woman."

"So what's new?" Mary asked, laughing.

"You know, honey, I think Frank's the horniest man I've ever known."

"He's not the horniest man I know," returned his wife kiddingly.

"Well, maybe the second," said Moore, reaching out toward his wife.

3

VENTURA, CALIFORNIA.

Lounging around the olympic-size swimming pool, behind Emerson's palatial home in the hills near Ventura, were Paul Ames, his son-in-law; Sallie Endorf, a friend of his daughter; General Moore and his wife, Mary; and William Emerson. His daughter, Alana, was swimming laps. She finally tired and climbed from the pool. Her father tossed her a towel.

"Thanks, Dad," she said, and began drying her long black hair. She flopped down in the lounge chair next to General Moore. "So when is this big war hero of yours getting here, Uncle Jim?" she asked casually. Moore was not her uncle, but she had called him that for as long as she could remember.

"Well, 'Lana, he should be here any time."

"You did say he was single, didn't you?" asked Sallie.

"Sallie," interrupted Alana, "I swear you'd go after anything with pants on. However, I can imagine General Frank Stevens, war hero: egotistical, pompous, overbearing, with an IQ of 55, and wearing a size 10 hat."

'That sounds like you're describing me," laughed Moore.

"Don't be silly, Uncle Jim. You aren't like that at all." She jumped up and sat on his lap, wet suit and all. With her arms around him she kissed him affectionately on the cheek. "You will always be my number-one hero!"

"I think you'll be surprised when you get to know Frank, won't she honey?" he said, turning to his wife.

"Frank is the finest gentleman I know," Mary said positively. "Although he is somewhat on the quiet side, he's far from being dumb, having two Master's Degrees. I think Frank is a most unusual person. He is different, but that's because of everything that has happened to him. He is a loner. Oh, he likes ladies, and they seem to go for him; but he never gets seriously involved. I wish he could find a good woman and be happy."

Sallie leaned toward General Moore: "Tell me more about him--he sounds exciting!"

Moore lit a cigarette and leaned back in his chair. his wife reached over and took it away and snubbed it out. "Nag, nag!" he said. "She's trying to get me to quit."

He coughed. "Well, first of all, Frank Stevens is the greatest soldier I have ever known. In combat I don't believe he has an equal--anyway, not in our Army. I have never seen him show fear. This used to bother me, but as I got to know him, I realized he was for real--the perfect fighting machine!

"I first met him at Ft. Benning in Georgia, in '61 when I commanded the Ranger Department, and he was a brand new second lieutenant fresh from the Academy. He took to Ranger training like a duck to water. I kept him on as an instructor. Within six months, he had mastered hand-to-hand combat, and he became our top instructor. He just seemed to outshine all of the other officers in everything he did. I saw then that he was a natural leader.

"Then I was transferred, and I didn't seem him again until I took over the Special Forces in Vietnam in '65. At that time, he was commanding a Mrong guerrilla unit in Laos. His combat operations along the Ho Chi Minh Trail already had made him something of a legend in the Forces. His unit had the mission of attacking Communist supply columns along the Trail and striking at their base camps deep in Laos. Most of the things that he did there still are classified, mainly because the United States didn't officially have any troops in Laos at the time. However, I will say that he was highly successful, so much so that the Commies had a $50,000 price on his head.

"In 1966, he and a small Special Forces Team jumped in-to North Vietnam on a special mission. Enemy agents tipped-off the commies, and the team walked into a trap. Frank and one of his NCO's were captured. The rest of the team were killed. Frank was a valuable prize to the enemy because he knew a lot about operations in Laos and South Vietnam. Most men never could have survived the tortures he went through, but Frank Stevens did. To this day he has never spoken a word to anyone about what happened in that prison camp. When he returned, he even refused to talk about it to our Inteligence debriefing team. I found out the details from the sergeant who was with him.

"One night Frank overpowered his guard and escaped, but not before killing every North Vietnamese in that camp. He and the sergeant were picked up 10 days later, more dead than alive. When I learned that, I put him in for the Distinguished Service Cross, but he came to me and begg-ed me to cancel it, which I did."

Moore paused, and took a sip of his drink. It was evident from the silence that the group was eager to hear more. The retired General purposely omitted the part about how the Communists killed Frank's wife. He didn't think it was the time nor the place to discuss that gruesome detail of the young General's life.

William Emerson shook his head. "Unbelieveable! How many did he kill while making his escape?"

"No one knows for sure," answered Moore, "but we believe 10 or 12. I'm sure even Frank doesn't know. Brax-ton, the Sergeant, said that Frank was out of his head at the time."

Moore leaned forward in his chair and reached for his drink. He toop a sip and continued. "There was a distinct change in Frank when he returned from the hospital. It seemed all he lived for was to kill Communists, and he soon developed a reputation for cold-blooded efficiency. He led several raids into Laos and even a raid back into the North. Twice he commanded relief forces that went to the aid of beleaguered Special Forces Camps.

"Eight months after he rejoined me, one of his reconnaissance teams was cut off, inside enemy territory, with their radios inoperative. Frank rappelled from a helicopter at night, with radio and ammunition on his back, and located the patrol. He led them through enemy lines and fought a two-day game of hide-and-seek, until finally he got them to a hill within range of our artillery with a landing zone for helicopters. The Communists caught up with them, and the small force fought all night long. Finally, with all of his men out of action, Frank called in artillery and air strikes, including napalm, right on top of his own position.

"Several times during the night I tried to land relief forces, but the enemy fire was just too heavy. At first light I decided to attack; but having lost radio contact several hours before, I fully expected to find all of the Americans dead. When my helicopter approached the hilltop, I saw a sight that I'll never forget. The hill had been blasted bare of all vegetation, and the tree stumps and charred limbs still were smoking from the napalm. Enemy bodies were strewn all over the hill. It was unreal! --something you read about or see in the movies but never would believe that you'd see in person.

"Then I saw Frank! He was standing on a boulder, in plain sight and fully exposed, daring the enemy to try to kill him. The North Vietnamese survivors were moving toward him, in a group, and were within 30 meters of him. Yet, they couldn't hit him! It seemed as if he was being protected by some unseen force. Frank was firing calmly at the NVA closing on him. When our gunships attacked, the North Vietnamese broke and ran. I landed a few minutes later, and Frank still was firing into the pile of enemy dead in front of him.

"We counted over 200 enemy bodies on Hill 555. Frank later was awarded the Congressional Medal of Honor.

"I wonder what it is that makes some men rise to incredible feats of bravery during times of crises?" mused Emerson.

"All animals fight like hell if they are cornered," returned Moore, "And men are animals. But in this case, it was a little different. The Communists thought they had easy pickins'--thought they had the patrol by the tail, and they did. What they didn't know was that the tail had a tiger on the other end. Frank Stevens wanted them more than they wanted him. When they got to Hill 555, the tiger turned. All along, he was the hunter--not the hunted.

"Later, as a Major, he commanded an Infantry Battalion during the TET Offensive. His force fought alongside the Marines and spearheaded the assault on Hue. Altogether, he spent five years in Vietnam and Laos, and when he returned home he was America's most decorated soldier.

"But, his fighting wasn't over yet. He was selected as an exchange officer with the British Special Air Service (SAS). They are very much like our own Special Forces. He fought with them in South Yemen and won the British Military Cross, which is their second highest combat award. He returned to the States and commanded a brigade in the 82nd Airborne Division. After that, he worked for two years on a special project."

Mary interrupted him. "You should say that he worked for you on some super secret mission. Frank just disappeared for two years. Jim knows what he was doing, but he won't tell even me. CIA-types are very secretive."

Moore reached over and patted his wife's hand. "Yes, Frank worked on several classified operations for me." Moore could not tell them that Frank spent most of that time in the jungles of Angola, advising and fighting with the Anti-Communist forces of Jonas Savimbi. "Then six months ago he was given command of Fort Irwin.

"Yes, Frank is a very unusual man. He has more combat experience than any other officer in the Army. He's no phony; he's just one hell of a fighting soldier!"

"And, you love him like a son," inserted his wife.

"Yes, I love him like a son, just as you do," he admitted, gently clasping his wife's hand.

★ ★ ★ ★ ★

Frank Stevens drove up to the Emerson mansion at 6 p.m. The grounds covered a vast estate of several hundred acres. With the price of California real estate, he could only guess at its worth. There was a circular drive in front of the house, which surrounded an Italian-style fountain. In the center of the fountain was a statue of a young boy, Le Mannequin Pis. Any entrepreneur would have envied the quality reproduction of the famous Belgian statue.

A white-jacketed servant led him to a large foyer. The home was a repository of Persian rugs and portraits by great masters. Although not an expert, Stevens recognized that they were not copies. He followed the servant down a long hallway, out through wide doors, down several steps, and onto a large tiled terrace where the occupants seated around the pool were in various states of dress and undress.

General Moore rose to meet Stevens. After shaking hands, he clasped the young General's shoulder and guided him over to Emerson. "Bill, I'd like you to meet Frank Stevens."

Emerson grasped Stevens' extended hand firmly. "General, I'm pleased to meet you. Lord knows I've heard a lot about you from Mary and Jim. This is my family."

He gestured toward a beautiful black-haired girl wearing a white bikini. "My daughter, Alana."

She took Stevens' hand: "So, you are the famous General

Stevens?" Alana stared intently, studying his face. "You don't look a bit like your pictures. I expected you to be much older."

He noted that she was a stunning woman--beautiful! Her dark eyes held his, and he felt a strange stirring.

"This is my son-in-law, Paul."

The bubble burst, and Stevens felt his desire turn to envy. Her husband was the tall, blonde, all-American image.

Paul Ames appeared younger than his 40 years. His middle, once hard and muscular, was beginning to paunch a little. His hair was blonde and combed straight back. His face was smooth and soft-looking. His cheeks were slightly flushed--probably from liquor. His handshake was weak. Stevens felt revulsion as their hands touched.

"Hello there, General. I hope you had a pleasant drive down? May I get you a drink?" Ames asked smoothly.

"Yes, please. Bourbon and water," answered Stevens.

Ames walked over to the bar to mix the drink.

Alana pointed to the buxom blonde: "And this is Sallie Endorf, my classmate--oh so many years ago--and my best friend."

Sallie stepped toward him. Her hips undulated provocatively as she moved. Her soft blue eyes challenged Stevens. Her ample breasts filled her meager bikini. She was taller and heavier than Alana but still a beautiful woman.

"General, I'm charmed to meet you," she purred. "I've heard so much about you from General Moore." Her eyes talked to him as she openly flirted.

Alana continued, "And you know Mary?"

Stevens put his arms around Mary Moore and kissed her on the cheek.

Sallie seated herself by Stevens, thereby signalling that she was staking a claim. Alana couldn't understand her reaction, but suddenly she wished that her friend wasn't here. Stevens was a good-looking man, thought Alana. He exuded strength, and Alana found herself wondering what it would be like to have someone like him make love to her. "But how in the hell would I be able to compare?" she thought grimly.

Alana noted that Paul was standing beside her. As was the rule more than the exception, he already was well on his way with booze.

The conversation settled into generalities. Out of the corner of his eye, Stevens studied Alana Ames. She was the one thing that shone more brightly than anything else in the area. She was a breathtakingly beautiful woman. Her dark hair was long; her eyes seemed enormous, liquid and sensual. Her skin was satin-smooth, darkened by the sun. Her firm breasts swelled as she breathed; the nipples were visible through her bikini bra. Her waist was narrow, her legs long and elegant. There was a certain pride in her face giving the impression of great strength of character. She also gave the impression that she could be cold or distant.

Alana felt Stevens watching her and observed him over the rim of her glass. When he arrived, she had noticed that he walked with a slight, almost imperceptible limp. She wondered whether it was the result of a recent injury or if it was something permanent. He was dressed in Western slacks and a sport jacket, with brown cowboy boots. Well, O.K. That was stylish in California these days. He looked fit and tan. His body was physically trim. His face was taut; there was no smile. A small scar ran across his left cheek: a duel? He was handsome in a rugged sort of a way--slightly over six feet and perhaps 175 pounds. His nose was large and slightly crooked. His hair was short and neatly combed--definitely virile looking--that rare type of rugged man who was macho without acting so. He was quiet. When he did speak, it was often so low he hardly could be heard. There was a certain gentleness in his manner. No, he was not at all what she had expected.

What was it General Moore had said? "Frank Stevens is the nearest thing to a perfect fighting machine that I have

61

ever seen--the most deadly man-killer I know!" Well, his manner certainly belied his capabilities.

It was his gaze which caught and held her attention. His eyes were grey, clear, and cold. When he looked at her, she felt a loneliness to match her own.

Her marriage was on the rocks. She knew that. It was a wonder that it had lasted this long. Only the fear of hurting her father had caused her to continue it. She had met Paul in the swirl of New York society. She was the rich, well-educated daughter of William Emerson, and Paul was the highly successful, brilliant Harvard law graduate. The **New York Times** called him "the city's most eligible and sought-after bachelor." She had to admit that, at the time, his reputation intrigued her. Paul courted her rigorously until she finally consented. Her Dad was pleased. He was gaining the son he had always wanted. He thought that Paul would fit perfectly into the corporate structure of the Emerson empire.

It hadn't taken Alana long to find out that he wasn't the man she had thought he was. In fact, when it came to sex, he wasn't much of a man at all. There was always the nagging feeling of guilt that she was the cause of his sexual impotence, that perhaps her frigidity was the cause of his problems. She simply could not help herself. Her body would not respond to his advances. Sex had departed from her life long ago. She forced aside desire and replaced it with work.

Alana and Sallie excused themselves, returning a short while later wearing long dresses. Alana looked beautiful in a flowered Van Gant cocktail dress that showed off her tan and her supple body. Sallie looked sexy in a tight-fitting summer shift.

"Dinner is served," announced a servant.

Sallie put her hand on Stevens' arm and guided him into the house. Dinner was pleasant, but Sallie kept up a constant chatter. Occasionally one of the other persons at the table managed to get in a word edgewise, but Sallie definitely dominated the conversation.

"Other than General Motors, you are the first real live General I've met. I read a story about you in **Time** magazine several months ago. You know, the story about your action with the British Army?" She paused to catch her breath then resumed. "I just love the British, don't you? They have such a unique sense of humor . . ." "Alana and I have been the best of friends since college--almost like sisters, I guess."

Alana smiled and thought: "Dear, sweet, wonderful, frivolous Sallie! You really are such a nit at times."

Sallie went on. "I live in San Francisco, you know, and you really should come up and visit. I would love to take you to a stage show. 'The Best Little Whorehouse in Texas' is playing now, and I hear it is great!"

Stevens listened politely. Occasionally he nodded his head "yes" or "no." He thought: "I hope she runs down soon." He glanced up at Alana. She was staring at him and gave a slight smile of apology for Sallie.

Alana knew that Sallie came on strong once in a while, but tonight she was overdoing it. "While you were in Vietnam, Sallie and I were marching in anti-war parades at Berkeley," announced Alana. Now why did she say that, she thought to herself, too late.

Stevens looked at her and said quietly: "At least you were involved. Most Americans didn't care what was going on in Vietnam."

She said to herself: "Touche, General. You handled that beautifully."

Sallie wasn't sharp enough to leave it alone. "That must have been terrible to have been there with all of that killing and death."

Stevens spoke calmly. It was evident that he was uncomfortable with the trend of the conversation. "Only a soldier truly knows the horror of war, Sallie. The public just reads about it or watches it on TV, but the soldier experiences it. I think that is why we hate it so much!"

"But if there was another war, you would fight, wouldn't

you?" Sallie asked.

"Yes, of course," he admitted frankly.

"Why?"

"It's my job."

Although she really didn't understand, that seemed to satisfy Sallie, and she dropped the subject.

"Why don't we have coffee in the den?" said Emerson, rising from the table. It was more of a decision than a suggestion.

Sallie turned to Stevens and whispered, "I'll see you later. I'm not privy to the family business stuff you're going to discuss. I'll be down by the pool."

The rest followed Emerson into his study. It was a spacious, comfortable room, with leather sofas and chairs. Bookshelves covered two walls. A large mahogany desk dominated the room. On the desk were two photograhs: Alana and an older, very attractive lady--presumably Emerson's late wife. A servant followed them into the room and offered coffee.

Mary left with Sallie, but Alana and Paul joined the group for the meeting. General Moore flicked on a slide projector, and as he talked, he ran through a series of pictures concerning Saudi Arabia--equipment, facilities, and training that his people were conducting.

"Frank, as you know, my job in Saudi Arabia is as the Program Manager for Emerson Corporation which has a contract to modernize the Saudi Internal Security Forces. My work force consists of Americans, Koreans, Thais, Jordanians, Pakistanis, and Saudis. We are organized into a Training Directorate, Logistics Directorate, and Personnel Directorate. The program is now in its seventh year. We started with one battalion, equipped them with modern weapons, and trained them by using both the formalized school instructor method and the advisor system. So far we have trained one brigade, and now we're working on the second. Our goal is to train three Mechanized Infantry

Brigades and two Tank Battalions. At the same time, we're establishing a training and logistics base so that eventually the Saudis will take over our jobs.

"The basic fighting vehicle the Saudis are using is the V-150 Commando, built in Florida by Cadillac-Gage. There are several variations of the V-150, equipped with several different types of weapons systems. The V-150 is ideally suited to the desert environment of the Middle East. It is fast, highly mobile, and easy to maintain.

"This is big money we're talking about. The Saudis have purchased from the U.S., or have on order, over 22 billion dollars worth of military equipment. Therefore, the project is important to the U.S. economy --not to mention the fact that a stable government in Saudi Arabia is important to our country as far as peace in the Middle East is concerned. I might add, it is also important to keep this oil flowing in our direction.

"Next year we're going to be organizing a modern Saudi Tank Battalion, but the Saudis haven't decided which tank to buy--the U.S. Abrams, the British Chieftain, or the German Leopold. Naturally we want them to buy the Abrams. At a price of over $5 million each, it would be a healthy shot for our economy.

"I have a good work force. Most of the Americans are retired military, with a heavy preponderance of ex-Green Berets. Most of the blue-collar workers--mechanics, clerks, and drivers--are Koreans and Thais, and they are damned good. The interpreters are Jordanians and Egyptians. The average age in the organization is about 40, so you see that we have a lot of experience.

"Now, you may be wondering where you come in. Well, you don't, as far as the modernization program is concerned. However, in cooperation with the Saudis and with backing from our own State Department, Emerson Corporation wants to organize a squadron of mercenaries who will specialize in desert warfare." Moore paused and looked at

Stevens. "Frank, we want you to command this unit."

Alana noted that Stevens displayed no reaction to this announcement. He sat there stone-faced.

Moore continued. "This organization will have a multi-faceted mission. Since Saudi Arabia will be footing a large part of the bill, the Saudis will have first say on the use of the force for maintaining internal order. The idea of using mercenaries is not new to the Arabs. They have done it for hundreds of years, and now the Saudis certainly can afford it. It's important to our country that the Saudis have a stable government, because we cannot afford another Iran.

"Secondly, both the United States and the Saudis have certain allies that we might want the squadron to help--the Sudan, Egypt, and Morocco, for example--and there is the possibility of trouble with South Yemen and their Communist Government. In fact, there are several possibilities of out-of-country deployment.

"Third, as you know, the biggest business in the world right now is arms sales. Last year it finally surpassed the oldest profession, prostitution, as the biggest money-maker. Also last year, for the first time in history, the Russians out-did us in arms sales. We want to close that gap. This squadron will give us an ideal opportunity to show off American arms, either in actual combat or by demonstrations staged for interested friendly nations. And last, but not least, we will be able to test new weapons and concepts.

"Now, don't misunderstand me. Although the driving force behind this venture is a stable government in Saudi Arabia and furtherance of our own government's interests in the Middle East, economics is still a major factor. The Emerson Corporation is in the arms sales and Army-building business, and we want to make money. We want to sell weapons to Saudi Arabia and other friendly nations in the Middle East, and we want to sell our technical expertise along with it.

"It's going to be a big job, Frank. There are many

unknown factors, but we think you are the man for the job. Are you interested?"

Stevens was a little stunned by the offer. He still was digesting the General's briefing, but the idea was intriguing. "Of course, Sir, but what about my military status?"

"Well, Frank, this is strictly a civilian venture, and officially you would have to retire."

"What about my personnel?" asked Stevens.

"We'll continue hiring for my project and siphon off interesting ones to you. The members of your squadron will receive a fat bonus. I'm sure there will be a number of ex-British SAS-types interested, and there are a lot of Rhodesians and South Africans out of work. You've worked with the SAS and the Saudis, so you know them and should have some good contacts yourself."

It didn't take Stevens long to make up his mind. First of all he was bored stiff with his present job. His physical being craved action, just as an addict craves dope. His military career appeared to be in limbo. He knew that the two years he had spent working for the CIA was frowned upon by many of the more senior, parochial general officers, so why not make a change? Then, too, the offer was coming from General Moore, and Frank Stevens would do anything that man asked of him.

"O. K., Sir. I'll take the job," he announced positively.

Emerson had been silent during the briefing, studying Stevens from under lowered brows. He slapped his knee, jumped up and shook Stevens' hand. "General, I'm glad to have you aboard." He pushed a button at the side of his desk, and a few minutes later a servant appeared with a bottle of champagne; after filling the glasses, he left the room, closing the door behind him.

Emerson raised his glass. "Gentlemen," then looking at his daughter he corrected himself, "and m'lady, I propose a toast to our new colleague, General Frank Stevens, Commander of Emerson Corporation's Desert Legion!"

They discussed details for another hour, and then they adjourned to the patio. Sallie came over and sat beside Stevens. "Well, General, I understand you are going to work for the Corporation?"

"Please call me Frank. Yes, it looks as if I have taken on a new job," he answered.

By 9:30, Paul Ames was feeling no pain. He liked his martinis dry and had been drinking steadily since Stevens' arrival. "Never was in the service, myself," he announced. "After law school I went right into the firm. Now I handle the legal contracts for the Corporation." He slurred his words and leaned across to Stevens: "They tell me you're quite the hero, General. How many men have you killed?"

There it was, thought Stevens, the old question. Sooner or later at parties or on dates, when people found out about his background, someone always asked how many people he had killed. Nine times out of ten, the question came from a well-meaning drunk. He suddenly felt a visceral dislike for the lawyer.

Stevens looked coldy at Ames. "I never counted them. Besides, Mr. Ames, at parties I make it a point never to discuss my religious or political beliefs, sexual preferences, nor war experiences."

Ames started to press the point. Alana reached over and nudged his arm. Her eyes met Stevens' with an apology. "Paul, I think it's time for us to go to bed." She pulled him up and led him into the house.

Stevens felt a little twinge in his belly when he thought of Alana gong to bed with that man. He was intrigued by her. Several times during the evening he had caught her looking at him, but Sallie was doing more than that right now. Her hand was squeezing his thigh.

"Paul is a drunk and a bore," she said. "I don't know how she puts up with him. Did you bring a bathing suit?" she whispered. Stevens nodded. "Then let's take a swim when everyone else goes to bed?"

68

Alana lay awake, feeling miserable and frustrated. It had been the same old story. Paul climbed on, lasted a few minutes, finished, apologized drunkenly, and went to his own room. They had been married for eight years, and Alana hadn't felt any emotional satisfaction for the last five.

During their courtship Paul had been the perfect gentleman. She had not thought it odd that he never tried to go all the way with her before marriage. However, the honeymoon was empty. There were no fireworks, no shooting stars, and for her, no satisfaction. Most of the time Paul wasn't interested in sex, and when he was, he acted as if it were something to be done quickly and gotten over with. He left her feeling unsatisfied, disgusted, and dirty. At first she tried various ruses to be sexy to try to turn him on. She desperately wanted a complete life. But, nothing worked, so after a few months she gave up. Most women would have turned to a lover, but not her. She turned, instead, to her work.

There had been no children. Her tests were O.K. "There's no reason why you can't have a child," the doctor had told her. "Better have Paul come to see me." But Paul refused. She wanted children, so it was a bitter pill to swallow, and it widened the rift between them.

Alana couldn't sleep. She lay staring at the ceiling. Insomnia was another of her problems, and lately it seemed to be getting worse. "What you need is a good lay once in a while," Sallie advised, aware of Alana's sexual problems with Paul. "If that stuffed shirt can't take care of you, you should get someone else."

Today, when she met Stevens, she had reacted strangely-- at least for her. There was something about him that disturbed her. During the evening, she found herself watching him more and more. He was damn distracting! His cold, sad eyes stirred her. She would like to see him smile--just once--but he hadn't, all evening. She lay in her bed wondering where he had been, what he had seen, what he had done. Uncle Jim had talked about him, but that was indistinct. It had only mildly stirred her curiosity. One thing was for sure; there was something vital and compelling about him.

It was a warm night, and she had left the door open to her balcony. She heard a muffled giggle outside. She got out of bed and crept out onto the balcony. In the darkness below, she could see Stevens and Sallie in the pool. Sallie was lying back in the water, and her legs were wrapped around Stevens' lean waist. Alana could see Sallie moving back and forth against his muscular body. "My God! said Alana to herself, "he's taking her right in our pool!"

She started to scurry back into her room--sex was a private thing and shouldn't be watched by outsiders. Instead, she turned back and looked, feeling a little guilty. She heard Sallie gasping--it was evident from her gyrations that she was enjoying herself.

Alana felt a warmness between her legs. She reached down. Ever so gently she touched herself. She was moist. Then she did something she hadn't done for years, but had thought about. She began to massage herself as she watched Stevens and Sallie. Sallie pushed violently against Stevens; her legs went limp. Her low squeals hid Alana's own moans. Sallie had had her first climax of the evening, and Alana had had her first orgasm in five years!

★ ★ ★ ★ ★

Stevens crawled out of Sallie's bed at 0600. It had been a boisterous night. They had made love for hours. Sallie heard him stir and opened her eyes. "My God, General. That was one helluva night. You must have a built-in generator! I'm so sore I can hardly move. I think I'll just lie here for a while, if you don't mind? But before you go, can we do it just one more time? A short one?"

70

Afterward, Stevens went down the hall to his own room, showered, shaved, and put on swim trunks. Then he headed toward the pool for a swim.

Alana was already at the pool, swimming laps back and forth. She glided through the water like a seal. Her tanned body, although small, was muscular--not an ounce of fat. Evidently she kept herself in good shape.

Stevens stood watching her, captivated by her beauty and the smoothness of her strokes. She absolutely was the most stunning woman he had ever seen. His desire was smothered by the realization that she was married to Pretty-Boy--that smug, self-centered bastard. If he were in the Army, we would call him a REMF (Rear Echelon Mother-Fucker), mused Stevens.

Alana pulled up at the end of the pool and climbed out. He tossed her a towel.

"Thanks, General." Her big eyes held his. She has dangerous eyes, he thought. A man could get lost in them.

She looked at his hard, muscular body. He was lean and tan. There were visible scars across his chest and stomach. A large white scar went halfway around his left thigh.

He dove into the pool and began a long, smooth crawl. His back caused her to walk to the edge of the pool and stare. There were pencil-thin white scars criss-crossing his back like the scratches of barbed wire--the kind of scars a person only could get from an excruciating experience. She wondered how it could have happened. Then she recalled Jim Moore saying that Stevens had been tortured by the Communists. She felt a cold chill run down her spine.

Despite the evidence of injury, his back muscles rippled as he swam effortlessly. She felt an erotic sensation, and she remembered last night. Suddenly, for reasons she couldn't understand, she wanted to know this scarred warrior more intimately.

After 30 minutes, he climbed from the pool. Toweling himself, he joined her at the poolside table.

71

Alana looked at his hard, lean body. His scars seemed to accentuate his toughness, as if they were trophies to be worn with pride. She poured him a glass of orange juice.

"Thank you, Mrs. Ames."

"Did you sleep well, General?" she smiled, mockingly. "You must have worn Sallie out, for she usually is an early bird."

He looked her straight in the eye and replied: "Yes, to the first question; no comment on the second. Sallie is a most charming lady. I enjoyed her company."

His eyes held hers, and she shivered. "I'm sorry," she said, "I had no right to question you."

"Apology accepted," he said. Toasting her with his orange juice he said, "Truce?"

She changed the subject. "I am really glad that you are going to be joining the company, General. Dad is a great guy to work for. Of course, I'm a little bit prejudiced."

"I'm looking foward to it. For me, the Army has grown a bit stale."

"You mean there is no war--no one to fight--don't you?"

"Perhaps," he admitted.

This man is no phony, she thought. She found herself feeling relaxed and enjoying his company. They began to eat breakfast in silence.

She felt cheated by the interruption when Paul walked up with a Bloody Mary in his hands.

"Good morning, General." He leaned over and kissed Alana on the cheek. "Dear," he said. His breath smelled of stale liquor. She made a face and turned away.

About 11:00, General Moore and Alana began a tennis match. Afterward they all sat around the pool and made small talk.

Sallie showed up about noon. She came directly over to Stevens and sat down on his lap, put her arms around him, and kissed him. "Good morning, Frank." She pulled him out of his chair and gently pushed him into the pool. Then she dove in behind him and swam over and whispered in his ear: "Again, please?" Stevens gently ducked her.

Later, while the men sat talking business, Alana and Sallie were alone. "Sallie, you're being a little obvious, aren't you?"

"What do you mean?"

"With Frank--you know what I mean--and wipe that silly grin off your face. You look like the Cheshire cat that ate the golden canary."

"No--last night he got my golden canary," laughed Sallie.

"Sallie Jones! You are horrible!"

"I know it, 'n ain't it grand? What a man! I think he's the most man I've ever met. Last night was the most fantastic night I have ever spent. It felt like I was giving birth to a covey of quail, and every third one was a turkey! Imagine!"

Alana shook her head and smiled. Sallie was Sallie! She would never change, but Alana loved her like a sister, anyway.

"Lani, I think you are jealous! You are, aren't you? You're jealous of Frank."

"No, of course not. To me he's just another one of Dad's employees."

"But a great lover--don't forget that," chided Sallie.

"O.K., if you say so Sallie. I, for one, never intend to find out." Alana wondered why the words sounded unconvincing, even to herself.

"I'm going to spend this weekend with him," Sallie said.

Alana felt a stab of envy. Why should she care? They both were free, consenting adults. She looked over at Stevens, deep in an animated conversation with her father. Yes, quite a man, she thought.

4

Immediately upon returing to Fort Irwin, Stevens called the General Officer Branch, Department of the Army, and informed them of his intention to retire. Two hours later he received a call from the Chief of Staff's office, ordering him to report to the Chief ASAP (as soon as possible). The next afternoon, he was ushered into the Chief's office.

General Cunnings shook his hand. "Sit down, Frank."

Cunnings sat down at his desk and lighted a cigar. "The minute I heard that you wanted to retire I sent for you. I was all set to ream your ass and talk you out of such nonsense; however, I received a call from the State Department this morning. It was highly suggested that I not interfere. What is this damned nonsense, Frank?"

Stevens explained the details. General Cunnings listened intently.

When Frank finished, the General took a deep puff from his cigar, coughed, and snubbed it out in the ashtray. "Well, Frank, I hate to see you leave. We had something planned for you. But, just remember this--Generals never really retire. I can tell you one thing for sure. If we get into another shootin' match, I'll have your ass back in uniform so fast you won't know what hit you!"

After assuring the Chief that this was exactly what he wanted to do and thanking him for his concern, Stevens left the Pentagon. He caught the next plane back to California.

Stevens set about the innocuous task of retiring and the critical task of selecting his team for the Saudi Project. The first name on his list was David Braxton. The black giant, who had stood beside him in many battles in many places, was serving as the Sergeant Major of the Special Forces at Fort Bragg, NC. The two soldiers were closer than brothers. Their friendship had been forged in battle and tempered by blood, sweat and gunpowder. Stevens would no more think of going on a critical operation without Braxon than he would without a weapon.

The second man was Tom Purdy. Purdy, now retired, was the General's Executive Officer when Stevens commanded the 1st Ranger Battalion. Tom Purdy was an experienced expert in special operations and, even more important, he was a brilliant manager and organizer. Stevens wanted Purdy as his second-in-command.

The third man was British. Percy Winters was Stevens' Commander when the American General served with the British in South Yemen. An original member of the Special Air Service, Winters had fought in Korea, Malaya, Africa, South Yemen, and Northern Ireland. Winters was a bona fide expert in counterinsurgency.

The fourth man was another Brit--Lieutenant Colonel James Brolin, an expert in gathering intelligence. They had met when Brolin was the Regimental Intelligence Officer in South Yemen. He possessed an uncanny knack for producing reliable and current information. His work in Northern Ireland had moved him to number three on the IRA hit list. After retirement, he changed his name, for security reasons, to Arthur Devlin, and he became a civilian instructor at the United Kingdom Staff Officer's College. Brolin was small, wiry, and looked as if a decent wind would blow him away. However, his appearance was deceiving. Brolin was a martial arts expert, an avid marathoner, and tough as nails. He still covered over 100 miles a week in training. His other skills were better suited to the field than to the classroom.

Brolin's basic prisoner interrogation philosophy was "if the information will save our chaps' lives, I will get it!" An avid student of psychology and an expert in mind manipulation, Brolin seldom resorted to brutality. However, if it were necessary, if there wasn't time enough to go through the longer process, he also was an expert in the art of inflicting pain. Brolin usually started an interrogation by saying: "By Jove! I hope I don't have to crush your balls. That's rather messy, you know?"

FORT BRAGG, NORTH CAROLINA

Command Sergeant Major David Braxton was not the type of man one could forget easily--six foot five in his stocking feet and 290 pounds of solid muscle. Braxton kept himself fighting fit by practicing karate and weight-lifting. His muscular black body was toned to perfection. A Master Parachutist with over 700 jumps, he was an imposing figure in his uniform: jump boots, green beret, and five rows of combat ribbons.

When he received the call from General Stevens saying, "I need you," there was no hesitation. The fact that he would have to retire from the Army to go with Stevens didn't faze him. He knew the General well enough to realize that there would be action, and Stevens wouldn't dare go into a firefight without him! This welcome call to arms was just the tonic he needed after nearly two years of inactivity. His adrenalin started pumping in anticipation of a "last hurrah"!

SAN FRANCISCO

Tom Purdy, Professor of Psychology, Stanford University,

read the telegram again:

TOM I NEED YOU FOR JOB IN SAUDI ARABIA. GOOD PAY COME SEE ME ASAP.

FRANK STEVENS

Twenty-four hours later, Purdy walked into Stevens' office, shook the General's hand, and eased his bulk into a chair. With a sigh, he reached down and let his belt out a notch. He had gained forty pounds since hanging up his battlegear. Damn Eleanor! His wife had taken up gourmet cooking since he retired. If he didn't know how much she loved him, he might think she had some bizzare scheme to fatten him to death. He concluded she must be as bored as he was with their present situation.

Stevens looked across the desk at his massive friend. "Tom, you're getting fat!"

"I know it, General," returned Purdy. "It's the damned candy-assed civilian life I've been leading. I find it really difficult to stir up the incentive to trim down."

"Well, Tom, if you want this job you're going to have to lose weight fast."

After Stevens explained the operation, Purdy readily accepted the job as Executive Officer. "When do I leave?" he asked eagerly.

"Just as soon as you lose 40 pounds and get your personal affairs in order. I want you to get over there, get the camp set up, and start selecting damned good men."

DEVONSHIRE, ENGLAND

Percy Winters was trying, but not too successfully, to be a country gentleman. He stomped into the kitchen, leaving a trail of mud on the tile floor, and muttering under his breath. He took the cup of steaming tea from his wife.

"Why Percy," his wife chirped. "Whatever is wrong?"

"It's those bloody-fucking sheep again!" he stormed in his heavy cockney brogue. "They've gotten through the bloody-fucking fence again, and now they're in that bloody-

77

fucking Haversheim's garden again!"

Long ago Nora had become accustomed to his crude language and stormy antics. Somehow they had muddled through a loving marriage and had seven children in the process. Because his career kept him away from home much of the time, the burden of rearing the children had fallen upon her.

The last time he returned, it was to stay. His left arm had been blown off by an IRA booby trap. Not used to having him underfoot all the time, he was beginning to wear on her nerves.

She reached into her apron pocket and withdrew a folded paper. "By the way, Dearie, this tele arrived for you this morning." She unfolded the paper and held it out to him.

PERCY: I NEED YOU AS MY OPERATIONS OFFICER IN SAUDI ARABIA. THE OLD DESERT LEGION IS GOING TO RIDE AGAIN. IF INTERESTED, WIRE ME, AND I WILL SEND PLANE TICKET TO COME AND DISCUSS THE OPERATION.

FRANK STEVENS

Percy read the telegram and exclaimed, "Great God in the morning--I'm saved!"

His wife read the telegram and thought: "Great God in the morning--I'm saved!" She turned to him. "Well, you'd better get your bloody-fucking sheep out of Haversheim's garden before you go."

During the Korean War, Percy had started out in the ranks. He moved to officer status strictly by process of elimination. At the end of three months on the front lines there were no officers left, and Percy found himself commanding the company. He served with such distinction that he was given a direct commission. After Korea, he fought the Communist guerrillas in Malaya. It was here that his reputation as a guerrilla fighter was established as his company conducted one successful operation after another.

It was Northern Ireland that had ended his career. Fighting the IRA was a frustrating assignment for the British Colonel. It was almost like brother fighting brother. The enemy was faceless and of his own race. The foe could be the 12-year-old on his bicycle, the old man pushing a car, or even the young mother carrying a baby in her arms. This was a difficult war: the ambushes, the assassinations, and the bombings--especially the bombings where innocent bystanders were killed and maimed. A bomb is an impersonal weapon; anyone in the blasting radius can get hit.

One morning as Percy opened his car door to drive to work there was a horrible, blinding, deafening explosion. The car erupted in a ball of flame, throwing him back against a nearby building. He sat up dazed, realizing that he was lucky to be alive. Then, when he tried to push himself up with his left hand, he fell over. His arm was gone--blown off above the elbow! They found him like that, lying on his face, unable to get up, his life blood pumping out of his stump in great spurts.

Percy survived. He fought medical retirement, but he lost. His beloved Army put him out to pasture, and his 25 years of experience in fighting guerrillas and terrorists was being wasted raising sheep.

FORT IRWIN

Jimmy Brolin and Percy Winters were reunited after a five-year void. Percy peered over his whiskey at Stevens. "I say, Frank, do you think we can get the bloody-fucking wogs to fight?"

"First of all, Percy, you've got to quit calling them bloody-fucking wogs!"

"Ah hell, you know me, General," Winters smiled sheepishly, "I call everything bloody-fucking."

Stevens knew this was true and that old war dogs like Percy didn't change their spots. One thing for sure, this was one "old dog" that the General wanted on his team.

★ ★ ★ ★ ★

His selection of key personnel was completed when, following the advice of General Moore, he chose retired Lieutenant Colonel Scott Warner as his Logistics Officer. Although Stevens didn't know Warner, the ex-Army officer was a two-year veteran of the Saudi Modernization Program and a known figure, respected by the Saudis. Already being in the area, Warner could commence organizing the supply and maintenance aspects of the venture.

He selected three Americans and one Rhodesian for his troop commanders. He didn't know the Rhodesian, but the ex-Major had an impressive resume, with seven years experience as a troop commander with the Gray Scouts fighting the "Ters."

With his selection complete, Stevens set about the business of retiring. He would miss the Army. It had been a way of life since he was 17. At the same time, he felt stagnated. He needed a new direction--a new challenge. The fact that General Moore was involved was the major deciding factor. If Jim Moore needed him--then there was really no discussion involved. Besides, he had a "gut feeling" that it was the thing to do; and he had learned a long time ago to always go with his intuition.

5

On the morning of Stevens' retirement, the sun rose bright in a cloudless, blue sky. Winter in the California desert is the most scenic and pleasant time of the year. The nights are cool, and the days are warm and comfortable. The crisp mornings call for a light jacket until about 10:00 a.m. The desert looks alive and vibrant. Small flowers cover the desert floor and bathe it in a kaleidoscope of bright colors. A great time for photo-bugs, hikers, campers, and lovers. A great time of the year to have a retirement ceremony.

The thick grass that covered the parade field was dark green. By mid-July, it would be burned brown by the hot desert sun.

This was not to be the usual retirement ceremony, for the soldier being honored was not an average soldier. He was Brigadier General Frank Stevens, Medal of Honor recipient and the most decorated soldier in the Army--the man the newspapers called "the greatest fighting man since Audie Murphy!--a genuine American hero!"

The 3d Brigade, 82d Airborne Division--which he once commanded--the 82d Airborne Division Band, and a battalion of the U.S. Special Forces were flown in from Fort Bragg to do the honors. No one less than General Robert

Mace (the CG, U.S. Army Forces Command, the four-star in charge of all U.S. Army combat forces in the United States, Alaska, and Panama) was on hand to be the reviewing officer.

General and Mrs. James Moore, William Emerson, and Alana drove from Ventura to attend the ceremony. Alana was hesitant to accept the invitation since Paul was in Washington on business, but Mary Moore convinced her to go. Alana never had seen a retirement parade, and she was awed by the spectacle of soldiers marching onto the field in camouflaged battle dress. The paratroopers were wearing maroon berets, and the Special Forces were in their green berets.

They were seated in the front row, to the right of the reviewing stand. According to Mary, this space is reserved for immediate family. On the way from Ventura, Mary had confided that Frank was just like a son to them and that he spent the holidays with them whenever he could.

"Doesn't he have a family?" Alana asked.

"No. No one now. His parents died when he was very young, and an Uncle raised him. His Uncle died a few years ago, so I guess that Jim and I are the closest thing to a family that he has."

Alana noted that the end chair on the left in their row was vacant and was draped with a black cloth. She leaned across the others to read the nametag: "Nuyen Stevens."

Mary explained. "Nuyen was Frank's wife. She was killed while Frank was a prisoner. It's a long story, which I will tell you sometime if you're interested."

Mary's statement peaked Alana's interest in this legendary soldier. Ever since she had met him, he had been on her mind. She found herself thinking of him more and more. She was drawn to his name. She could shut her eyes and see him naked--in the pool with Sallie. There was something about him that stirred strange feelings within her--feelings that she didn't understand. He certainly was different than

82

any man she had ever known. Maybe that was it, she thought. Maybe it was because he was so different. Maybe that was why he confused her emotions.

★　★　★　★　★

As Frank Stevens and General Mace stepped onto the reviewing stand, the band sounded "Attention." After moving his staff members to their correct positions, the Commander of Troops brought the soldiers to "Present Arms," then he faced about, saluted the reviewing stand, and announced: "Sir, the Command is formed."

General Moore returned his salute, and the Troop Commander faced about and gave several commands which finally brought the formation to "Parade Rest."

Stevens and the four-star general moved from the stand, joined the Commander of Troops, and marched out to the formation. As the band played "Colonel Bogie's March," they passed in front of the assembled soldiers.

"This is called 'Reviewing the Troops'," General Moore explained to Alana. As they marched in front of the assembled soldiers, each unit commander saluted, and the men stood at attention, their heads and eyes turned to the right to follow the two generals as they passed in front of their formation. After circling the command, Generals Mace and Stevens shook hands with the Commander of Troops and returned to the stand.

The Commander of Troops marched over and brought the flags forward to stop 15 feet in front of the reviewing stand. The Army Flag, with its multiple battle streamers blowing in the light breeze, was an emotional sight. The announcer asked the audience to stand while the National Anthem was played. There were tears in Alana's eyes as she listened to the stirring music.

After a series of commands, the troops were back at "Parade Rest." Stevens moved out and stood at attention in front of the colors. General Mace stepped forward and pinned a medal on the retiring soldier as the announcer read the citation for the Distinguished Service Medal. He followed this by reading the Orders for Retirement.

The two Generals returned to the stand. First, General Mace read a letter written by the Army Chief of Staff lauding Stevens' bravery and his contributions to the country. Then Mace gave a personal speech discussing the retiring soldier's many accomplishments.

Alana glanced at the program she had been holding. There was a picture of Frank in his green uniform. Around his neck hung the blue-ribboned Medal of Honor, and his chest was covered with many other awards. Quite a dashing figure, she thought!

She read his biographical sketch:

"Brigadier General Frank Stevens enlisted in the Army in 1956, at the age of 17, and was selected in 1957 to attend the U.S. Army Military Academy. He was commissioned a lieutenant in the Infantry in 1961. . . ."

"General Stevens has a Master's Degree in Political Science from Auburn University and a Master's Degree in Personnel Management from Harvard University."

Alana skipped through his various assignments and looked at the last paragraph:

"B.G. Stevens' awards include the Congressional Medal of Honor, two Distinguished Service Crosses, three Silver Stars, three Legions of Merit, five Bronze Stars with 'V' for Valor, five Meritorious Service Medals, 12 Air Medals, and six Purple Hearts."

[There were numerous lesser awards listed.]

"His foreign awards include the British Miltary Cross for Valor, and four awards of the Vietnamese Cross for Gallantry."

Alana couldn't be sure, but it looked impressive to her!

After General Mace concluded, Frank Stevens stepped over to the microphone. His speech was surprisingly short. He thanked the troops for their participation and complimented them on their appearance. He thanked the spectators for coming. He concluded by saying that it had been an honor to serve his country.

When he finished speaking, the colors were marched back to the formation. Then a drummer began a slow, steady roll. The announcer said: "At this time, the Special Forces soldiers who served with the General in Vietnam wish to honor the memory of Mrs. Stevens who was killed in action while aiding the Special Forces in that country."

Seven soldiers, wearing green berets, marched toward the reviewing stand. They were led by a giant black man whose massive hand dwarfed the bouquet of red roses he was carrying. They stopped ten paces in front of the Generals. Command Sergeant Major David T. Braxton moved forward and placed the roses in front of the vacant chair. Then he stepped back and saluted. The band struck up Sergeant Barry Sadler's "The Ballad of the Green Beret."

General Stevens trained his eyes on Braxton. His face was taut and bare of expression or emotion. Then Alana saw a single tear slowly run down his cheek, and his lips quivered slightly. She was overcome with an emotion she did not understand. She felt tears welling up in her own eyes, and she stifled a sob. She turned to Mary, who was crying unashamedly. Even General Moore was moved by the unusual touch in the ceremony. He took his handkerchief from his pocket and passed it to his wife.

The Sergeant rejoined the small group of Green Berets, and they all saluted the General. Stevens moved off the reviewing stand and shook hands with each one of the soldiers. Then he stopped in front of Braxton, who held out his hand. Stevens ignored it and put his arms around the Sergeant. Then he stepped back, and in a voice loud enough to be heard by most of the dignitaries, he said: "I love you, you big ugly son of a bitch!" Stevens returned to the stand.

The command was given: "Pass in Review." The troops stepped off, led by the Commander of Troops and the Band. They marched past the reviewing stand. As each unit came by, its Commander saluted and ordered: "EYES RI-GHT!"

The unit guidons went up into the air, then dipped in a salute. As the last troop unit passed, the Band played the "Army Song," and a flight of phantom jets screamed low over the field with a thundering roar.

Then three C-130's flew over in tight formation, and the 2nd Ranger Battalion jumped, in honor of their first Commander. The sky was filled with 500 paratroopers in full battlegear.

William Emerson turned to Moore. "That was the most impressive ceremony I have ever witnessed."

"Don't forget, Bill," returned Moore, "the Army is saying goodby to its greatest living legend."

Alana turned to Mary. Both women were dabbing tears from their eyes. "Whew," she sniffed. "I'm glad I'm not married to a soldier. I don't think I could stand too many ceremonies like that!"

"It's something you never get inured to," said Mary. "They are all tearjerkers, but this ceremony was just a little more touching than most, especially for Jim and me."

Retired Brigadier General Frank Stevens finally extricated himself from the throng of well-wishers and moved in their direction. He picked up the roses and handed them to Mary Moore, who promptly hugged them.

Stevens, his face impassive, nodded to Alana. Then, shaking Emerson's hand, he said: "I'm glad you could come." Any emotion he had shown on the reviewing stand had disappeared.

The huge, black NCO joined him, and he introduced Braxton to Emerson and his daughter. For just an instant, Stevens' cold gray eyes settled on Alana, and she felt disturbed. A cold chill edged down her spine, and she was aware of the magnetism of his presence. His eyes were overpowering. She wanted to reach out and touch him, but she gained control and chided herself for her weakness. Stevens turned and walked to the waiting sedan.

The wind picked up, and Alana glanced at the vacant chair. The black cloth rippled angrily in the breeze.

6

Dressed in his pale blue Bedouin robes, the Libyan leader looked up from his paperwork as his Chief of Intelligence entered the office.

Colonel Amak, once thin and tough, was beginning to show the rigors of the good life. His paunchy stomach drooped over his too-tight uniform trousers, and the buttons of his shirt strained against his growing bulk. Before entering Khadafy's office, he had eaten several mints to conceal last night's excessive quantity of liquor. He knew that if he were caught drinking, the punishment would be severe. Amak handed a manila folder to his leader. "Your Excellency, we may have a problem developing in Saudi Arabia. According to reports I have received, the CIA has persuaded the Saudis to allow them to station a unit of mercenaries at Riyadh. One of the CIA's top agents, Brigadier General Frank Stevens, has been selected as the commander. The primary mission of the unit is supposed to be to help the Saudis maintain internal order, but the unit also will train with battalions from Saudi Arabia, Egypt, and Sudan."

Khadafy sat quietly for a minute, pondering the information. He riffled through the papers in the folder, then he looked up at his Intel Chief: "Mustapha, this could cause trouble. Any strengthening of the Saudi Forces may delay our plans. What do you know about this Stevens?"

"He's a well-known war hero in America, Your Excellency, and he has worked for the CIA on several special missions. The Russian KGB has a file on him, and I'm trying to get a copy."

"That's good. Find out all you can about him. He can only do us harm. Do you have any agents in Riyadh that you can assign to watch him?"

"Yes Sir," answered Amak, "one of the best."

Khadafy thought for a while, then he spoke: "I think we should plan to eliminate Stevens the first chance we get. Do not kill him inside Saudi Arabia--that would be politically dangerous. Get him the first time he leaves the country."

★ ★ ★ ★ ★

RIYADH, SAUDI ARABIA

The Saudi Airline's 707 began its long, gradual descent into the Riyadh Airport. The plane bucked and shook as it hit turbulent desert thermals caused by a sandstorm on the desert surface. Visibility was poor, but the American pilot decided to try to land anyway. Just before touchdown, the pilot realized that they were going to miss the runway. He reversed the flaps and gave the huge bird full power. The nose of the 707 turned skyward and, with a great shudder, began to climb. The next 20 seconds were long and frightening as the sand and swirling winds tried to push the plane back onto the ground. Finally, the struggling cabin crew fought the bird above the turbulence and headed back to Dhahran.

Stevens well-remembered the fierce desert sandstorms from his first visit to Saudi Arabia. They were called Zawabeis. They came fast and sometimes lasted for several days. A 50-mile-an-hour wind picks up the fine desert sand

and blows it with such force that it feels like thousands of little pins stabbing at your face. At times, the desert traveler is unable to see three feet ahead. The roaring, swirling dust sometimes is several miles deep and thousands of feet high. Like many things in the desert, the Zawabei can, and does, kill! There is an old Arab saying: "Death rides on the winds of a Zawabei."

After a three-hour delay in Dhahran, the airliner returned to Riyadh. The Zawabei had subsided, and they made a safe landing.

Jim Moore was on hand to meet Stevens, and after collecting his luggage, they began the 45-minute drive to Camp Emerson. Stevens was impressed by the changes in the Saudi Capital. Three years ago, the tallest building in the city was five stories high. Now there were scores of eight- and ten-story structures dotting the downtown lanscape. New buildings were going up everywhere, and hundreds of tall construction cranes jutted up into the sky like TV antennas in the Bronx. General Moore read Steven's mind: "They say the national bird of Saudi Arabia is the steel construction crane."

Stevens could believe that. There surely must be a plan, thought Stevens, but it looks like runaway construction.

The other sign of rapid modernization was the thousands of cars crowding the streets. Out of every 1000, it looked like 999 were of Japanese make. Toyota pickups were everywhere. "I'll be damned!" exclaimed Stevens. "The Japanese really have cornered the automobile market here."

Just ahead of them a Mazda sedan smashed into the side of a white Toyota pickup. Traffic never slowed; it merely detoured around the smashed vehicles.

"Last week," declared Moore, "I counted 164 wrecked cars between my home and the Training Directorate--a distance of nine kilometers. When a car is wrecked, the Saudis just pull it off the road and leave it. Once in a while, if the King or one of the Princes is going to drive along a certain road, there is a crash cleanup campaign. Just a few miles east of Riyadh is the largest pile of wrecked cars I have ever seen."

"The small Japanese cars don't seem to hold up too well in accidents," observed Stevens, looking at the mangled hulks on the side of the road.

"No, I think the American car manufacturers are losing out here when they could be taking over the market," said Moore, as their driver swerved the car to avoid a Mercedes truck. "It's apparent that the larger American cars are holding up better, and with gas 17 cents a gallon, there isn't a great need for the small cars. Hell, by conducting a simple, honest advertising campaign pointing out the advantages, I think the Saudis would go for the larger, tougher U.S.-made cars."

As they neared the compound, Moore turned to Stevens. "By the way, Frank, we are invited to the Emersons for dinner tonight, if you feel up to it. Bill and Alana arrived yesterday from their home in Athens."

Stevens nodded, then wondered why he felt a desire to see Paul Ames' wife again.

The compound was a cluster of cement block buildings. Three modern high rises were under construction. Just inside the gate were several family-style quarters, where Moore and his directors lived with their families.

"We have 1,200 personnel living in the compound," offered Moore, "and 300 living in villas downtown. During the last few months, we have made a significant improvement in the quality of life for the employees. We have cable TV, an outdoor and indoor movie theater, a nice swimming pool, two tennis courts, a small gymnasium, outdoor volleyball and basketball courts, a billiards room, lapidary shop, library, and a compound exchange--all of the comforts of home, almost! Alcohol absolutely is forbidden in the camp."

On the way to dinner, Stevens thought about Alana. For

reasons he couldn't quite fathom, Mrs. Paul Ames had been much on his mind of late. He could close his eyes and see her long, raven-black hair and her huge brown eyes. It was not like him to give a second thought to a married woman. His steadfast credo was that he never messed around with anyone's wife. However, there was something about this cold, aloof woman that attracted him.

Moore broke into his thoughts as the driver stopped the car in front of the quarters. "Mary and I would like you to stay with us tonight. I'll take you over to your job site tomorrow."

Alana was in the kitchen busily preparing dinner. She was dressed in a blue silk cocktail dress, with a white apron covering her gown. Her growing anticipation of seeing the lean, stone-faced General again bothered her.

Her father walked in. "My, aren't we becoming very domestic? Where is that hard-headed business executive of mine?" He opened the oven and sniffed the prime rib. "Um! Smells good!"

William Emerson could be called a self-made man. A graduate engineer, he was drafted during World War II and advanced to command of a heavy Construction Battalion in the Engineer Corps, specializing in building airfields. After the war, he started his own construction company. His first major contract was building an Army base in Thule, Greenland. Several fat government contracts followed, and he made his first million three years later. At 61, he was lean, fit, and tanned. His thick white hair was unruly and belied his otherwise usually neat appearance. He never lost the common touch. He still enjoyed rolling up his sleeves and getting into the saddle of a giant D-9 bulldozer.

His wife had died when Alana was 10, and he never remarried. There had been plenty of women--Emerson still was very sexually active. He never had the son he wanted, so Alana became his whole life. He sent her to the best schools and was proud of the business sense she had developed. He had been pleased when Alana and Paul were married. In him he hoped to find the son he had always wanted. He immediately brought his new son-in-law into the corporate structure and began grooming him to become the Vice President. Paul had turned out to be a disappointment. The man was weak. Before long, Emerson realized he never could turn the company over to him. Paul was a good lawyer, and capable in that field, but the boy lacked business sense. On the other hand, Alana was strong--too strong for her husband, and she quickly outperformed him in the decision-making end of the business. Emerson began giving her more and more responsibility. To the outside world she was his administrative assistant, but in reality she helped to run the business.

Paul was a proud man, and Alana's achievements hurt him. Bill was well-aware of Paul's womanizing and his increasing drinking problem. He also was aware that Alana had never gotten pregnant, and that she and Paul slept in separate bedrooms. She was fast becoming a frustrated, hard woman, who lived only to work. At times she treated her husband like an employee. It was to the point that she had Paul hardly spoke to one another anymore.

Lately he had noticed a change in his daughter--ever since Frank Stevens had entered their lives. This morning she began to get ready at 8 o'clock. She had been buzzing around all day, checking this, then that. Twice she had changed dresses. He was certain that even she was not conscious of her change of attitude. At any rate, something, or someone, was putting a sparkle in his daughter's eyes, and she was acting years younger. Emerson was sure he knew the answer but pushed it from his mind as none of his business.

General Moore, Mary, and Frank arrived at 7 p.m. They were ushered into the spacious Emerson villa by a Filipino servant smartly dressed in a white serving jacket and black trousers.

Emerson shook hands with the men and kissed Mary on

the cheek. "As you know," he smiled wickedly, "I can't offer you booze because alcohol is forbidden in the Kingdom, but I think you'll like my tea."

The Filipino brought in a tray. Stevens' tea turned out to be a fine American bourbon with a dash of water.

Alana floated into the room. She looked more alluring than ever. The blue silk dress set off her hair and her enormous eyes to perfect advantage. She kissed General and Mrs. Moore and extended her hand to Stevens. Her touch gave him a tingling sensation, and her eyes captured his and lingered for an instant. Stevens remembered a verse from an old poem:

"Her eyes stole into my heart
and petrified my soul."

Over dinner, Alana was vivacious and charming as she and Mary discussed the role of women in the Saudi society.

"I think the thing that bothers me most," said Mary, "is that we can't drive a car. I miss just jumping in the car and taking off."

"Not Alana," interposed Bill. "She can't stand the fact that she can't put in her two-cents worth when I'm having a business meeting with the Saudis."

"You're right, Dad," Alana agreed, "and one of these days the women here are going to stand up for their rights."

"Maybe--in about 200 years," added her father.

"Well, I'm glad we don't have to have four wives," mused Moore.

Mary leaned over and said to her husband: "You mean you would like to have four wives, don't you?"

"Hell no, Honey. I have enough problems trying to take care of the one I have!"

As they were having coffee, Stevens complimented Alana. "That was an excellent dinner. You are a lady of many talents."

"Alana is really quite a good cook, as well as an outstanding executive," seconded her father. "In the old days she used to do all of the cooking."

Stevens turned to her. "I just can't picture you slaving away in the kitchen." The fact that Alana Ames, heir to her father's millions, could cook had never occurred to him.

"Why not? Good cooks run in our family. Dad is the best backyard-barbecuer in California. You should taste his barbecued tri-tips. Just last month, the President offered Dad a job as official White House Barbecuer," she kidded.

She looked over at Stevens. "What do you hear from Sallie?" She immediately regretted her question and wondered why she had blurted that out.

"I had dinner with her in San Francisco before I took off. She sends you her love."

When the others went into Emerson's recreation room to play billiards, Stevens found himself sitting alone with Alana. He became acutely aware of a sweet and gentle fragrance. He felt strangely uncomfortable with her nearness. He sensed her loneliness. After meeting her husband, he understood why. He also sensed fear. Alana was afraid of him!

Alana was uncomfortable too. Whenever he looked at her she felt numb, and definitely uneasy. It was almost as if he could read her innermost thoughts. It bothered her pride that he could disturb her so much.

Finally she broke the awkward silence. "You don't like me very much, do you?" She spoke in a low voice so the others in the next room could not hear.

Stevens was surprised at her question. He stared at her in silence for a few seconds, trying to form an answer. He finally answered a question with a question: "What on earth gave you that idea?"

"Well, the way you look at me," she stammered. "It is impolite, and it bothers me!"

He lowered his eyes, then speaking slowly he said: "I'm sorry; I never realized that I was disturbing you."

"Well--you do!" she snapped back.

Stevens stood up and looked down at her. "You disturb

me, too, Mrs. Ames. You disturb me because you awaken feelings that I had thought were long dead. If you have seen anything in my eyes, I can assure you that it wasn't dislike. I'm sorry, and I'll make every effort not to bother you in the future."

He turned and walked into the other room.

Alana smarted from his words. She was more confused than ever.

7

Stevens was happy to be back with combat troops again. Tom Purdy and the staff had been busy. The key personnel were all on board, and the squadron would soon be up to strength. General Moore had been correct; there was no end of volunteers. The major problem was weeding out unacceptable personnel.

When the selection finally was complete, the squadron was composed of 300 Americans, 100 British, and smaller numbers of South Africans, Rhodesians, Koreans, Thais, and Jordanians.

The average age of the mercenaries was 37, and almost all were combat veterans. Since the men were experienced soldiers, the most important aspect of Stevens' job would be to mold them together as a team.

By the time Stevens arrived, Purdy had organized the squadron, and the units were busily engaged in range firing, physical training, and familiarization and maintenance of the V-150's.

The Cadillac-Gage V-150 Commando is an ideal vehicle for desert warfare: fast (55 mph on highways) and maneuverable, with a 25″ ground clearance to help in cross-country operations. Special "run-flat" tires allow more than

25 miles of travel, even after a bullet puncture. The vehicle is amphibious, and one of the best aspects is that it is easy to maintain.

The V-150's proved themselves to the Saudis in 1979, when a well-armed group of religious fanatics took over the Al Haram Mosque in Mecca--the holiest place in Islam. The Grand Mosque, with its myriad of corridors, tunnels, and storerooms and built of thick concrete, made an almost impregnable fort. The Saudis were reluctant to use heavy artillery or air for fear of damaging the holy place. The fanatics held out for 20 days, until the Saudi National Guard, using V-150's as firing platforms, moved into the Mosque and blasted them out. Several weeks later, in three different cities, the 69 survivors had their heads chopped off--on the same day.

The mercenary squadron was composed of several variations of the V-150 Commando, including:

--Forty-one Armored Personnel Carriers, each carrying an 11-man rifle squad and mounting a .50 caliber heavy and a 7.62mm light machine gun. Firing ports at the sides allowed the squad to fire their individual weapons from the vehicle.

--Twelve V-150's were Dual Machine Gun Vehicles, carrying a crew of four and mounting a .50 cal. and a 7.62mm machine gun.

--Nine of the V-150 Commandos carried 81mm mortars and a crew of four. They were to provide close-in indirect fire support.

--Nine Commandos, fitted with 90mm high velocity direct fire guns for use against armor and heavy fortifications.

--Three V-150's armed with 20mm Oerlikon cannon, effective against light armored vehicles and fortifications.

--Eight Command vehicles carrying a crew of four and armed with a .50 cal. and a 7.62mm machine gun. These cars were fitted with beefed-up communications for command and control.

--Six Commandos carrying the TOW missile system provided the primary anti-tank protection for the squadron.

--Six armored cars, armed with 20mm Vulcan Gatling guns which fire 3,000 rounds per minute. This weapon system is excellent against low-flying aircraft and devastating against personnel and soft-skin vehicles.

--Eight V-300's, each carrying a 105mm howitzer, provided artillery support. This vehicle is a stretch-version of the smaller V-150, 36 inches longer and having six wheels rather than four.

--Other V-150's modified for use as ambulances, recovery vehicles, and communications vehicles.

The squadron of 860 men was organized into three rifle companies and one artillery battery, supported by a headquarters company composed of maintenance, communications, mess, medical and reconnaissance sections.

The three rifle companies had a strength of 164 men mounted in 25 V-150 Commandos. Each company was organized into three rifle platoons, an anti-tank platoon, and an 81mm mortar platoon.

Later Stevens' force would train with three Mounted Infantry Battalions from Saudi Arabia, Egypt, and Sudan. After the training period, the Sudanese and Egyptian Battalions would return to their own countries. If the mercenary squadron was ever deployed to those countries, the Battalions would join them.

On his first day, Stevens had a meeting with his officers at 1400 hours. It was almost a family reunion since he had served before with many of them. Purdy called for silence, and Stevens rose to speak. "Gentlemen, this will be a short speech because I'll make a more detailed talk to the entire squadron sometime next week. It's good to see so many old friends here. I don't like that word 'old,' so let me correct myself. It's good to see so many of my experienced friends here. You are the leaders of the squadron, and your job is not going to be easy. The fact that this is a multinational force adds an extra challenge. Since most of us already are professional soldiers, our most difficult task is going to be to weld our men together as a team.

"At this stage in life, each of you has developed your own leadership styles. I'll accept that as long as it gets the desired results and as long as it doesn't clash too much with the mission. You are all being well-paid for your experience, so I expect first-rate performances.

"The men under you have varying degrees of experience; they speak different launguages; and they have many different customs. I expect you to treat them as individuals and to respect their customs.

"While we are on operations, we will live under the same conditions as the men. There won't be any frills for the leaders.

"We are going to build a unique force that will have an important part to play in maintaining stability in the Middle East. I'll withhold any further remarks until I speak to the whole squadron. We all know our jobs, so let's do them.

"What are your questions?" Stevens spent the better part of the next hour giving the answers.

When Alana and her father arrived at the Moores' for dinner, they found that Frank Stevens wasn't there.

"Frank called, and he has to work tonight," explained Moore.

Alana doubted that was true. She believed he probably was avoiding her because of their verbal exchange a few nights before. She felt a quick stab of disappointment because of his absence, and she cursed herself for caring. She wished she had never met this man who disturbed her thoughts and dreams.

After dinner, Mary Moore dug out one of her old photo albums to show pictures of her and Jim in their early years together. Among them was a photo of young Frank Stevens when he was a lieutenant.

"I almost didn't recognize him with a smile on his face," stated Alana.

"That picture was taken before the war," volunteered Mary. "Frank was a fun-loving person then, always joking and kidding; but, I guess things and time changes all of us," she said sadly. "When you see as much violence and death as he has, a person is bound to change somewhat."

Jim Moore broke in. "That's true, Honey, but Frank changed in that POW Camp in North Vietnam. When he returned, he was a different person. I don't know of any man alive that could go through what he did and not change."

Bill Emerson's curiosity was peaked. "Jim, just what happened to Frank in that camp?"

"Frank was quite a catch for the Communists," began Moore. "He had a lot of valuable information. Once they got him into that camp, they went to work on him with cold-blooded oriental efficiency in order to break him."

Jim Moore explained in graphic detail the tortures used on Stevens: the beatings, water torture, electric shock treatment, etc.

"Sergeant Braxton watched the beating that scarred his back," said Moore. "It was done with a metal rod, and each blow split the skin like a knife."

Alana sat transfixed, listening to the horrible details. She tried not to show any emotion; but she was shocked, and her hands trembled. As Jim Moore explained Frank's ordeal, she tried to imagine the pain he must have felt--but she could not, for pain is a difficult thing to imagine.

"They worked on him for 10 days," continued Moore, "but they couldn't break him. Then when his body was broken and his spirit weakened, they played their trump card! His wife, Nuyen, had been kidnapped in South Vietnam on her way to the airport where she was to fly to the States. Somehow they spirited her out and took her North, probably by boat. The Communists in the South received over half of their supplies by sea, so it wouldn't have been difficult to take her out by sampan."

General Moore paused and took a drink of his bourbon. Alana was mesmerized. She sat on the edge of her seat, still not quite understanding why she was so anxious to hear about Frank's wife.

Moore set his glass down. "Frank thought his wife was safe in the United States, waiting for him. When they produced her and tortured her as he watched, the shock was too much for him and he broke! In a desperate effort to save her, he confessed to false war crimes, and he told them everything they wanted to know. It was no use, for they tied him up and then tortured her to death in the hut next to him. Braxton said that she died very slowly--screaming most of the night."

Alana's hands were shaking. She realized now what was tormenting Frank's soul.

"My God!" exclaimed Emerson. "Can you imagine the torment he must have gone through, hearing his wife's screams? It's a wonder he didn't go completely insane!"

"I think he did," Moore said heavily, "and that's probably what saved him. There is no stimulus equal to revenge. Sometime during all of his pain and anguish, he went over the edge, and his heart grew cold. Every thought except revenge was forgotten.

"Somehow, he overpowered his guard; then, he went to the North Vietnamese Commander's hut and killed him. After freeing Braxton, he moved from hut to hut in a silent rage, killing them all. When it was over, he collapsed. Braxton loaded him into a truck and they headed south. When they ran out of gas, the sergeant carried him. Somehow they made it into South Vietnam and were picked up by a friendly patrol. By this time, they both were in pretty bad shape.

"Frank spent four months in the hospital in Japan. When he was discharged, he refused to go back to the States, so I put him back to work. However, this was a different Frank Stevens. He was a man obsessed--a man filled with guilt. He blamed himself for his wife's death, and he felt guilty about breaking under pressure. Frank became a cold-blooded fighting machine, not caring whether he lived or died. He took risks that others wouldn't. But, it seemed he possessed a talent that cannot be learned--the ability to survive under any circumstances. Instead of getting himself killed, his exploits just added to the legend."

There was a short period of silence, then Emerson spoke: "I don't see how he could have gone through all of that and still worked himself up to general's rank. He certainly is a remarkable man!"

"After several months," said Moore, "his blood-lust subsided, and he took over an Infantry Battalion. I believe the heavy mantle of combat command was just what he needed. He seemed to settle down into a somewhat normal military life. Frank deserves every honor he has received, including general's rank. In fact, he has done things for his country that no one will ever know about."

Alana was flooded with mixed emotions. What she had heard was shocking, but why should it affect her this much? She had read and heard other stories of man's inhumanity to man, so why was this so differrent? Her throat was dry. She took a sip of her drink, but it didn't help her relax. Her heart ached for Frank Stevens. She looked at her hands-- they were shaking.

Her father broke the deep silence. "I wonder why he has never remarried?"

"Well, he hasn't exactly been a monk as far as women are concerned," spoke up Moore. "There have been many who chased him, but I think he treated them as one-night stands. None of his affairs seemed to last very long."

"I don't think he'll ever love anyone again," interjected Mary. "I think he was hurt too much the first time to become emotionally involved again. But, I may be wrong." Her eyes fell on Alana. "He seems to have changed a bit lately."

Later that night, Alana lay in her bed, staring at the ceiling. Frank's cold, gray eyes haunted her. She was disturbed by the hot rush of her blood, and she felt a fierce hunger for the quiet soldier. She told herself that what she was feeling was pity.

The mercenaries milled around as they waited for their new commander to make his first appearance. It was only 0700, and the hot summer sun already was bearing down on the desert. A few of the "mercs" had served with the General before; most were aware of his exploits; and all knew the reputation of the legendary soldier.

Brigadier General Stevens stepped up to the microphone. He was wearing camouflaged fatigues and a green beret. There was no insignia nor rank on his uniform. The men stopped talking without a command and waited for Stevens to speak.

Finally the General broke the silence. "Men, I won't keep you long, but I thought it was time we became acquainted. I've studied each of your records, and I'm impressed. Each of you has been screened and selected for your particular military specialty. Your leaders are the best. They have been handpicked because of their demonstrated ability to command men in combat. It might interest you to know that, combined, we have over 10,000 years of military service and nearly 3,000 years of actual combat time. I don't believe any other military organization in the world can compare.

"Our mission will be to help the Saudis maintain order within the Kingdom. A healthy, stable government in Saudi Arabia is important for keeping peace in the Middle East

103

and for serving as a bulwark against the expansion of communism. We cannot afford another Iran in Saudi Arabia. Last, but not least, we will be helping to insure the continued flow of oil to the Free World.

"We are mercenaries, and that means we're getting paid to fight for a government other than our own. We are unique, because we are a multinational force. We must respect our differences if we are to survive and succeed.

"I know your reasons for being here vary. Some of you like to soldier and don't want any other life. Some of you are looking to fight communism. All of us are here for the money--and that's good. The only thing I can promise you is hard work and good pay. You will be the highest paid soldiers in the world, and I'll expect you to work hard to earn it.

"We're all subject to the laws of Saudi Arabia. Some of these laws are rather strict. Perhaps that's why Saudi Arabia has the lowest crime rate in the world. Handouts have been passed out explaining these laws in detail. You can be beheaded for crimes of murder, rape, and adultery. Most of you know that two Filipinos were beheaded in the public square just last week. For serious crimes of robbery and theft, you can loose a hand. Lesser crimes are punished by flogging and confinement. The making, selling, and drinking of alcohol is prohibited in the Kingdom. Now I would be foolish to tell a group of soldiers not to drink; so just let me say, if you get caught, you will be fired. If you get drunk and are picked up by the Saudi authorities, you will be in serious trouble. There will be very little that we can do to help you.

"Let's talk about reward and punishment within this outfit. For infractions of military discipline, you can be fired or fined. There'll be no medals for bravery or gallantry. If you excel, I will be able to give you a monetary reward.

"Since we are mercenaries, we will live by the 'Code of the Brotherhood,' similar to the pact made by pirate bands many years ago. You each will sign a pledge dedicating your allegiance to the people that pay us, to your leaders, and to your brother mercs. Any man that breaks the pledge will be tried by a group of men picked from the squadron. Under this code, for now I'll only set punishment for an act of cowardice in battle or for an act causing the death of a fellow merc. The punishment will be death by firing squad! I'm not trying to scare you, I just want you to know what you're getting into when you sign the pledge.

"I think that you will find that serving in this organization will be a unique and rewarding experience. I've been a soldier all of my adult life and have been fortunate enough to command several elite military units, but none with the experience and background that we have assembled here. I consider it an honor to be your commander, and I know that you are going to keep me hopping. Now, let's get to work!

8

Alana lay in bed waiting. She knew what was going to happen, and she dreaded it; but it wouldn't do any good to feign sleep. Paul had arrived that morning from the States, and as usual he drank heavily all day. After dinner, while Alana was in the kitchen, her father had finally spoken to Paul about his increasing drinking problem. They ended up in a heated argument. She had heard parts of it but did not join them.

"Paul, you should seek professional help," her father had suggested.

"I don't need it. I'm fine. I can stop drinking any time I want to. Have you seen anything wrong with my work?" Paul snapped back, defensively.

"No, Paul, not yet, but I'm afraid you might say something you shouldn't to the wrong people when you are drinking. This new venture is delicate, and--"

"Do you think I'd give out Corporation secrets?" interrupted the lawyer. "You should know better than that."

"Not when you're sober, son," said Emerson with growing impatience. "But when you're drinking, you talk too much. I would prefer that you go back and stay at the home office for the next two months."

"And what about Alana?" Paul asked angrily.

"Well, that's up to her, but I do need her here right now," answered the contractor, "at least until we finalize the contracts with the Saudis."

"She'd like that!" Paul shot back. "It would give her a chance to be near that soldier-boy."

"Now you're talking stupid, Paul. There's nothing going on between Alana and Frank."

"The hell there ain't!" Paul snarled, downing his drink. "I've seen the way they look at each other."

William Emerson was getting fed-up with his son-in-law. He was beginning to realize that not only was Paul a drunk, but he was also a first class bounder. He felt a growing dislike for him. Suddenly he realized that he wanted Paul out--out of the Corporation, out of the family, and out of his life. He really had never trusted the lawyer, and he knew that Paul was making Alana's life miserable. If she ever was to have a chance for happiness, then she would have to rid herself of the burden of Paul Ames. It was a frustrating situation, and Emerson was in a dilemma as to what to do about it. He didn't want to interfere in his daughter's life, but at the same time, he couldn't stand by any longer while his daughter was so unhappy.

★ ★ ★ ★ ★

Alana heard Paul coming down the hall. He went into his room. Several minutes later, as she knew would happen, the door connecting to her room slowly opened. "Are you asleep, Alana?"

"No Paul. I've been reading and have just turned out the light. Shall I turn it back on?"

"No, leave it off." He leaned over and kissed her on the cheek. There was a heavy odor of liquor on his breath. He slipped out of his robe.

A few minutes later he was finished. He got up and put

on his robe. "I'll be back a little later, honey." He went into his own room and closed the door.

Alana lay on her back, fists clenched, angry and frustrated. "The god-damned rabbit!" she said, half out loud. She felt cheated. There had to be something more to sex than what she had. She got out of bed and went into the bathroom. She bathed, douched, and the warm water relaxed her. She felt cleansed, but dissatisfied. Afterward she stood looking at herself in the mirror. What was the matter with her--was she frigid? A wave of revulsion swept over as she thought about Paul pumping away on her unfeeling body. She felt guilty about her lack of response to his love-making. No, it wasn't love-making. There was no foreplay, no tender words or caresses. He just climbed on, did it, and left. Maybe she was partly to blame, but she also knew that Paul simply was inadequate in bed--at least in her bed.

Sallie as always bragging about her orgasms. "Super. Indescribable!" she had said. According to her, an orgasm was a moment of "sweet death." She said that sometimes she lost complete control of her body with the ecstacy of multiple orgasms. Alana believed that she herself evidently was incapable of such a feeling. She had never experienced a multiple orgasm; she never felt like crying out; and her legs never quivered for an hour afterwards.

Several days ago, Alana conjured up enough courage to ask Mary if she and Jim had a good sexual relationship.

"Fantastic!" Mary admitted, "And it seems to get better with the years. I keep telling Jim that he is like good bourbon--just gets better with age."

"Alana, good sex in marriage isn't the only thing, but without it there is no real marriage. Sex between two people that love each other can be the most beautiful and precious happening in the world. Why all Jim has to do is touch me, and I still get all goose-pimply. Two touches and I'm ready to make love."

Alana was just a little embarrassed by the conversation,

108

but since Mary seemed willing to talk about it, she asked: "How often do you and Jim make love?"

"Oh, usually three or four times a week, but sometimes we do it every day. It always has been a spontaneous thing with us. If I'm in the mood, I have a particularly sexy black negligee that I put on, and it works every time."

Mary turned the conversation. "Alana, you and Paul are not happy, are you?"

Alana shook her head. Then she confessed her marital problems to Mary. She had been holding them in for so long, and she needed to talk to someone. Mary had become a mother-figure to her. Tearfully, the years of frustration flooded out: the childless marriage, Paul's jealousy over her business ability, the separate bedrooms, Paul's increasing drinking problem, her disgust with attempts at love-making, and her growing disrespect for her husband.

Mary put her arm around the younger woman, comforting her. "You have the wrong man, honey. If I were you, I'd get rid of him," she advised.

"But what about Dad and the company?" blurted Alana.

"Your father would understand. Don't you think he knows what's happening? Besides, to hell with the company. Think of your own happiness. Alana, you are the classic case of an emotionally depressed and sexually frustrated woman, and things aren't going to improve as long as you stay with Paul."

"What you need," continued Mary, "is to wrap your legs around someone like Frank Stevens. His lady friends have told me that he's quite a stud!"

"Why would you say that?" asked Alana, surprised at Mary's suggestion.

"Alana, lately I've noticed a change in Frank. He looks at you with a hunger in his eyes that I've never seen before. He reminds me of a tiger about ready to pounce. I've also noticed the way you act around him. I think you two are falling in love and that neither of you realizes it."

"Don't be silly, Mary. I have no romantic interest in Frank at all!" She tried to sound convincing, but her words were false-sounding, even to herself. "And, he doesn't think of me romantically, either. You said so yourself: 'Frank will never really care for anyone again.'"

"I was wrong, Alana, and you're wrong. I've known Frank for a very long time. He may not realize it yet, and he may even be fighting it, but he's falling for you. I used to think that no woman could ever rouse him again, but I believe that you have. Frankly, I think it would be good for both of you. What a team you two would make! I love you both, and I believe that you could make each other happy."

"Mary, I honestly don't know if I could satisfy any man. Paul was my first and only lover, and I haven't been able to respond to him. I feel inadequate. Just the thought of sex makes me feel sick. I guess I am just a frigid person."

"Nonsense, Alana!" replied Mary, positively. "You're a beautiful, healthy, normal female, and you should have a healthy sex life. Honey, just remember, there is no such thing as a frigid woman--there are just inept men. Inside every woman is a hot-blooded sex tigress. It just takes the right man to bring it out. I don't believe for one minute that the problem is you--Paul is the one who has problems."

"I can't stand to have him touch me any more," Alana admitted frankly. "I don't know if I can ever enjoy any man's touch."

"You're wrong, Alana, and someday you'll know that what I've told you is correct."

Alana walked away from the mirror and climbed into bed. She remembered Mary's words: "It just takes the right man."

She closed her eyes and thought about the night in Ventura when she had watched Frank and Sallie making love in the pool. She tried to imagine that she was Sallie. A warm feeling came over her. She could imagine Frank's lean, muscular body, moving in and out. She touched herself and she was wet. Tears came into her eyes.

On a sudden impulse she got out of bed and walked over and opened the door to Paul's room. "Are you asleep Paul?"

She heard a muffled, sleep, "Huh?"

"You're never going to touch me again, you inconsiderate bastard!" she yelled, and slammed the door.

Half-asleep, and half-drunk, Paul Ames raised up from his pillow, confused--then he lay back down and commenced to snore.

Several miles away, Frank awakened from a troubled sleep, drenched in sweat, his heart pounding. He got out of bed and poured himself a half-a-glass of bourbon. It was the same dream again. Nuyen was tied to a stake on a hill, her assailants circling her, striking her with bamboo poles. He was cutting his way to the top of the hill with a knife. Every time he would cut down a shadowy figure in front of him, another would take his place. His hands and arms were sticky with blood. He was screaming at them, but no sound came from his mouth. Finally he reached the top, only to find that Nuyen was gone and only her clothes lay at the foot of the stake. Her white dress was drenched with blood. He fell to his knees, weeping. At this point he always awoke.

He took a deep draught of the bourbon. His ears were ringing and his mouth was dry. No one knew the personal torment that went on in his mind--the sleepless nights, the dreams, the pain, the feeling of guilt and failure.

Nuyen still lived and suffered in the deep recesses of his mind. He was haunted by her tormented ghost and by that night conceived in hell. He lived with the realization that she had died because she loved him, and when she needed him the most he was unable to help her. He could still hear his wife's screams as they tortured her--hear her tormented, anguished cry as she called out to him in her agony. Then the silence--the awful silence when he realized she was dead.

That morning after they killed her, he awoke and found himself lying on the floor of his cage in his own filth and blood. He lay there all day, feeling a despair bordering on insanity, drifting in and out of consciousness. Sometime during that day, his spirit hardened and the pain dissolved. Strangely, as the pain and fear slowly disappeared from his tormented mind, it was replaced with a new deadly resolve, and his strength returned. He was sedated and strengthened by the opiate of revenge.

That night he heard the guard coming to check on him. He lay still, not breathing, as if in death. With his flashlight in his hand, the guard leaned in the cage to feel the pulse in the prisoner's neck. With almost super human strength, Stevens reached up and choked the life out of the hapless guard. The body slumped across him. Disregarding the AK-47 assault rifle, he removed the knife from the sheath on the guard's belt. It was Stevens' own Randall fighting knife! Stevens knew it was razor sharp. For some strange reason, fate had placed his own knife back into his hands. The hellish night was about to begin!

He staggered out of the door and stumbled across the compound, falling twice before he reached Major Phoung's hut. He knew it well, having spent many painful hours there. He opened the door and entered. The Major was sleeping peacefully beneath a mosquito netting. The bright moonlight cast eerie shadows through the bambo bars in the windows. Stevens placed his hand over the Major's mouth. Phouhg awakened with a start but lay still as he felt the knife edge piercing his throat. Stevens grabbed a sock and pushed it into the Major's mouth. He jerked Phoung out of bed and dragged him over to the center pole. There already were ropes hanging from the rafters to tie him to. After tying up the NVA Major, Stevens walked over and turned on the light.

On the table was a roll of adhesive tape which he used to secure the sock in the Major's mouth. Beads of sweat stood out on Phoung's forehead, and his eyes were wide with fear. He made small moaning sounds as he tried to cry for help.

Stevens spoke quietly to Phoung. "I'm going to kill you, you son of a bitch! But first I want you to remember the night you killed my wife. I want you to remember her screams and how you showed no pity. You enjoyed it, didn't you?"

Phoung's head moved back and forth in denial. He knew his end was near; he could see it in the American's eyes.

Stevens pressed the sharp point of his knife against the Major's chest, just below the collar bone, then slowly he cut to the bone with a long slice down and across. The knife bounced across the ribs.

The Major strained against his bonds in pain as the blood ran freely down his stomach and dripped on the floor.

Then the Green Beret reached up and sliced off Phoung's right ear. He followed by finishing the X across his chest.

Phoung screamed and squirmed. His muscles were taut with pain, his eyes wide with fright! His body was quivering.

Stevens stuck his face close to Phoung's and spoke slowly and distinctly. "I'm going to cut off your balls and let you bleed to death, and I want you to think of my wife as you die!"

Phoung's eyes bulged. Low whimpers and animal sounds came from his muffled mouth. His body twisted as Stevens sliced away his shorts. He trembled as the knife was placed next to his groin, and he tried to hold his legs tightly together.

Stevens flicked his wrist, and Phoung writhed in agony, blood spurting from between his legs. The avenging American reached down and picked up the bloody sac and held it in front of the Major's eyes. That was the last thing Phoung saw in this life. Unable to restrain his hatred any longer, Stevens plunged the knife up under the rib cage and into the Communist's heart! As he ripped out the knife, he was covered with Phoung's blood. The room smelled strongly of blood, shit, and death!

From that moment, until he awakened in a hospital three weeks later, the dark side of his nature took command. Everything that happened was a bloody blur. He didn't remember freeing Braxton or going from hut to hut looking for his wife's body, killing as he went. Killing and killing-- silently, and with bloody efficiency.

Stevens took another drink and walked out of his door. He stood looking up at the star-studded sky. The vision of Alana Ames entered his troubled mind. He could shut his eyes and see her long black hair and her beguiling eyes. She was the first woman to touch his feelings since Nuyen, who was beyond his reach. He finished his drink and went back into his lonely room. He refilled the tumbler. Booze sometimes can be the anodyne for pain, loneliness, and guilt.

9

TRIPOLI, LIBYA

Colonel Muammar Khadafy sat cross-legged, meditating, in his black Bedouin tent, in the desert wastes a few miles south of Tripoli.

The cursed Russian missiles had proven ineffectual against the American ships and planes. He needed to get the more advanced SA-7's and 9's. The Soviets had been reluctant to sell him the newer missiles--but now they would have to, because the short battle had made their technology look bad.

The Libyan leader knew what he had to do. Now was the time for revenge. The Pig Reagan must pay for his terrorist attack. Khadaffy picked up a notebook and pen and wrote:

Contact our agents in Western Europe and Lebanon. Direct them to attack Americans wherever and whenever possible. Make the world run red with American blood!

★ ★ ★ ★ ★

Paul Ames sat nursing his third martini of the day. A half-empty pitcher sat in front of him on the desk.

Ames was a pyramid of inadequacies. He was inadequate

as a husband and lover. Unable to satisfy his wife, he turned to prostitutes. He needed to dominate a woman completely to enjoy the act of sex. Alana was not the kind of woman that could be dominated, nor could she be physically intimidated. With hookers, premature ejaculation meant nothing. Besides, one didn't have to try to satisfy a whore. If you paid them enough, a little physical abuse also was tolerated.

He was inadequate as a businessman and a disappointment to his father-in-law. Paul was not a manager. Having been miserably spoiled and brought up with a silver spoon in his mouth, he was not used to cooperating with people. He lacked the confidence and experience to get out and deal with a labor force. Over the years, William Emerson had placed his reliance on Alana--not Paul--to help run the business. This made Paul turn away from his wife and view her as a competitor.

His drinking problems had developed gradually. Alcohol gave him a feeling of confidence; he even believed it increased his potency as a lover. Gradually it became his crutch. It was the one thing he could count on to make him feel adequate as a man.

He realized he was on the verge of losing his wife and the Emerson fortune, and sometimes he didn't care. He blamed Alana for emasculating him, for holding him back from his true potential. He was beginning to hate his cold wife.

He fantasized that his future lay in politics, not the Emerson Corporation. However, he planned on using Alana's money to help him move into the political arena. He would start out as a State Senator, like his father, then perhaps on to Governor. Why not? Paul drained his glass and poured himself another.

Now he had a more serious problem--one that could affect his political future. He had received the envelope full of photographs at his New York office. The 8 x 10 photos showed him and the girl in several compromising positions. The most damaging picture showed her lying naked across his lap, with him spanking her with a belt. There was no note with the photos, nor had he been contacted, but he realized that he was about to be blackmailed.

Several weeks ago, in Las Vegas, he had met a prostitute and had gone to her apartment. It had been a stupid mistake, because obviously there had been a hidden camera.

He was afraid! He needed alcohol to synthesize his frayed nerves--to give him courage.

"It's a little early, even for you, isn't it?" Alana had walked in and startled him.

"I've only had a couple," he lied.

"Paul, I think you should slow down. We are going to have guests tonight."

"I really don't give a damn! Anyway, they're your friends, not mine," he snapped angrily.

"Paul! How can you say that? They're your friends, too."

"Not really," said Paul dryly--the drinks giving him false courage. "Especially your General. I don't like him. Don't think I haven't noticed the way he looks at you."

"Don't be silly," said Alana, holding back her anger. "You should have more sense than to talk like that." Alana's voice began to raise in anger. "I'm getting sick and tired of your attitude lately, and I won't put up with it! You're beginning to act like a typical drunk."

"Well, you're no great shakes as a wife, either," blurted out Paul savagely. "Making love to you is like trying to screw a cold duck!"

"Maybe it would be best if we got a divorce," said Alana, feeling desperately hurt. "We haven't had a real marriage for several years, and I'm sick of your drunken antics. I don't ever want you to touch me again! You make me sick." She walked out of the study and slammed the door. Paul drained his glass and threw it across the room.

When Frank arrived, he was met at the door by Alana.

She was breathtakingly beautiful. Their eyes met and held just an instant too long. He followed her into the livingroom where Prince Mohamad rose to meet him.

Stevens addressed the Prince in Arabic: "Assalama Alaikum, Saadatekum." ("Peace be upon you, Your Excellency.")

The Prince extended his hand: "W'alaikoum Assalam, General." ("And upon you, General.") "Kaif Halak?" ("How are you?"), he asked. "Ana Mabsout, Shokran" ("I am fine, thank you"), returned Stevens.

Alana looked surprised and turned to Stevens, questioningly: "I didn't know you spoke Arabic."

"I went to language school in Monterey several years ago, but I'm afraid I'm a little rusty now."

"Your pronunciation is excellent, General Stevens," said the Prince in English. "What do you think of Saudi Arabia? Have things changed much since your last visit?"

"There are many changes, Your Excellency, especially in construction. It's almost beyond my comprehension. Much of the architecture is beautiful. I'm most impressed with the rapid growth that's taking place. I only hope it's not too fast."

"I know what you mean," the Prince said, reaching for his tea. "I also fear we are moving too rapidly. If we didn't subsidize them, many of our old ways would die out rapidly. The government actually is paying people to raise camels so that the tradition will not disappear. It wouldn't be Arabia if one couldn't see an occasional herd of camels. Our major problem is to modernize without losing our treasured customs and traditions. It is a very difficult task."

After a time they moved into the dining room. Filipino waiters served an excellent dinner of lobster and steak fillets.

Prince Mohamad looked across the table at William Emerson and smiled. "I have been trying to talk Alana into divorcing Paul and becoming one of my wives."

Alana laughed, "You know you only have one wife, Your Excellency, and she would shoot you--and me--if she heard you say that."

"Ah! but to add such a beauty as you to my harem might be worth a small wound. Don't you think so, General Stevens?"

Stevens nodded in assent.

Emerson added, "I don't know Prince, these American women are pretty independent. I believe you can handle the Kingdom, but I'm not sure that you could handle my daughter."

"I'm sorry Nuri could not be here, Your Excellency," commented Alana.

"Yes, so am I," returned the Prince, "but she probably is buying all of the most expensive dresses in Paris. She will be back next week."

The pleasant bantering continued throughout dinner. Paul was unusually quiet. Stevens figured it was because the lawyer didn't have a drink to bolster his courage. What was noticeable was the strained relationship between Alana and Paul. The tension could have been cut with a knife.

The Prince leaned over and whispered something to Alana which caused her to burst out laughing. Watching her, Stevens was positive that he had never seen a more beautiful woman.

After dinner, Emerson asked Stevens: "Frank, how does your organization look?" The Prince put down his cup and shifted his attention to Stevens.

"It's beginning to take shape. We are almost at 100 percent in personnel, and all equipment is on board and has been issued to the units. We have a strong group of officers and senior NCO's. As you might suspect, we have some tough characters. You'll find them in any mercenary outfit. However, that doesn't mean they aren't good soldiers. It simply means that the leaders are going to have to make sure their energies are channeled in the right direction."

"Money is the main incentive, and the men are receiving good pay. When the time comes, most of them will fight for that reason alone. Add to that the fact that they are mostly professional soldiers. We should have a good outfit. So far I'm happy with the way things are going."

After dinner Paul disappeared to fortify himself with alcohol. The rest refrained from drinking in deference to the Prince.

Stevens looked across the room at Alana. She had been watching him, and their eyes met again. He felt his pulse quicken, and a feeling of desire engulfed him. He got up and walked out onto the patio.

Alana watched him go, then in response to an unexplainable impulse, she followed him. She found him standing in the garden looking up at the star-filled sky.

"It's a beautiful sky, isn't it?" she asked quietly.

"Yes," he answered. "I never get tired of looking at it."

He could smell the soft scent of her perfume. Her hair shimmered in the moonlight.

Alana looked up into his lonely eyes. "Do you think of her often--your wife?"

"Yes. I guess I do," he answered truthfully.

"She must have been a very special women to hold your love for so many years."

"Yes, she was," he said positively.

"Why have you never remarried?"

"I guess that I've never found the right person."

"Someday you'll meet someone and fall in love again."

He looked down at her radiance. The nearness of her was too much for him. He reached out and enfolded her in his arms. His mouth found hers and crushed it. She struggled for a moment, trying to resist. She felt his body against hers, and she experienced a sensation she had never felt before. She felt an overpowering urge to become a part of him--of his body. She involuntarily pressed closer. Her arms went around his neck; she held him with all of her strength. They stood in close embrace, with their lips pressed together in a long, passionate kiss.

Suddenly, without understanding why, she pushed him away and stepped back. Her breasts rose and fell rapidly with her breathlessness. Her legs felt weak and rubbery. "No, Frank, don't!" she gasped, as he reached for her again.

He stood there for a moment, looking at her strangely, hurt by her rejection. Without a word, he turned and strode back into the house.

Alana wanted to call after him. She regretted her reaction. She had liked the feel of him. Her body had responded as it never had before. Tears rolled down her cheeks as she tried to sort out her confused thoughts. Maybe she was frigid? Maybe her fear of not being able to enjoy sex caused her to push Frank away? She needed to talk to him, to try to make him understand. She dried her eyes, and hurried after him, but she was too late. He had already departed.

The following day, Stevens took his unit to the field for a month's training.

Alana's reaction to his advances had startled him. She was married, but it was evident that she was not happy. Her eyes had indicated loneliness. Stevens still could feel the warmth of her body and remembered the smell of her perfume. He tried to push thoughts of her away and concentrate on his work.

10

Muammar Khadafy, the world's most visible symbol of terror--and the most vocal tormentor of the United States--escaped the rain of death. However, the terror from the skies had hit close to him--his 15 month old adopted daughter was killed and two of his sons were injured!

The Libyan leader cleared his throat and leaned toward the microphone. This was to be his first public broadcast since the raid. His voice was almost hysterical, and there were tears in his dark eyes: "President Reagan is a murderer of babies. He should be tried as a war criminal and executed! I call upon all Arab people to join with Libya in a bloody vengence--against the American terrorists and those people that support them. Americans and their friends will not be safe anywhere in the world. Libyans will hunt down Americans in their own streets. We are ready to die, and we are ready to carry on fighting and defending our country."

Mustapha sat listening to his leader. His heart ached for the Colonel--the raid had been a great personal loss for Khadafy. Also, it came as a surprise. Khadafy did not think the Americans would attack. He said, "America lacked the national resolve to back up its threats and was afraid of world opinion."

When the Americans attacked, Brother Colonel was in his black tent behind Army headquarters and one of the bombs had hit within 150 yards of where the Colonel was sleeping. It had been a close call--but Allah had saved the Libyan leader. It was a good omen!

Major Mustapha Amak, Khadafy's Chief of Intelligence and primary liaison to "Terrorist International," had been a busy man since the Gulf of Sidra Battle in March. He had delivered grenades to Turkey in his diplomatic pouch, and he had personally contacted several special teams in Europe and the Middle East and given them the "green light" to attack American targets. Brother Colonel wanted American blood to flow. The most successful attack was on the disco in Berlin by a Libyan team from East Germany. The Americans used it as an excuse for their murderous raid on Libya.

Mustapha's thoughts were interrupted when his Executive Officer tapped him on the shoulder and handed him a decoded message. It was from Al Ward (The Rose), his agent in Riyadh:

> BG STEVENS WILL FLY TO CAIRO TOMORROW ON SAUDI AIRLINES, FLIGHT 207. HE WILL BE STAYING AT THE SHEPHERDS HOTEL FOR TWO DAYS. HE IS TRAVELING UNDER HIS OWN NAME.

Mustapha stood up and signalled his Executive Officer to come with him. They walked out of Khadafy's office and across the hall to the Major's office. Once inside, Mustapha closed the door and turned to his Exec: "Salim, send a coded message to General Rashan in Cairo. Inform him that General Frank Stevens will arrive in Cairo tomorrow on Saudi flight 207, at 1400 hours. The General will be staying at the Shepherd's Hotel for two days. The General is to be eliminated. However, he must not be killed until Wednesday night-- repeat, must not be killed until Wednesday night."

The Executive Officer wrote the instructions on a note

pad and read the message back to Mustapha. The Major nodded his head and Salim hurried out of the office. It was as good as done!

Mustapha sat back and rubbed his hands together, as if washing them. A smile of satisfaction played at the corners of his mouth. He leaned over and opened the bottom right-hand drawer of his desk and withdrew a shiny metal flask. He saluted the picture of his leader on the wall with his flask and took a deep swig. The bitter liquid burned--but he liked it.

Khadafy would be pleased when the American General was dead. The Colonel wanted American blood --so he, Mustapha, would give him Stevens'. "ALLAH WAS GOOD, ALLAH WAS GREAT!"

The Saudi Arabian 747 lifted off from the Riyadh airport and turned toward Cairo. Stevens was reading the details of the American raid in Libya in the English language version of the Riyadh Daily News.

"It is about time we acted," he thought. "The only thing a madman like Khadafy understands is force. The only way to fight terrorism is to strike at its roots--and to make it too costly for the terrorists to engage in. So far, Khadafy has been paying only money for his terrorist activities--now suddenly, with the American raid, the price has gone up."

His thoughts were interrupted by a pleasant voice at his shoulder.

"Hi, you are American, no?" asked the female voice with a slight French accent.

Stevens looked up from his newspaper at the girls seated next to him. He had been reading when she sat down, and he hadn't noticed. He was greeted by a charming smile. The girl was small and curvaceous. She had a pouting mouth, large blue eyes, and her auburn hair was cut close in a pixie-style. She appeared to be in her mid-twenties.

"Why, yes, Miss. I am an American, and you are French. Correct?"

She smiled and her eyes twinkled. "I'm French by birth, Italian by nationality, and now I work in Riyadh." She extended her hand and he took it. "My name is Gabrial Deveroux, but my friends call me Gaby."

"I'm Frank Stevens," he returned, still holding her hand. "Are you going to Cairo for a holiday?"

"Yes, I'm only staying for a couple of days, just to get away from Riyadh and have some fun. How about you?"

"I guess you might say mine is a combined business and pleasure trip," he answered. "Where do you work?"

"I teach French at the Women's College, but I've only been there three months. Where do you work, Mr. Stevens?"

"I work for a private company that has a contract with the Saudi Government, and I've only been in the country a short while myself."

Gaby was a friendly, but somewhat talkative, traveling companion. Stevens found out that she was staying at Shepherd's Hotel also, and yes, she would be delighted to have dinner with him.

Cairo in the early evening was awash with a flood of humanity. During the hot afternoon, businesses close and people remain indoors. Now the city was coming to life again.

East meets West and old mingles with new in this cosmopolitan city on the Nile. With nine million people, Cairo is Africa's largest city. The dress was a mixture of old and new; Eastern and Western; Arab robes and Western business suits; turbans, fezes, and baseball caps; desert boots, sandals, tennis shoes, and bare feet.

The Nile River is the heart and soul of Egypt. It dominates

the life and history of the country. It was, and is, Egypt's major highway. Along its extended oasis, a lifestyle emerged that still is basically unchanged after 5,000 years. The most lasting of all great civilizations developed here where the Pharoahs ruled for 30 centuries.

Stevens and Gaby took a cab to the Flange Restaurant which was up the Corniche from the Shepherd's Hotel. The Flange, a four-star establishment, is famous for its Middle Eastern cuisine and seafood. They ordered a tasty beef shish kabob, pilaf, and two bottles of Core de Lange, an excellent French champagne.

"That was delicious!" exclaimed Gaby, smothering a ladylike burp behind her napkin. "Excuse me," she giggled. "It's the champagne bubbles."

For a small gal she could really put away the food, he thought.

She answered his thought. "Most of the time I starve myself to stay thin; but now I am on vacation, so I plan to live it up." She looked boldy across the table at him and touched his glass with hers. "Eat, drink, and make love, for tomorrow, who knows?"

His eyes held hers. "Those are my sentiments exactly." He held his glass up, saluting her. "Here's to a very charming young lady."

Again she touched her glass to his, "And to a very handsome and somewhat mysterious man. Are you sure you're not some sort of spy?"

"Would you like to dance?" he asked, changing the subject.

"I would love to, but only just the slow ones until my dinner settles."

As they swayed to the soft music, he was conscious of her leg between his. She moved forward and slowly began to rub her pubic mound against his leg, at first very lightly. He could feel her small, firm breasts pressing against him. His own hardness dug into her leg. It was a pleasant, sen-

126

sual sensation, for both of them. She looked up, her eyes soft and sexy, and he leaned down and kissed her lightly on the lips. After a while, he whispered in her ear, "Are you about ready to go back to the hotel?"

"Only if you tell me that the evening is not over," she said, still pressing close to him.

"My dear young lady--it hasn't even started," he promised. "Now if I can just walk out of here decently, we'll see what lies ahead."

In the taxi he took her in his arms. Her mouth was hot and demanding. She reached down and gently squeezed him. He moved his hand up under her dress. He began rubbing her through the silken garment. Gaby began to breathe heavier, and spread her legs inviting him to probe further.

She started to tremble, then grabbed him: "Oh, kiss me-- kiss me quick!" she whispered breathlessly. "Oooh! It's here!" She put her mouth to his, and their kiss covered her moans as her body jerked in spasms.

The driver would have had to be deaf not to know what was going on, however he gave no indication. He just stared straight ahead, darting in and out of the turbulent traffic.

Gaby pulled back, trying to catch her breath. "Wow!" she exclaimed, "You'd better get me to the hotel quick before I rape you right here!"

At the hotel, Stevens stopped by the front desk and ordered a bottle of champagne to be sent to his room. Once inside the door, they kissed briefly, then Gaby excused herself and disappeared into the bathroom. Seconds later, Stevens heard the sound of the shower.

When she emerged from the bath, wrapped in a big blue towel, he had the champagne opened and two glasses filled. They each took a sip, then set their glasses on the nightstand. Gaby stepped back and let the towel fall. She was small, but well-proportioned. Her small breasts stood out firm and proud. She had a boyish figure, like a gymnast. Her body was wiry and, for her slight height, her legs were long and sensuous.

"Do you approve?" she asked, her eyes never leaving his.

"Very beautiful. I like," he murmured as he unbuttoned his shirt and slipped it off. Then he removed his trousers, and soon they stood naked together.

"You are tremendous!" she said. She put her arms around his neck, and standing on her toes, she kissed him. Her body moved seductively against his. He was pleasantly conscious of her fresh, clean smell.

Stevens swept her up and carried her to the bed. They kissed deeply, lying side by side. He kissed her neck and shoulders as he gently rubbed her breasts. Her breathing became hot and rapid as her passion rose. Her tongue darted into his ear. She began to stroke him slowly. She moaned with pure delight. "Oh Frank, that feels so damn good!

He moved slowly down her stomach, kissing and lingering here and there. Her body writhed in anticipation. As she spread her legs for him, he moved on and her body jerked as his love-making drove her close to a climax.

"Oh, Frank, now! Do it now!" she sobbed.

She had lost all control. "Oh, you sweet wonderful man!" she screamed as the spasms enveloped her.

She was still trying to catch her breath when he moved up between her thighs and entered her. "Oui, faster. Faster! I'm coming again. Come with me, Frank. I want to feel you come!"

Stevens moaned aloud in the convulsive climax, and he felt his strength churning out of him. He rolled over on his back and pulled her on top of him.

He pulled her down and entered her. She threw her head back and shuddered violently, then went limp and rolled off of him, lying on her stomach.

Later, sipping champagne and smoking a joint she had in her purse, she said: "You are something else. Did you know that? Never have I had a man like you. You are unbelievable!"

Stevens lay back, feeling the warm glow of a man who has satisfied a woman and been satisfied himself. Then, unexpectedly, he thought of Alana Ames.

Stevens was picked up early the next morning and driven to the 1st Brigade Headquarters. Before leaving his room, he promised Gaby to call her when he returned to Riyadh. The prospects looked good for some pleasant diversion. Gaby was young enough to be his daughter, but as long as she didn't mind, why should he? Besides, she was damn good, and the only thing he really was hooked on in his lonely and sometimes violent life was sex.

The Brigade Commander, Colonel Andwar Habab, was to leave his command soon and become Stevens' Liaison Officer in Saudi Arabia. He met the American General and escorted him out to his Second Battalion. The Battalion was outfitted with American M-113 Armored Personnel Carriers and a company of obsolete British Half-tracks. Stevens could see a potential market here for the V-150 Commandos and the new Abrams tank. He was given a briefing, met the battalion officers, and toured the base camp to watch some of the training. The Battalion recently had several skirmishes on the border with the Libyans, so there was a sense of urgency in their training.

He had supper at the Colonel's quarters and then returned to his hotel. He opened the door to his room and stepped inside. As he closed the door and turned on the lights, he was startled by a voice behind him: "Don't move, General!"

Stevens felt the pressure of the gun on the right side of his back. The gunman made a classical mistake by jamming the revolver against him. The American reacted instinctively with the perfect reflexes of the well-tuned fighting machine that he was. First, he raised his arms as if surrendering. Then, in a blur, he twisted his upper body to the left. This first move put the gun barrel parallel to his back. The gunman fired, and the bullet plowed into the wall.

Stevens' left hand swung down in a vicious karate chop. There was a loud snap as the gunman's arm was broken. The gun fell to the floor. Stevens' turning movement continued and, with the fingers of his right hand slightly bent, his arm sprang forward and the heel of his hand smashed with a resounding crunch into the bridge of his assailant's nose. There was a snapping sound as the man's nose was broken and driven through the base of his skull, forcing splinters of bone into his brain. He fell like an axed steer and was dead before his body hit the floor.

Out of the corner of his eye, Stevens saw another man enter the room with his weapon drawn. The man evidently had been hiding in the bedroom. As his new adversary fired, Stevens threw himself to the floor and snatched up the dead man's .45 automatic. He fired three times as he continued to roll. The three shots were so close together that they sounded like one. The gunman was hit squarely and driven back through the door, three holes in the center of his chest.

Stevens quickly checked the bedroom. There had only been two assassins. He went through their pockets and removed their wallets, which he stuffed under his mattress. By this time, people were knocking on the door.

He asked the hotel manager to call Colonel Habab, and the Colonel arrived shortly after the police.

The police deduced that it was a simple robbery attempt. With Habab's assistance, Stevens didn't have to go to the police station. When the police left, Stevens turned over the wallets to Habab.

Stevens was given another room. Habab placed two soldiers on guard at his door.

The next morning, General Moore arrived at the Emerson residence carrying a TELEX he had received from CIA agents in Cairo. Emerson met him at the door and ushered him into the study.

"Somebody tried to kill Frank in Cairo," Moore announced, handing Emerson the TELEX.

Alana was in the kitchen and heard his statement. She hurried into the study, visibly upset.

"What's happened? Is Frank all right?"

"Yes, he's O.K.--not a scratch."

Alana snatched the TELEX from her father.

LAST NIGHT AT 2300 HOURS AN ATTEMPT WAS MADE ON THE LIFE OF GENERAL FRANK STEVENS BY TWO UNIDENTIFIED GUNMEN. AS THE GENERAL ENTERED HIS HOTEL ROOM, ONE OF THE ASSAILANTS PLACED A GUN AT HIS BACK. B.G. STEVENS DISARMED HIS ATTACKER AND KILLED HIM. THE SECOND ASSAILANT THEN FIRED AT STEVENS, WHO, USING THE GUN OF THE FIRST MAN, RETURNED FIRE, KILLING THE SECOND ATTACKER. BOTH ASSAILANTS WERE DEAD WHEN POLICE ARRIVED. POLICE BELIEVE IT WAS A ROBBERY ATTEMPT. HOWEVER, WE THINK OTHERWISE. BOTH MEN HAVE BEEN IDENTIFIED AS PROFESSIONAL ASSASSINS. NO OTHER INFO AVAILABLE. STEVENS O.K. WILL KEEP YOU INFORMED.

Her hands shaking, Alana handed the TELEX back to her father. She returned to the kitchen and tried to pour herself a cup of coffee. It spilled from the cup over her hand.

Moore and her father had followed her. Emerson put his arm around his daughter. The two men exchanged knowing looks. They didn't have to ask her about her reaction; her obvious concern was their answer.

General Moore said, soothingly, "Don't worry about Frank, Lani. He's indestructible."

"Nobody is indestructible," she muttered.

The two men left her and returned to the living room. Emerson frowned. "Jim, we have a problem. It looks like someone is onto our game."

Moore nodded in agreement. "But who?" Then he gestured toward Alana in the kitchen: "It looks as if we have another problem."

Emerson shrugged. "It was inevitable!"

11

TRIPOLI, LIBYA. AN UNDERGROUND BUNKER NEAR THE CITY.

Someone indeed, was interested in their game, because he feared it might interfere with his own game. He was a dark, moody, brooding man whose name was Ghadafy, Qaddafi, Khadafy, Gadhafi or Ghaddafy, depending on which newspaper one read--a man whose life had changed abruptly since the American attack in April. Khadafy knew exactly who the Americans were after, especially when a "Smart" bomb went into the front door of his residence, and he lived in constant fear of another attempt on his life. Since the bombing, he had been under constant watch by a "praetorian guard" of East Germans commanded by Karl Haensch, an East German secret policeman.

However, Khadafy was still confident because he still had his ace-in-the-hole--nuclear weapons. The Prophet of Terror knew that the time for his revenge was growing closer--it was Allah's will!

Brother Colonel's face turned darker as he read the message his Chief of Intelligence had handed him. He tore it into scraps, rolled it into a ball and made an excellent one-handed bank-shot off the wall into the wastebasket. He looked up with his dark eyes ablaze. "Mustapha," he said, tight-lipped, "I thought these men were supposed to be good."

'Brother Colonel, General Rashan said they were two of the best. He has used them many times before, and they have never failed," answered his very nervous intelligence chief.

Khadafy leaned back in his chair. "Well, apparently they weren't good enough. I think you have underestimated this General Stevens." He sat forward abruptly and picked up the manila folder on his desk, which contained a file on Stevens furnished by the Russian KGB. He shook it at his Chief of Intelligence and asked, "Have you read this file carefully?"

"Yes, your Excellency, I have."

"I mean, have you really studied it? This Stevens is no ordinary man. He is a talented warrior! He has killed many men. Also, I think he is a very smart man. I have a bad feeling about him. We cannot let him consolidate his plans in Saudi Arabia. When we strike, the Saudis must be neutralized. If he is not stopped, he could delay our plans."

"We will watch him closely, Your Excellency. The next time he leaves Saudi Arabia, we will be waiting for him."

Khadafy touched his fingertips together and leaned his elbows on the desk. "He must be stopped as soon as possible. Do not fail the next time!"

Mustapha saluted and left the office with the ominous threat hanging over him. His stomach churned with fear. What he needed was a good stiff drink.

These were tense days in Libya. Everyone went to bed each night with the fear of Americans coming in the night. There was even internal pressure to ease off in supporting international terrorist activities. However, Mustapha was more afraid of his boss than he was of the Americans. He saw first-hand what happened to the three Army officers who tried to organize the coup after the American raid. The Koran, as interpreted by Khadafy, has a special fate for traitors of the Islamic Revolution. And now, Brother Colonel placed the blame for the failure to kill Stevens directly on his shoulders. Mustapha knew that if he did not succeed the next time . . . the Major shivered!!

KHARTOUM, SUDAN.

Colonel Abdulla Sabeh, a tall, thin, Sudanese, met Stevens at the airport. The Colonel looked sinister with three knife scars of the Beberini slashed on each cheek. However, things had suddenly changed. The Sudanese Colonel informed Stevens that his government had changed its mind and would not be sending any units to train with the Saudis.

Stevens had been afraid that something like this might happen. During the last few months, the Khartoum government had begun to cool toward America. There was an increasing, heavy, sinister Libyan influence in the Sudanese capital.

"I am sorry for what is happening in my country," apologized Colonel Sabeh. "Khadafy's money is buying out my government. If things continue, I am afraid that I will have to leave my own country."

Stevens left on the next plane, after his short conversation with the Sudanese Colonel. Sabeh had made it clear that the American General was not welcome in his country.

When he returned to Riyadh, he found a note from Gaby: "Frank, thank you for a wonderful evening! Please call: 487-7224."

Remembering their pleasant interlude, he picked up the phone and dialed her number.

During the next six weeks, Stevens spent most of the time in the field with his squadron. Occasionally he would return to Riyadh and take Gaby to dinner, and to bed. She was an excellent companion who helped to keep his mind occupied. He tried not to think of the beautiful raven-haired Alana Ames. After all, she was married, and their worlds were light-years apart. Alana travelled in the high society cicuit of the super-rich; and he was a soldier, not used to the bright lights of Broadway nor the white beaches of the Riviera. When he reached for her that night on the balcony, he had tried to reach across too great a distance in lifestyles. Still, she affected him as had no other woman since Nuyen.

The squadron trained in the large desert south of Riyadh called the Rub al Khali (the Empty Quarter). They practiced tactical movements, navigation, aerial resupply, and general desert living and survival.

Almost one-third of the Kingdom is covered in sand, and the vast Rub al Khali is the largest continuous area of sand in the world, covering some 564,000 square kilometers. This desert sand, because it is bone dry, can be swept along by winds up to 60 kilometers per hour, which can pile up vast dunes often rising several hundred meters high. The dunes form a variety of shapes and forms. They resemble a vast, turbulent sea, captured at one moment in time by a stop-action camera.

It is a challenge just to survive and move in these shifting sands, let alone try to train for combat. The desert will seize upon any weakness and turn it into a fatal error. One cannot fight the desert and win. One must learn its ways.

The hot desert sun shows no mercy, climbing to 160 degrees Fahrenheit in the open. Considering that roast beef is "medium-well" at 170 degrees, that is hot! During the days of the Zawabei, the strong northwesterly winds whip the sand at 50 to 60 MPH, causing whirling sand clouds that often reach hundreds of feet into the air, and cover miles on the ground. During these sandstorms, movement is impossible, and gauze masks have to be worn to keep the fine dust particles out of the lungs. Goggles protect the eyes from being scratched and cut. The fine sand permeates everything. It is a maintenance nightmare for the drivers and mechanics to keep the vehicles in operating order. The Cadillac-Gage fighting vehicles continue to prove that they are excellent for this type of environment.

The desert can kill in a matter of hours. The intense ultraviolet rays will sear exposed skin and literally fry the body like an egg. The extreme heat boils away the body chemicals and creates confusion and disorientation. Shortly afterward, dehydration occurs--then death.

Water, the essence of life, particulary in the desert, is a continuing problem. To help alleviate this, one V-150 armored car in each company was rigged with a 500-gallon watertank. The squadron was taught desert survival by their Arab Bedouin counterparts. Perhaps the most important thing they learned was how to make a "desert still."

This simple, but ingenious, device can produce a pint of water in about three hours. A pit is dug in the sand, about two feet deep and three feet wide. A receptacle to catch the moisture is placed in the center of the pit. Then, the pit is lined with vegetation, perferrably green. However, dry foliage can be used since it emits a certain amount of moisture. A sheet of clear plastic is stretched over the top of the pit and held down on the sides with sand and rocks. Then a small stone is dropped in the center, directly over the receptable, which stretches the plastic down at that point. Water will form on the inside of the plastic, and drip into the receptable. It is best to place a rubber tube in the receptacle and to run it out under the sheet. This allows one to drink water without disturbing the plastic sheet.

Each vehicle carried a camouflage net which not only helped to conceal it but also provided shelter for the crew when draped properly.

When the squadron finally returned to Riyadh, the men

were weathered, sun-baked, and trained into a highly mobile, combat-ready desert strike force. Stevens granted two weeks leave for all.

At his office, he found an invitation to a dinner party at the Emersons. Alana, her husband, and her father had just returned from a month's stay in the United States. Stevens called Gaby and invited her to go with him.

Dave Braxton took a healthy swig of his Johnny Walker Red. After six weeks in the desert without a drink, the scotch tasted good. He wasn't missing the Army. So far, he hadn't had time. Besides, he was doing the same thing as he had done on active duty. During the three months he had been in Saudi Arabia, he had been working long, exhausting hours. But, this was his life--the kind of work he enjoyed most.

And, the pay was good! His salary was non-taxable, and he could salt away 50 thousand dollars a year. Most of all, it was good to be back with the General again. The man he loved and admired most, next to God, was Frank Stevens.

Braxton took another pull on his glass and leaned back onto the soft sofa. When one of the British mercs invited him to the party with British nurses, he had readily accepted. He felt that he had earned a little R&R as the merc squadron Sergeant Major.

When he drained his glass and stood up to get a refill, he noticed that an attractive redhead seated at the other end of the couch was holding an empty glass. He leaned toward her. "May I get you a refill, Ma'am?"

She looked up at him and smiled. "Yes, please. Scotch and water."

A few minutes later he returned and handed her the drink. "Thank you," she said quietly.

He sat back down, thinking about her red hair and green

eyes. Finally, after fortifying himself with another scotch, he built up enough courage. He leaned across the sofa and asked, "Would you like to dance?"

She looked over at the black giant, surprised. Then she stood up. "I'd love to!"

She was tall, just under six feet, slim-waisted and full-bodied. As they danced, she looked up at him. "You are Sergeant Major Braxton, aren't you?"

"Yes, Ma'am. How did you know my name?"

"Oh, I've heard some of the men talking about you, and you certainly fit the description. My name is Maxine Davenport."

After dancing for a while she looked up at him. "For such a big man, you are a very good dancer."

He smiled down at her. "In America we call it natural rhythm."

After the dance was over they sat down on the couch and talked. He found out that her husband had been a Sergeant Major in the British SAS and had been killed in Northern Ireland. Maxine was head nurse in the Intensive Care Ward at the King Faisal Hospital. She had been in Saudi Arabia for two years. Like him, she had no children.

"And what about you?" she asked. "Is there a Mrs. Braxton?"

"There was, but she divorced me ten years ago. I guess she couldn't take the frequent separations."

"Well, I can understand that," returned Maxine. "I went through it, too. However, basically we were happy, and I never considered a divorce. Of course, I always had my job to keep me busy, and I think that made a big difference."

They danced and talked through the remainder of the evening. When it was time to leave, Braxton didn't feel ill at ease about driving her to her quarters. At her door, he took her in his arms, but she pushed him back.

"Please, Dave. Slow down," she asked.

Braxton had dated white women before, and usually they

were easy, because most of them wanted to add a little variety to their lives. It looked as if this lady was different.

He realized that he wanted to see this beautiful lady again. "Would you have dinner with me some evening?"

Without hesitation, she said, "I would like to. Just name the night."

12

While Dave Braxton was in the process of making the acquaintance of Maxine Davenport, Frank Stevens sat alone in his quarters nursing a glass of bourbon. His thoughts were disturbed by Alana Ames, and he wasn't sure that he liked what was happening to him. She was beginning to invade his private thoughts--to disturb his years of solitary mourning for his dead wife.

He felt the urge for a cigarette. He stood up, walked into his bedroom, and opened the drawer of his bedside table. There, next to the pack of cigarettes was a blue velvet box. He opened it and looked at the blue-ribboned Medal of Honor.

Nightmares were not unusual for him. Some nights he wakened drenched with perspiration after dreaming about his maddening experience in the POW Camp, but he never dreamed about Hill 555 and the night he had won the medal. Over the years, he had come to realize why. During that period of his life--the year after his escape--the year he killed out of blood-lust for revenge, he was insane! While he was a prisoner, he felt an almost constant, overpowering fear. Then, when they killed his wife, it stopped. During the terrible battle on Hill 555, he couldn't recall having been afraid for one moment. Anyone that does not feel fear in combat has to be crazy!

He reached out and touched the medal. He was proud of it. Winning it was the greatest achievement a soldier could hope for. In 1945, President Truman told a group of awardees that he "would rather have the Medal of Honor than be President."

Stevens shut his eyes and moved back in time.

PLEIKU PROVINCE, REPUBLIC OF SOUTH VIETNAM. AUGUST 1967.

Major Frank Stevens, Commanding Officer, U.S. Special Forces Detachment, Pleiku, was awakened by a loud knocking at his door. He opened it to find his Operations Officer standing there with a worried look on his face. "Sir, we've lost radio contact with Alpha Three!"

Alpha Three was the radio call-sign for a five-man reconnaissance patrol operating along the Laotian border, northwest of Pleiku. The patrol, led by Sergeant David Braxton, had the mission of reporting on Communist troop movements in the area.

Stevens began dressing in his battlegear. "Have my C&C (Command and Control Helicopter) crank up. I'll go out and see if I can make contact. Maybe all they need is to have some batteries dropped in."

One hour later the Huey was circling over the last known position of the patrol.

"Sir," the pilot said over the intercom, "I see a light blinking off to our right."

They flew down and hovered above the light.

"It's an SOS signal," declared the pilot.

Stevens could only assume that the patrol's radio was out. The area was triple-canopy jungle, and there were no open areas that would take a chopper landing for 20 miles. He made his decision quickly.

He began to rig the rappeling rope. "Take her down as

close as you can. I'm going to take them a radio. When you get back, notify Colonel Moore that we'll move to Hill 555 in Sector Bravo." Hill 555 was within the range of friendly artillery from the Nam Lang Special Forces Camp and had an open area on top where helicopters could land.

With his AK-47 assault rifle slung across his back and a radio and a carton of small arms ammo strapped to his backpack, Stevens hooked his snap-link to the rope trailing below the helicopter and stepped backwards, out into the blackness. He was greeted on the ground by the grateful and helping hands of the patrol and the whining crack and snap of enemy automatic weapons fire.

Without speaking, his men helped him take off the equipment and distributed the load. Braxton whispered in his ear: "Glad to see you, Sir. Our radio's shot, and Charlie is all around us."

"How're the men?" Stevens whispered back.

"Burns has a facial wound, but he's mobile. The rest are O.K."

"Dave, we want to move to Hill 555 for extraction. Do you know how to get up there?"

"Yes, Sir," the Sergeant nodded. Then he moved from man to man, giving them instructions.

Enemy fire was still searching the area. The Communists didn't know their exact location, so they were firing blind-- and as usual at night--high, but they were closing in now, because the helicopter had been a pinpoint giveaway.

Braxton signalled, and the patrol moved out in single file toward the northeast, along a well-used trail. Enemy fire receded as they moved away from the link-up site. After moving rapidly up the trail for 30 minutes, they ran into an enemy patrol. The point man gave a cry of pain as automatic weapons fire cascaded down the trail.

"Straight ahead!" yelled Stevens, as he moved to the point, firing short bursts from his Kalishnikov. "We've gotta bust through!" He almost ran over two NVA blocking his way.

He shot them both at point-blank range, and their bodies flew to either side of the trail. Braxton brought up the rear, firing at the dark shadows coming up the trail behind them. They ran, stumbled, and fought, dragging the wounded point man with them.

"God-dammit, I'm hit!" yelled Braxton, grabbing his stomach.

Stevens moved to the rear and took Braxton's place as another patrol member put a field dressing on Braxton's gaping belly-wound. Stevens kneeled, squeezing off short bursts of automatic fire. He yelled over his shoulder: "Dave, can you walk?"

"Yes Sir, I think so," said Braxton between gritted teeth.

Stevens motioned for another of the patrol members: "Smitty, take the rear and cover us. We have to stay on this trail. The jungle is just too damn thick to try to go cross-country."

Stevens moved out. Now there were three of the five men wounded. They wouldn't be able to move very fast, and staying on the trail was extremely risky. They moved in bounds. One hundred meters--stop! Let Smith catch up. Tend to the wounded, then move out again. Stevens realized that they couldn't continue this much longer. Sooner or later they would run into NVA waiting for them on the trail. The Communists had radios, too!

Smith came stumbling up to them, clutching his left shoulder. Sergeant Jackson, the sole remaining able-bodied man beside Stevens, moved to cover the rear, as Stevens examined Smith's wound. He had taken a round in the shoulder-joint--a nasty wound, in an area where it was difficult to stop the bleeding. They couldn't go on like this!

Stevens moved over to where Braxton was leaning against a tree. The black giant was in great pain and weak from loss of blood. "Dave, I want you all to crawl into the jungle about 200 meters and lay dog. I'll try to lure them away. After I ditch them, I'll be back."

Braxton understood this was their only chance. He nodded his head.

Stevens continued. "If I don't make it back by 1100 hours tomorrow, get the men to Hill 555!"

Without further words, the patrol crawled into the dark jungle. Stevens took a branch and wiped away all signs of their movement. Then he took a hand grenade and tied it to a tree next to the trail. He attached a string to the safety-pin and strung it across the trail about three inches above the ground. On the other side, he took out another grenade and did the same. Then he moved on down the trail. About five minutes later he heard an explosion. His pursuers had found his booby trap!

Now he began a game of waiting, firing at the approaching NVA, then moving along the trail to a new position. After an hour of this, he came to a small stream. He moved upstream for about two hundred meters, leaving as much evidence as possible that he'd been there; then he returned, walking backwards, to a point 100 meters downstream from the trail crossing. From there he crawled into the jungle and began a slow movement parallel to the trail, back toward his men.

He linked up with his men just after daylight. He decided their only chance was to move cross-country through the thick jungle. The going was agonizingly slow as the two uninjured members traded off breaking trail and helping the wounded. They moved all day and most of the night, resting every 30 minutes. Early the next morning, Stevens called a halt to let the men sleep. About noon, a shot rang out to their rear. The NVA had found their trail, and their scouts were signalling. The chase was on again!

Late that afternoon, as they neared the base of Hill 555, the Communist scouts closed in on them. Stevens took Jackson's M-14 sniper rifle and sent the men on ahead. The jungle had opened up considerably, and the long range weapon would allow him to bring the enemy under the gun

145

at some distance.

About 200 meters up the hill, he took up a position between two trees. He could hear his men laboring their way toward the hilltop. Three NVA came out of the jungle just below him. He centered the cross-hairs of his scope on the chest of the third in line and gently squeezed the trigger. The shot echoed loudly through the jungle, and the NVA was flung backward where he lay still. Stevens quickly moved to another target as the two remaining NVA sprinted toward the jungle cover. His second shot took one of them in the back and sent him on his face. The third made it to cover.

Stevens bolted up the hill as heavy enemy fire from below searched for him. It wasn't long until he caught up to his slow-moving patrol.

He went to ground again about 200 meters from the summit. The NVA were approaching more cautiously this time, using all available cover and concealment. He caught a glimpse of khaki through the trees, and his snap-shot brought a cry from below. It was beginning to grow dark, but he could hear the NVA approaching. A noise off to his left indicated that they were trying to flank him. He tossed two grenades down the hill. The explosions were answered by a sprinkling of enemy fire which gradually began to build. He opened fire and squeezed off a full clip, then he bolted up the hill as bullets began richocheting off the rocks and trees around him. He reloaded as he scrambled upward.

He stopped about 100 meters from the tip to catch his breath. An artillery smoke round exploded in the jungle below him. Good old Braxton! The Sergeant was already zeroing in the artillery from Nam Lang Special Forces Camp. As the first rounds of HE (high explosive) began falling below him, he sprinted for the summit. Bullets thudded into the soft ground around him and whined off nearby rocks. When he turned to fire at his pursuers, a hard blow smashed into his stomach, doubling him over and knocking him backwards. He grabbed at his belly and felt the warm sticky blood. Holding his stomach, he gathered his waning reserve of strength and sprinted toward the top. His men were firing to cover his dash. Miraculously, he made it through the gauntlet of enemy fire without being hit again and stumbled into the tiny perimeter that Braxton had set up on the top of Hill 555.

Jackson bound up Stevens' wound, as Braxton brought artillery crashing into the enemy positions below. A round had entered on Stevens' left side. There was no exit wound, so the bullet was still inside. Stevens had no way of knowing the extent of his injury, but he didn't feel like it was a killing wound.

Hill 555 was part of a long ridgeline running north-south. There were a series of peaks, with 555 being the highest. The western slope they had climbed was steep until the last 100 meters, then it leveled off. The best approach for the enemy would be to attack along the ridgeline from the south. The patrol was situated in a bowl formed by boulders--a natural fortification.

Stevens' mental estimate of their chances was interrupted by Braxton: "Sir, Colonel Moore's on the radio."

Stevens picked up the mike: "Warmonger Six, this is Hunter Six, over."

Moore's voice came back loud and clear. "Hunter Six, this is Warmonger Six. Alpha Three filled me in on the situation. Will get relief force to you ASAP. Have requested air support. What is size of enemy force?"

"This is Hunter Six. Size unknown."

The conversation was interrupted as the hollow thump of mortars leaving the tube was heard from below. "Incoming!" warned Stevens, as he tried to cram himself between two boulders. The quiet was shattered as a sheath of mortars exploded with deadly accuracy on the top of the hill. Then whistles began to blow, and cries of "Xung Phong!" (Forward--kill!) echoed up the hill.

Braxton called for artillery and illuminating rounds. As the first flares went off, night turned into day. The defenders looked down the hill and saw a chilling sight as hundreds of khaki-clad NVA surged up the hill toward them.

Stevens' men opened up. Braxton walked the artillery up the hill in 50 meter barrages. The first wave of enemy crumpled like ripe wheat cut by a scythe as the defenders cut them down and artillery ripped into them. The second wave surged forward, and enemy grenades rained on the hilltop. Stevens was knocked down by a concussion grenade.

Then the NVA were on top. Stevens rose to one knee and shot four, one after another. Then, as quickly as they had come, the enemy faded back down the hill. As they departed, the NVA mortars opened up again. Twenty minutes later, the mortars ceased and the hill grew quiet.

Stevens was puzzled. The enemy force was much larger than he had expected; if they had not broken off the attack so suddenly, it would have all been over by now. He called Colonel Moore and told him that he estimated the size of the NVA force to be about a battalion (normally around 300 men). He added that since the NVA had the hilltop covered with mortar fire, it would be impossible to get helicopters in to pick them up.

The patrol was a ghastly sight. Had the enemy pressed the attack, they easily could have taken the hill. Jackson was dying, his stomach ripped open with his entrails lying exposed. He tried vainly to poke them back into place, but there as no way of holding the bloody, slimy mass. Finally he gave up and lay on his side, screaming in pain. Stevens took five morphine syrettes from the aid pack and jabbed them in Jackson's arm. Jackson died without feeling any further pain.

Braxton was the next worse-off. A bullet had entered just below the rib cage on the right side and exited above his hip. He was weakening fast and occasionally lapsed into periods of unconsciousness. Smith's left arm hung uselessly at his side. His back was peppered with grenade fragments. Torres' left arm and side had been shredded by a mortar. Earlier, Burns had been hit in the face, and he now lay unconscious from the blast of a concussion grenade. The patrol had had the course! It no longer was a fighting force--they could not withstand another assault.

With the help of Smith and Torres, Stevens cleaned out the brush and loose rocks from a crevice formed by two large boulders. They dragged the unconscious Braxton and Burns over and placed them in the shelter. "O.K. You two crawl in there too!"

Smith and Torres protested, but Stevens stood fast. "I'm going to call for artillery on top of this position when they come in again, so get in the shelter!"

With his men all inside the small cave, Stevens then dragged up several enemy bodies and placed them over the opening. Just before the explosions of mortars signalled the next assault, Stevens heard helicopters approaching in the distance. After a few minutes, the mortars ceased, and hordes of NVA streamed up the ridgeline from the south.

Stevens reached for the handset and called artillery at Nam Lang: "This is Hunter Six. From last concentration, drop 100. Fire for effect--and keep it coming."

A faraway voice came back: "That puts it right on your position. Do you understand? Over!"

Stevens yelled into the mike: "God dammit! That's where the enemy is! Pour it on, and keep it coming!"

The world came down on top of him in a deafening roar as the artillery plowed into Hill 555. Bodies and parts of bodies were tossed around like rag dolls. Stevens operated alone in a vacuum. He was oblivious to danger. The screams of the NVA echoed through the night.

The radio crackled again as an Air Force FAC (forward air controller) came on his net. A southern voice drawled: "Hunter Six. This is Birddog Four. Over."

Stevens picked up the handset. "This is Hunter Six. Over."

"Ah, Roger there. I have a flight of two, carrying fire. Where do you want us to put it? Over."

Stevens took a small strobe-light from his pocket, turned it on, and placed it on the rock above him. "Birddog. Do you see the blinking light?"

"Roger that, Hunter Six. Where do you want the strike?"

Stevens replied, "About three meters south of the light."

Two minutes later the jets screamed in, and Hill 555 erupted into a ball of flame as the napalm rolled across the top. The flaming gasoline washed over the rock he was lying behind and miraculously missed Stevens and his men. When the jets had passed, the hill became silent. Their radio had been destroyed by the airstrike, so now Stevens was out of radio contact with American Forces. Several times during the night helicopters tried to get into the hilltop, but each time heavy enemy ground fire drove them off.

Stevens climbed atop the nearest boulder and looked at his battlefield. The ground was littered with enemy dead. Mangled bodies of dead NVA were strewn across the slopes and top of Hill 555. They looked like broken, grotesque carcasses torn apart and scattered haphazardly over the landscape. The area looked like a slaughterhouse after a busy day.

The gray light of dawn began to cover the battle area. Hill 555 would never be the same again. It bore an inexpungible stench of death and destruction.

Then Stevens saw the enemy, coming along the ridge line from the south. The stubborn bastards were going to make another assault. This time he wouldn't be able to call for artillery. This time it was between him--and them. He had been waiting for this moment for ten months. He felt no fear, no pain. His only emotion was a dark, boiling thirst to kill. He was back in the prison camp, and these men had killed Nuyen. Now they were being delivered into his hands!

Stevens picked up Braxton's shotgun and checked the load. He chambered a round in his .45 and stuck it in his web belt. He climbed on top of a large boulder and stood in plain sight, waiting for the enemy.

When the NVA spotted him, they stopped. Then they boiled forward. Bullets richocheted off the rocks around him and sighed in the morning air. The shotgun began to buck in his hands when they were about 30 meters away. He felt exhilarated as adrenalin pumped through him. He was posessed with a deadly resolve to kill them all.

He did not hear the incoming choppers.

13

Alana regarded her naked self in the full-length mirror. She always had been proud of her body, and she exercised regularly to keep trim. Her skin was sleek and unblemished, her flesh firm, her stomach flat. Her waist was narrow, her breasts full, ripe, and firm. Her legs were long--the muscles taut and supple. And yet, Paul called her a cold bitch. She wondered what could be wrong with such a perfect body?

The last few weeks had been a nightmare. All of the years of their bad marriage had come to a head. Paul had been drunk almost every day. In New York, he had disappeared for three days. When he returned, he hurt her terribly when he announced that he had been with a woman who knew how to make love. Again, he had called her a cold bitch.

Alana couldn't believe that she ever could have seriously loved Paul. There was no doubt that he was an alcoholic, but he wouldn't listen to anyone, not even her father. She now realized that Paul Ames was a very sick man--mentally sick.

She hadn't brought up the question of divorce again, but the thought was on her mind. She glanced at her watch. Their guests would arrive soon. She looked in her closet, trying to decide what to wear. She looked again in the mirror and asked herself: "Who am I trying to impress?" Then, she answered her own question: "Frank Stevens."

Alana met her guests at the door. Stevens' heart missed a beat when he saw her. She was radiantly beautiful. Her black cocktail dress hugged the contours of her body like a sheath.

At the sight of him, Alana's heart beat faster. Frank looked thinner, and his face was darkened by the hot desert sun. He reminded her of a tawny jungle cat. Her first impulse had been to throw her arms around him and kiss him, but looking at the lovely young girl beside him, she felt instant jealousy and disappointment.

"Alana, I would like you to meet Gaby Deveraux. Gaby, Alana Ames."

The two women shook hands, and then Alana led them into the living room. Gaby radiated a certain youthful charm that was difficult to resist. Soon William Emerson was asking her all about her work at the Women's College.

"She is young enough to be his daughter," thought Alana, irritably.

After dinner, they adjourned to poolside. Alana turned on some taped dance music. Gaby took Frank's arm and led him out to the tiled dance area.

"Nice young lady," Emerson murmured to his daughter.

Alana usually drank moderately, but because of her marital problems and disquieting thoughts about Stevens, she drank more than usual this night. She was beginning to feel the effect. She looked at Stevens and Gaby. The young girl was pressing provocatively against the General.

"She's young enough to be his daughter," she snapped angrily.

"Alana," chided her father, "I do believe you are jealous."

"Don't be absurd, father," she returned--really trying to convince herself. She felt angry with Frank for flaunting the young girl before her.

She spoke again to her father. "She's not the sweet, innocent young thing she pretends to be!"

Emerson asked Mary to dance. Jim Moore was dancing with Gaby, and Paul Ames was standing at the bar. Alana and Frank were sitting in awkward silence at the table. Finally, forced by the situation, he asked her to dance. He took her in his arms, and they both felt a strong current flow between them. As they danced, without talking, he was conscious of a sweet and gentle fragrance. That, and the warmth of her body, made him feel slightly intoxicated. They danced effortlessly, wordlessly, slowly becoming oblivious to those around them. She felt his strong arm about her waist, holding her close. Without realizing what she was doing, she pressed her body closer. The contact ignited an electric current between them. Alana felt a warm longing and an almost uncontrollable urge to drop her composure. At that moment she realized that she wanted this man! This quiet, scarred warrior from a different world, this killer of men, had moved into her world and caused something to happen. When he tightened his arm around her waist, it sent shivers down her spine. The music had stopped, and the others were returning to their seats before Alana and Frank were aware that the dance was over. They returned to the present and broke apart.

Paul was about as drunk as usual, but he was sober enough to see what everyone else saw. As Frank sat down, Paul came over and demanded accusingly: "Have you been sleeping with my wife?"

A heavy mantle of silence fell over the group. Alana was first to break the quiet. "Paul, how could you say such a thing? What on earth is wrong with you?"

Paul lurched, spilling his drink. "Hell, anyone can see what's going on between you and the General."

Stevens said quietly, restraining his anger: "Paul, you're way off base." He stood up. "Mr. Emerson, if you will excuse us, we must leave." He reached down, took Gaby's arm, and ushered her toward the door.

Paul shouted after them, "Hey, General. Where are you going? You're not so brave without your Army to back you up, are you? You're nothing but hired help, and way out of your element here."

"Paul, sit down and shut up!" ordered Emerson. Alana's father had tried to stay out of their problems, but even he was sick of the way Paul was acting. He followed Stevens and put a hand on his shoulder. "I'm very sorry, Frank. Paul's drunk. He doesn't know what he's saying."

Mistaking Stevens' quick departure for capitulation, Paul continued to press his advantage. Having gained false self-confidence by Stevens' apparent retreat, he moved menacingly toward the young General.

"The hell I don't know what I'm saying," he spat out. "You stay out of this, old man. I'm sick and tired of your interfering bullshit!"

Moore had been quiet, watching the situation develop. "Better back off, Paul," he warned.

Alana ran and grabbed her husband's arm. He shook her off and, turning suddenly, he slapped her across the face. "Bitch!" he yelled. The sound of the slap cracked through the room. Alana staggered backward, hand to her face, tears forming in her eyes.

Paul raised his arm to strike again, but a vice-like hand grasped his arm, spun him around, and he was facing a blazing Stevens. The General's face was as hard as granite, his eyes cold and penetrating. Ames swung at him, but his doubled up fist was stopped in midair. There was a loud snap as Stevens' hand moved in a blur and broke Paul's wrist. Ames screamed and stumbled back.

What Alana saw in the soldier's eyes frightened her as she had never been frightened before. She ran and grabbed Stevens' arms from behind. "No, Frank. No more!" she sobbed. She felt his hard muscles loosen.

He walked over to Paul, who was holding his arm and moaning. "If you ever touch her again, I'll kill you!" There was no doubt that he meant what he said.

"Alana, I'm sorry this happened," Stevens said quietly. He turned and walked out of the house. Gaby followed, running to keep up.

General Moore turned to Paul and examined his wrist. "Come on, you idiot, I'll take you to the hospital."

Paul pulled away angrily to face William Emerson, who was livid with rage. "Paul, get out of this house. Now! You are finished with this family, and with my company."

Paul hurried out of the front door, escorted by Moore. "I'll see that his arm is cared for," said the General.

Alana put her arms around her father: "Daddy, I'm going to divorce him. I can't stand to live with him any longer!"

"I know, dear." He patted her back. "I've known for a long time. Paul is a sick man; and we can't help him, but I'll find him a doctor. Also, I'll call a lawyer for you."

Later, Alana lay in bed thinking back over the evening. Frank had fought for her! No one ever had fought for her before besides her father. She could shut her eyes and see the look on his face and see his angry eyes. She wondered what would have happened if she hadn't stopped him? She still could feel his iron-like strength when he held her as they danced.

★ ★ ★ ★ ★

"I'm sorry that happened, Gaby," Stevens said as they were driving home.

"It wasn't your fault, Frank."

"I know, but I have never liked that pompous drunk. Maybe I should have handled it differently."

Gaby was quiet for a while, then she said: "Alana's in love with you."

"Don't be absurd," he said, "we're from two different worlds. Actually, we hardly know each other."

"Women can tell such things, Frank. She was so jealous

156

of me that she could hardly stand it. Her eyes never left you all evening. Do you love her?"

"No. Well, I've never even thought about it," he lied. "She is just the boss's daughter, and I'm one of the hired hands, like Paul said."

"Anyway, you need someone like me to take care of you dear General," she purred. "I know what you need."

Gaby reached over and put her hand on his leg and began rubbing gently. Stevens put his foot on the brakes to avoid hitting the car in front of him. "You're going to make me wreck the car," he said.

Gaby giggled and leaned over to whisper in his ear, "You tend to your driving, Mon Cheri, and I'll tend to you."

"You know that you are a little sex maniac, don't you young lady?"

"Ah yes, but do not forget I am French," she laughed.

★　★　★　★　★

The next morning, Stevens was sitting in General Moore's office having coffee. Moore sat down his cup and looked over at his friend. "Frank, I'm glad you didn't hurt Paul any worse. He's nothing but a worthless drunk. Emerson once had high hopes for him, but Paul has turned out to be an embarrassment. During the last year, he has completely gone overboard: chasing women, gambling, making stupid business decisions. At first, Emerson blamed himself for keeping Alana away from home so much, but now I think he realizes that it wouldn't have made any difference."

Stevens took a sip of coffee. "Ames knows too much about our operation. I'm worried that he'll say something to the wrong people."

"No, I don't think so Frank. He knows the Old Man would kill him. Besides, he doesn't know enough details to harm us. After all, the fact that we are organizing a mercenary outfit for the Saudis is no secret. It's just something that we don't want blasted all over the front pages. Some of our future operations may get a bit touchy."

"I really feel bad about what happened, but I couldn't stand there and let him hit Alana again."

"You really like her, don't you Frank?"

"Well, I know that we have very different backgrounds, and that she's married, and that she never could understand an old war horse like me. But, she is the most attractive woman I've ever met--not just in looks, but also her personality and intelligence."

"You know Frank, Paul was right about one thing. There is some sort of an attraction between you and Alana. Hell, anyone can see that."

"General, I once swore that I would never allow myself to fall in love again. The hurt was too great. As you know, if it hadn't been for me, Nuyen would still be alive. I have to live with the knowledge that I caused her death."

"You're still blaming yourself, aren't you? Well, Frank, that's where you're wrong. Nuyen has been dead for a very long time, and her death wasn't your fault. She was a soldier, just like you. You have punished yourself long enough. Don't you think that it's about time that you buried her and got on with life? If you want Alana, then reach out for her!"

★ ★ ★ ★ ★

Maxine Davenport had never met anyone quite like Dave Braxton. He was the only black man that she had ever dated, and she would be the first to admit that initially she dated him out of curiosity. The curiosity had turned to friendship and admiration, and finally to love. Dave was the perfect gentleman. He also was somewhat of a romantic. He was kind, gentle, and considerate. Each time he came to pick her up, he brought her a single red rose.

However, she was just a little puzzled at his behavior, because after a dozen dates, he still hadn't tried to make love to her. Still, she felt that he liked her a great deal--maybe even loved her. Maxine was not a prude; she was a mature woman with a strong sexual appetite. She found herself wanting this American soldier to make love to her. She decided to take the initiative. She offered to prepare a meal at his quarters and gave him a list of groceries that she needed.

When Braxton came to pick her up, she was carrying a small overnight bag. He glanced at it with a puzzled look on his face.

"Well, I am going to stay all night, aren't I?" She smiled.

"Ah, yes, if you want to," he said, surprised.

"I want to!" she said frankly. "Now shall we go?"

Later, as she sat across the table and watched Braxton eat a third helping of beef stroganoff, she mused: "I haven't cooked for a man for a long time."

"It was delicious! You are an excellent cook," he said, wiping his mouth with his napkin.

"I like to cook for a man. I miss it," she admitted.

After the meal, he put on an apron to help her with the dishes. She laughed: "That apron doesn't do much for your macho image."

"It's not for looks, my dear; it's practical."

When the dishes were finished, she stood on her tiptoes and kissed him. "Please excuse me? I'm going to change my image." She returned 20 minutes later wearing a floor-length black negligee. She also had on black bikini panties, but no bra. The outline of her full, ripe breasts were plainly visible through the thin material. She stopped in the middle of the room and did a pirouette. "Any comment?"

"Beautiful!" he answered.

"Will you make love to me?" she asked in a husky voice.

It took Braxton three strides to close the distance between them and take her in his arms. Their lips met in a long, passionate kiss. Finally they parted, and he looked down at her. "I love you."

"And I love you," she returned. She took his hand as they

moved toward the bedroom.

Facing him, she slowly unbuttoned his shirt. She reached up and peeled it off, then ran her hands over his muscular torso. She had never seen him without a shirt before. He was built like a weight-lifter, and his muscles stood out like burnished ebony. She kissed his chest. He reached over and pulled the straps of her negligee from her shoulders to let it fall to her waist. Maxine pushed it past her hips and stepped free. She hooked her thumbs in her panties and slid them off.

Braxton stepped back, undid his belt, and pulled off his trousers.

"Is that all you?" she asked with an amazed look on her face. "You're magnificent!"

They lay down on the bed, and his large hands caressed her tenderly. She moaned and moved to his touch as her passion heightened.

"Be gentle, honey. Don't hurt me," she pleaded, reaching down to help him.

He was caught in a vise as she moved faster and faster. "Oh my gawd," she cried, and her body shuddered.

Braxton could feel himself ready. He groaned aloud.

Later, Maxine lay next to him, feeling satisfied and thoroughly loved. Suddenly she began to giggle.

"What's funny?" he asked.

She raised up on her elbow and looked at him. "Have you ever seen that Alka Seltzer commercial where the guy says 'I can't believe I ate the whole thing'?"

"Yes," he answered, puzzled.

"Well," she laughed, "I can't believe I took the whole thing!"

He reached out and touched her cheek. "I didn't hurt you, did I?"

"No, my sweet. It was wonderful. I loved it, and I love you!"

14

On the morning of 17 July, a Motorized Infantry Regiment from South Yemen moved into the Southern Province and occupied the city of Abar in the region of the Dhan Oasis. The Emir of Abar proclaimed the province an Independent State under the protection of South Yemen.

A few hours after this proclamation, Stevens was summoned to a special meeting in General Moore's office. There he joined Prince Mohamad, William Emerson, and a Saudi General who introduced himself as Suleman.

The Prince was somber, and plainly worried. There was pain in his dark eyes. He spread a map on the conference table. "We have trouble in the Southern Province," he announced. "A military unit from South Yemen has crossed the border and occupied the city of Abar." He pointed to the location on the map. "The Emir of the Province, along with some Shiite fanatics, has joined in proclaiming independence from the Kingdom. There also appears to be trouble in Al Hasa. We were expecting problems in these areas, but not so soon. It is imperative that we settle these problems as soon as possible to prevent the revolt from spreading. The National Guard has been alerted at Al Hasa."

The Prince paused and turned to Stevens. "My friend,

we would like you to take your squadron, along with the Second Saudi Combined Arms Battalion, and go to Abar with all haste. Use whatever force necessary to put down the rebellion. If you decide the enemy force is too large, engage them, and keep them contained until we can get more military units into the area. Unfortunately, it probably will be three or four days before we can get the 2nd Brigade to Abar from the northern border."

"General Suleman will accompany you as my representative in negotiations with the rebels. He will give them a chance to quit the city and to pull back into South Yemen before you use force. If you have to attack, General Stevens, try to keep civilian casualties to a minimum." He stared evenly at Stevens. "Now, my friend. How soon can you leave for Abar?"

Four hours later, a cortege of iron-skinned pachyderms moved out of the cantonment area near Riyadh and entered the Rub Al Khali (the Empty Quarter, one of the most foreboding and least explored sand deserts in the world). Abar lay 450 miles south. At first, the V-150's moved rapidly across the hard desert floor, but as the surface turned to churning sand, the movement slowed. Massive red sand dunes loomed in the distance, looking like great waves in an angry sea. The column wound its way in between the great dunes as the Rub Al Khali swallowed them up. They traveled all night. The next morning the sun appeared--splendid in a cloudness sky. By 1400 hours they were less than 160 km from Abar. Stevens called a halt and ordered his force to go to ground. Camouflage nets were draped over the Commandos, and the men ate their rations and rested. By 1500 hours, it was 160 degrees in the boiling sun.

Stevens sat under the sloping hull of his V-150, deep in his own thoughts. Sweat trickled in rivulets down his face and dripped onto the map he was studying. He tried to plan, but it was difficult in the stifling heat. He dozed and dreamed of Nuyen. Nuyen became Alana. They were beating her. Her face turned to him, pleading for help---. He awakened, drenched in his own perspiration. For years his dead wife had troubled his mind, and now Alana had joined her. A man dreams of two things: what he is most afraid of and what he most wants.

At 1700 hours, Stevens ordered the column forward, slower this time for they were nearing Abar and chance of running into a rebel position or patrol also increased. Stevens moved up to the Scout Section, well-ahead of the main body. He called a halt at 2200 hours, not daring to take his main force any closer without first reconnoitering the rebel stronghold.

He took Braxton and Devlin with him in his Commando. With the Scout Section, they moved forward, cautiously, to check out the approach to Abar. The main force remained behind, hidden by the contours of the land.

The moon lighted the desert like a giant torch. It was so bright that Stevens could read the map without a flashlight. At 2400 hours, Stevens and Braxton were lying, belly-flat, atop a sand dune about 1,000 meters northeast of Abar. From this vantage point they had an excellent view of the village and of the surrounding terrain. Abar was encircled by a series of low, hard-earth hills on the north and red sand dunes on the east and south. To the west, the desert stretched out flat and open as far as the eye could see. There were about 800 meters of open ground between the hills on the north, the dunes on the east, and the village. This would permit the defenders an excellent field of fire on anything approaching. The main road, which his force had carefully avoided, entered the village from the north. Another road ran from the village to the south, toward South Yemen. There was a shallow wadi 500 meters north of the village. Abar, a village of 2,000, was nothing more than a collection of mud-brick structures, sprawled haphazardly around an oasis.

Stevens glanced at his watch. The luminous digits showed 0030. Looking through his field glasses, he couldn't detect any military preparations. The village hardly looked worth fighting for. However, there was water, and since water is the lifeline of the desert, it made the location important. Now it was more important than ever because the rebels had chosen the site to challenge the rule of the Saudi King.

Stevens pondered the consequences of failure. The future of his squadron was at stake; the impact upon Saudi-U.S. relations would be enormous; and the likelihood of another Iran in Saudi Arabia was possible. There could be no question of failure--they had to succeed.

There didn't seem to be any rebel strong-points in the surrounding desert. It appeared as if the enemy would defend the village. If so, it was a mistake, because that would limit their maneuver capability. and they would not be taking advantage of the terrain.

After returning to his Task Force, Stevens called a meeting of his commanders. In the sand he sketched a model of the village and the surrounding terrain. When they were assembled, he issued his order. "The 2nd Battalion will move and occupy the high ground north of Abar. The Merc Squadron will move in behind the sand dunes, east of the village, and remain hidden, with the 3rd Company continuing on and establishing a blocking position astride the road running out of Abar to the south. The artillery will support from here." He pointed to the location on the map.

"All units must be in position by first light. At 0600 hours, General Suleman will approach Abar under a flag of truce and demand that the rebels surrender. If that fails, we attack. The artillery will initiate the attack, and the 2nd Battalion will provide supporting fire from their positions on the high ground. The Merc Squadron will deploy on line formation but remain hidden behind the dunes. On my order, the 2nd Battalion will assault from the north and move as far as the wadi. From there they will support with fire as the Merc Squadron attacks from the east. Hopefully, the 2nd Battalion attack will cause the rebels to concentrate their defense to the north, and the Squadron can hit them from the flank. Inshallah!"

By daylight, all units were in position. The command group--Stevens, Purdy and Braxton--were located atop the same dunes where Stevens had studied the village earlier. From the village they could hear the cry of the Iman (Holy Man) calling the faithful to morning prayer:

"Allaho Akbar." (God is most great.)

"Ashadu an la Ilaha Illa-Allah." (I testify that there is no God but God.)

"Ashadu anna Mohammadan Rasoulo-Allah." (I testify that Muhammed is the Prophet of God.)

"Hayya ala Assalah." (Come to prayer.)

"Hayya ala Alfala." (Come to salvation.)

"Assalato khairon mina annowm." (Prayer is better than sleep.)

"Allaho akbar." (God is most great.)

"La Ilaha Illa-Allah." (There is no God but God.)

At 0630 hours, General Suleman approached Abar from the north with his V-150 flying a white flag. A land rover drove from the village to meet him. There followed a 30 minute discussion. Finally, Suleman returned. Stevens could tell the results of the parley by his face.

"They refused!" he announced, angrily. "I gave them one hour to allow the noncombatants to leave."

Within a half-hour, streams of people carrying what belongings they could began to pour from Abar. Some were in cars, some on foot, and some were herding goats or sheep. Some went south; others moved north. Now there was nothing to do but wait. This was the worst part of battle for the soldier--the waiting. This was when all doubts and fears flashed through a commander's mind. Stevens thought of everything that could go wrong. What if the opposition was larger than he had calculated? Had their scouts picked us up miles back? Are we walking into a trap? Are there more units waiting in the hills to pounce on us? Do they know that the Merc Squadron is hiding to the east? Are there still women and children in the village? Are the men ready to fight? Will the Saudis fight? All of these questions, plus many more, were running through Stevens' mind. They wouldn't be answered until the last shot echoed across the desert.

Inside the village of Abar, Abdul Rashid, the leader of the rebel forces, also was thinking with deep concern. His troops were a mixture of regular South Yemen soldiers and hastily organized Shiites from the surrounding area. He hadn't expected the Saudis to arrive for two more days. By that time, he would have had 20,000 men occupying Abar. However, he wasn't too concerned because there was only one Saudi Battalion, and the V-150's were no match for his tanks. He decided that the Saudis must have come through the desert, because his agents along the Riyadh road had not reported their approach.

This was just the beginning, he thought. Soon the Shiites throughout the Kingdom would be up in arms. Already they should be in revolt at Al Hasa. In a few days, the Bedouin tribes in southern Saudi Arabia would be flocking to his banners. The time for the destruction of the Saudi monarchy was at hand!

Abdul Rashid was the nephew of the leader of South Yemen, Sherif Ben Abr Rashid, and had been selected by the old Sherif to strike the first blow for the Arabian Empire. Rashid had no doubts that his Russian tanks and artillery could destroy the flimsy Saudi Battalion. He ordered his artillery to open fire. The morning stillness was shattered by the crash of his guns.

The firing was inaccurate at first, most of it falling well to the rear of the Saudi positions. After ten minutes, they shortened the range, and the rounds commenced to fall dangerously close.

Stevens sniffed the morning air and turned to Braxton. "Dave, it's as good a day as any to die." Then he turned to his artillery forward observer: "O.K., Johnny, soften 'em up!" With those few words, Stevens had started his desert war. The game was opened--there was no turning back.

Two spotting rounds were fired, and some minor adjustments were made. Then over the radio the forward observer ordered: "Fire for effect!"

The heavy "crump" of the attacker's artillery shook the sand-packed desert, and the city of Abar began disintegrating into spouts of broken mortar and sand.

Stevens moved his commando, skirting the sand dunes, and joined his Squadron to the east of the city. He ordered the Saudi Battalion to stay on line and commence firing. The chugging of the heavy 20's and 50's and the chattering of the light machine guns gradually built into a frenzied crescendo. With their zipping sound, the Vulcan Gatling guns had a devastating effect upon the mud-bruck buildings, literally grinding them to pieces. The whining "whoosh" made by the high-velocity 90mm shells before they exploded on the target was nerve-wracking.

Gradually the din of battle built up. Smoke curled over the desert. The air smelled of cordite. Three Russian-made M-72 tanks moved to the northern edge of Abar and tried to pick off the Saudi vehicles. However, the Saudis were firing from hull-defilade behind the ridgeline, making themselves difficult targets. A Saudi TOW-gunner zeroed in on one of the tanks. The wire-guided anti-tank missile scored a direct hit, and the tank exploded. The remaining tanks scurried back to the protection of the village.

Stevens ordered the Saudis to move forward to the wadi north of the village. They sped up and over the hill and headed toward Abar with their weapons blazing.

So far, the Merc Squadron remained uncommitted. Stevens believed their presence still was unknown to the defenders.

He glanced at his steel-hulled paladins: on line, engines running, weapons primed, ready for his command to send them to victory or to death.

As the Saudi fighting vehicles moved downhill toward the wadi, two were destroyed by the defender's tanks. The rest made it to the protection of the wadi.

Stevens ordered the artillery to smoke the village in an attempt to blind the defenders. As the smoke began to drift solidly over the village, he ordered his Merc Squadron to attack. With his Commando leading, the line of iron-skinned monsters shot forward. The Squadron roared up over the sand dunes, leaving trails of dust behind.

Stevens was at home now. His senses were in tune to everything that was taking place. There was no fear in him--the time for fear was past. Enemy shells cracked overhead and pinged off his armored vehicle. Squeezing the trigger, he sent streams of .50 caliber bullets smacking into the mud houses as he drew nearer.

Abdul Rashid's world was crumbling, just as the village of Abar was crumbling under the devastating enemy fire. He had never seen a shot fired in anger before, and already he had a belly-full. Suddenly he heard firing coming from the east. What he saw paralyzed him with fear! A long line of armored cars were roaring toward the village, their guns spouting death! Along with his staff, he ran out of the concrete shelter and headed toward an undamaged truck.

Back on a sand dune where he could see all of the battle, Tom Purdy gave an order over his radio and fired a green smoke streamer. The Saudis ceased their supporting fire as Stevens and his Squadron of iron-replacements for the ship of the desert crashed into the village like ravenous beasts. Stevens spotted a group of rebels frantically scrambling to load into the back of a truck. He swung the .50 caliber around and squeezed the trigger. The heavy slugs hit the rebels like a bowling ball striking ten-pins. They went flying in all directions. He continued firing until one of his tracers struck the gas tank. The truck exploded in a plume of flames.

Rashid saw the armored car smash through one of the hastily erected barricades. Its heavy machine gun began chugging loudly, and Rashid could see the tracers dancing toward him. He felt a heavy hammer slam against his chest, and he was flung backward. He hit the wall of a mud-brick building and slowly slid to the ground. An ice-cold feeling climbed up his legs. He tried frantically to raise his hands to keep the blood from spilling out of the gaping hole in his chest, but he couldn't move. There was a second of fear as the on-rushing coldness covered his body. Then there was nothing!

The surprise of the attack from the east was complete. The shock of the tide of armored cars smashing into Abar with guns blazing was too much for the rebels. Vehicles and men were running out of the village, heading south. The stunned defenders began throwing down their weapons and raising their hands.

The American General called a cease-fire and ordered his Merc Squadron to fall back. At the same time, he directed the Saudis to come in and take over mopping-up and handling of the prisoners.

Firing from the south indicated the feeling rebels had run into the 3rd Company's blocking position. Within 30 minutes, they came walking back up the road with three Commando armored cars herding them. The scene resembled a herd of elephants shepherding a flock of sheep.

The victory was sweet and complete--a perfect example of the combination of surprise, firepower, shock action, and concentration of forces.

Tom Purdy came roaring up in his Commando, his heavy bulk jutting out of the Commander's hatch: "Well done, General--a neat piece of work. The fight went out of 'em fast!"

Stevens was occupied with reorganizing his forces. Working like a machine, he clicked off orders: "Tom, move the Squadron back to an assembly area. Have 3rd Company remain in their blocking position."

Purdy flipped a salute as his Commando moved out.

Stevens' losses were relatively small. The Merc Squadron had one Commando destroyed, with two men killed and three wounded. The Saudis had three V-150 Commandos destroyed, with nine men KIA and 12 WIA. The rebel count reached 160 killed, and over 600 prisoners were rounded up.

The devastated village smelled of blood, cordite, death, and sheep-dung. With the exception of the sheep-dung, Stevens had smelled the odors many times. The smell of death is unique: sweet, musty, and slightly pungent. There is no other smell on earth quite like it.

A helicoper landed amid a cloud of swirling dust. General Moore and Prince Mohamad stepped out. The Prince strode forward and gripped Stevens' hand. A broad smile covered his face. "Well done, General Stevens! This is a magnificent victory. I think the Yemenis will think twice before trying something like this again."

They walked over and looked at the destroyed Russian tanks. The TOW had proved that, properly employed, they could destroy heavy armor.

"They used their tanks all wrong," Stevens explained. "They should have come out into the desert after us. If they had, our casualties would have been much higher. Whoever was in command here was a complete idiot. I can't understand why he didn't have patrols out in the desert. The hills out there should have been defended. Hell, look at this place! They didn't even dig in! I'm sure they didn't know that we had a force east of the village. They concentrated their forces to the north, and we just rolled right up their flank."

The Task Force remained in Abar another day, then they were relieved by the 1st Saudi Brigade. Stevens called his men together and congratulated them. He left Purdy in charge and flew back to Riyadh with Moore and the Prince.

15

The Saudi Arabian news media hailed the Battle of Abar as a great victory for the Saudi Security Forces. There was no mention of Stevens and his mercenary force, and that was exactly the way he wanted it. A certain anonymity was necessary to insure the future success of his organization.

When the American General returned from Abar, he remembered that he was supposed to have a date with Gaby that evening. He was dog-tired, so he called her to beg off.

"I think I know where you've been!" she said excitedly. "I heard all about it on the tele. Was it bad?"

"Nope," he answered wearily. "Just like a routine field problem, only a little more exciting."

"Well, Mon General. You rest up tonight, and I'll come over tomorrow and fix you a great dinner." Then she added, "And stay longer, if you like."

★ ★ ★ ★ ★

When Alana saw the news report on the Battle of Abar, she instinctively knew that Frank was involved. She fretted all day, not quite knowing why. She could shut her eyes and feel Frank's strong arms around her, and she could see the fire in his eyes as he had gone after Paul. She felt a twinge of jealousy when she thought of Frank making love to that young girl. For some reason, the soldier excited her more than any man ever had. It was a fact that she couldn't keep her mind off of him.

When her father arrived home from the office, she asked with an obviously worried look on her face, "Was Frank at Abar?"

Emerson was in the process of mixing himself a drink. He looked up from his work. "Yes, honey. He was there. In fact, he commanded the entire shebang!"

"Is-- Is he all right?" she stammered.

Emerson walked over and put his arm around his daughter. "Yes, Frank's fine. Remember what Jim said. Frank's indestructible."

He could see the relief on her face. It wasn't difficult to see what was happening between his proud, self-willed daughter and the strong, quiet soldier. He had seen them looking at each other, and he sensed the longing they felt for one another. It would just be a matter of time before one or both of them tore down the barriers between them.

There were times when their relationship was almost laughable, as both seemed to go out of their way not to show their true feelings. Alana tried to avoid Frank and acted aloof when he was around. Frank took special effort to avoid her and to hide his feelings; he had even flaunted Gaby in her presence. Poor, young, innocent Gaby. Emerson wondered if she had any idea what was going on between Frank and Alana.

"Frank's quite a man, isn't he?" Emerson asked his daughter.

Alana's face flushed, feeling as if her father could read her thoughts. She turned and walked toward the kitchen, saying over her shoulder: "Oh, he's O.K. for a professional soldier, but he takes too damn many chances."

Yes, it was apparent that Frank and his daughter were on

a collision course. Emerson decided not to interfere. Better to let nature take its course.

★ ★ ★ ★ ★

Several days after the battle, Prince Mohamad, Stevens and his mercenary officers attended a victory celebration at the 2nd Combined-Arms Battalion. The meal (or kapsa) was the standard Saudi feast. A whole roast sheep was served on a bed of spicy rice, with side dishes of ox-tail soup, salad, and fruits. Prior to the meal, the participants sat in circle on rugs spread on the ground and drank tea and bitter coffee. At intervals, a soldier passed an incense burner to the guests. Each man leaned over and sniffed the sweet fumes. This tradition stems from the old days in the desert, where the smell of cooking sheep and unwashed bodies could get pretty rank inside the Bedouin tents.

The food was spread out on large serving trays placed on elaborately decorated carpets. The guests, all men of course (women never eat with the men on such occasions), gathered around the food and sat on the floor.

There were no eating utensils. All food is picked up with the right hand. The left hand is considered unclean since it is used solely for bodily functions. The guests tore off chunks of lamb and popped them into their mouths. Eating the rice was more difficult. It had to be squeezed and rolled into a ball before eating. The salad and oxtail soup was eaten by breaking off pieces of the Arabian flat bread to use as tweezers to pick up the food.

The American General thoroughly enjoyed the camraderie of the kapsas. He could speak enough Arabic to carry on a decent conversation, and there always were enough English-speaking Saudis present to help him over the rough spots.

In the midst of tearing off another chunk of sheep, Stevens turned to the Battalion Commander: "Latheith alham dulillah! Kalaf Allah Aleiukum!" ("It is delicious, thank God! May God return the favor to you!")

The Commander replied in English. "You are welcome. It is our pleasure to have you with us, General."

The guests moved to another tent and resumed their tea drinking. After a while, one by one, the officers excused themselves. Finally only Stevens and the Prince remained. For some reason unknown to Stevens, Mohamad wanted to speak to him alone.

"Frank," he asked casually, "what do you think of the Palestine situation?"

This was a heavily loaded question. There were two subjects that Americans shied away from talking to Saudis about--religion and Middle East politics. This question dealt with both issues. However, Stevens felt a growing friendship with the Prince, and he instinctively knew that he could speak honestly without committing an offense.

The Palestinian situation is a festering sore in the Middle East, and there never will be peace until the legitimate rights of the Palestinians are recognized and a reasonable solution found. The Arab nations all agree that the four million displaced Palestinians should have their own homeland, and they all give spiritual and financial backing to the Palestine Liberation Organization. However, none of them want the PLO in their country.

After the Second World War, there was a great international feeling of guilt and sympathy for the Jews because of their treatment by the Nazis. With pressure from other Western nations, Britain created a homeland for the Jews. In 1948, the British departed Palestine, leaving the Jews and Arabs to straighten things out. The Palestinian Arabs were driven from their homes and across the Jordan River to an area called the West Bank. This area was absorbed under the protection of Jordan. Gaza in the south went to Egypt, and the Golan Heights in the north went to Syria.

In 1967, the Jews attacked in a lightning war lasting only

six days. Their victory was overwhelming. They seized the West Bank and Jerusalem from Jordan, driving the Palestinians further into Jordan. A few months later, King Hussein, fearing that the PLO would dethrone him, used military force to drive them from his country. In the final analysis, in creating a homeland for one group of displaced persons, the world, in fact, created another group of displaced people.

"Your Excellency," Stevens began. "I'm afraid that it is almost an unsolvable problem. There never will be peace in the Middle East as long as the Palestinians do not have a home. I have to be honest and say that I always have admired the Israelis and the Israeli Army. However, like most Americans, I only knew one side of the story. In the last few years I have learned a lot more about the Middle East, and the situation is no longer simple for me. I also have come to admire the Arab people, and I feel a great sympathy for the Palestinians. I think the ultimate solution must be the creation of a Palestinian State in the area of the West Bank, in conjunction with recognition of Israel by all the Arab nations. But, I fear the only way a Palestine State will ever be created is through international pressure on Israel."

The Prince listened intently. He leaned forward, asking a question he already knew the answer to. "Why is it that most Americans are for the Jews?"

"I think there are several reasons. First of all, there still is a great national sympathy because of the Holocaust. However, the main reason is what I call the Jewish lobby. The Jewish-Arab problem is very similar to the Greek-Turkish problem. Turkey is a great ally of the United States, having an army of 400,000 men, and the Turks are good soldiers. That country is an important member of NATO, anchoring its southeastern flank. The Turkish people have great admiration for America. We, meaning the Western nations, need Turkey in our camp. There is no comparison, in my mind, between the relative importance of Greece versus Turkey. Turkey should be the obvious choice; however, most Americans are for Greece. Why? Because the Greek lobby is powerful. Every American knows a Greek. He is either their doctor, lawyer, or local restaurant owner. But, very few Americans know a Turk. They picure a Turk as a dark-complexioned man, with a great black mustache—a barbarian, brandishing a great curved scimitar. Of course this is far from the truth." Stevens paused and smiled.

"As you can tell, I have great admiration for Turkey and the Turkish people. The 1974 Arms Embargo we imposed on Turkey was one of the most foolish acts ever committed in foreign policy. It greatly weakened the NATO infrastructure, and almost caused us to lose one of our most staunch allies.

"In America, the Arab image suffers in much the same way. First of all, there are many more Jews in the United States than there are Arabs. They are doctors, lawyers, merchants, and in general, influential people. Very few Americans know any Arabs. The average American pictures an Arab as a rich Sheik, running around the country flaunting his wealth. Look at the bad publicity Al Fossi has caused. Most Americans consider him a nut. He throws money around as if he has it to burn. Then, there was that business of trying to bribe a city to vote against the President. He certainly isn't helping the Arab image.

"Also, there isn't much empathy for the Palestinians in America. The reason is because the word Palestine has become synonomous with the word terrorist. The PLO terrorist activities, whether right or wrong, have harmed the Palestinian and Arab images in America. Most Americans don't realize that out of four million homeless people, only a small handful have engaged in terrorist activities."

Prince Mohamad interrupted him. "You understand, don't you, that terrorism has become part of the arsenal of unconventional warfare? For years this has been the only kind of warfare the Palestinians have been able to engage in. And it is a fact that the first modern terrorist in the Middle East was Menachem Begin. In 1947, he blew up a hotel in Jerusalem, killing 19 British civilians. The Israelis started terrorism!"

"Yes, I know that," answered Stevens, "but the general American public does not. And as long as Khadafy and the PLO continue to use terrorism as a primary weapon-- Americans will be turned off. We have a new wave of conservatism sweeping America, and Americans want some action taken that will punish those that use, finance, and support terrorism."

The American General stopped and took a sip of tea. The Prince sat quietly, digesting the American's words and studying him. Then he asked: "Are you familiar with the Saudi Eight-Point Peace Plan that we recently proposed to the United Nations?"

"Yes, Your Excellency, I am," returned Stevens, "And I must say that I pretty much agree with the plan. Actually, it's very close to the plan recently proposed by our President. If I recall correctly, your plan called for the return of all occupied Arab lands and the creation of an Independent Palestine State, with East Jerusalem as the capital."

"That's essentially correct," said Mohamad, "and it also called for all Arab nations to recognize Israel."

"But neither the Jews nor most of the Arab countries have indicated an interest in such a plan," interjected Stevens.

"Unfortunately, no," the Prince said, shaking his head sadly. "We Saudis want to see a peaceful Middle East, and we realize that the Jewish state is already a fact of life." He cocked his head slightly to the left and looked at Stevens. "What do you think Saudi Arabia's role should be in the Middle East?"

"Well, I believe that your country should do exactly as you are," Stevens answered positively, "and that is to exert a moderating influence and to play the peace-keeping role. Saudi Arabia enjoys a unique position in the Arab world. You have financial power, you are the recognized leader of

OPEC, and you are the religious leader of the Muslim world. Unlike other Arab nations, you are at peace with your neighbors. These things combine to make you a powerful nation with political influence. I believe that Saudi Arabia holds the key to peace in the Middle East. That's why you must become stronger from a military standpoint--at least strong enough to handle an internal disorder. Any weakening of the Saudi family, at least for the forseeable future, would mean trouble for the Middle East in general, and for the United States in particular."

"Your ideas are very interesting for one who has only been here a short while," said the Prince thoughtfully. "You are a very perceptive man, General. If you could influence your country, what would you have America do?"

Stevens thought for a minute. "Well, first of all, we must support our friends again. Somewhere, after the Bay of Pigs and during the Vietnam War, we lost our national resolve. Now we are paralyzed by the fear of becoming involved in another Vietnam. Then Jimmy Carter came along and under the guise of human rights gave Nicaragua to the communists, Angola to the communists, the Panama Canal to a government friendly to Cuba, Iran to a group unfriendly to the U.S., almost gave El Salvador to the communists, and abandoned aid to Guatemala, Chile, and Ethiopia. Another four years of Carter, and we would have been speaking Russian."

The Prince gave an understanding smile; he knew only too well the impact of the weakening of American foreign policy.

The young General continued: "Things have improved under Reagan. He understands the communist problem and knows what should be done--but he's hamstrung by a weak, liberal Congress, that still thinks like Jimmy Carter. Here in the Middle East we need to take a more positive stand. We need to clearly identify our friends and back them. If America had to choose between Israel and Saudi Arabia, we would opt for Saudi Arabia. We can survive without

Israel, but at the present time we cannot survive without your oil. And your nation is more strategically located, and you exert a more positive influence in this part of the world."

The Prince was surprised by the General's statement. Surprised, and pleased. He was beginning to see something special in this American officer--a feeling of destiny.

Stevens continued: "I would like to see the U.S. demand that Israel withdraw from the occupied West Bank and insist that a Palestinian homeland be established there. However, I don't honestly believe that we have enough influence on Israel to help it happen. In return for Israel's cooperation, the U.S. would have to be willing to sign a treaty with Israel to help defend her with military force, if need be."

Mohamad had wanted to "feel out" Stevens' views on the Middle East. Actually, he had received more than he had expected. The Prince was impressed with the American's knowledge and personal beliefs. He could visualize a future for the American that even Stevens could not imagine.

16

Two weeks after the victory at Abar, Stevens, his Exec Tom Purdy, and Dave Braxton attended a special meeting called by General Moore. They were joined in Moore's conference room by Prince Mohamad, Emerson, and the Deputy Director of the CIA, Samuel Bertram.

Moore started the meeting: "Gentlemen, we were correct in suspecting outside complicity in the Abar revolt. Prisoners have confirmed that both Libyan and Iranian personnel have been operating in South Yemen for several months. Khadafy has been supplying arms and instructors, and Khomeini had sent hundreds of volunteers to beef up the Yemeni forces. However, the incursion and revolt may have been premature, or Khadafy may have used this as an excuse to test the waters. In any event, it was bad timing, and it was disastrous for them." Moore gestured toward the CIA man. "Sam, do you want to take it from here?"

Bertram sat back and lighted his pipe. Smoke rose around his face, obscuring his expression. "Khadafy is planning something big. We believe his ultimate goal is to take over North Africa and the Middle East. To accomplish this, he would have to destroy Israel and overthrow the Saudi monarchy. Khadafy sees himself as a 'Prophet' and the future leader of an Arab Empire stretching across North Africa and east to Afghanistan."

Stevens broke in: "That's pretty ambitious. His appetite sounds bigger than his stomach."

Bertram took a puff on his pipe: "It's not as far-fetched now as it seemed a few months ago. We have good reason to believe that soon he may have nuclear weapons!" He paused to allow his announcement to sink in. Everyone in the room realized the implications of his statement.

Bertram continued, his voice deadly serious. "He tried to buy them from the Russians and Chinese, but they both recognized the potential danger of having someone like Khadafy with his finger on a nuclear trigger. The other powers have been wary of selling anything to the Libyans that could be used to make a bomb, but it appears he is about to do it anyway. Evidently he finally has been able to assemble the necessary ingredients and the skilled technicians. He received much of the material through the terrorist pipeline. Last year, Uranium 235 was stolen from a plant near Antwerp, and Plutonium was taken from a nuclear reactor in Paris. There have been other unreported thefts. Khadafy has a secret nuclear reactor somewhere in Africa or the Middle East. We don't think that he has any nuclear devices ready yet. If he had, he surely would have used them when Israel invaded Lebanon. He must have been frustrated missing such an opportunity. As it was, he only could shout from the sidelines."

Emerson leaned forward and exclaimed, "Good God! He must be stopped. The damned fool could start World War III."

"Exactly," returned Bertram, "or, at the very least, cause a nuclear holocaust in the Middle East. His plan is the audacious scheme of a fanatical madman! If he develops a nuclear bomb, he's just crazy enough to use it."

"A fanatic perhaps," said Stevens, tonelessly, "but hardly a madman--he's not crazy. He's motivated by very strong religious beliefs, like the Ayatollah Khomeini, and that makes him doubly dangerous. There is nothing worse than fighting a religious fanatic. But you're right, if Khadafy has the bomb, he will use it."

Prince Mohamad spoke for the first time. "The danger is clear. We realize that Libya and Iran are actively conspiring to destroy the monarchy, therefore they must be stopped. As you know, we are not a strong nation militarily. However, we will give you whatever help you need as far as money, equipment, and bases from which to operate."

General Moore nodded his head, as if acknowledging the Prince's offer. Then he turned to Stevens. "Frank, here is our plan. We want Purdy to take over the merc squadron. This will free you to concentrate your efforts on locating and destroying Khadafy's reactor. You'll be provided with a headquarters and whatever personnel and equipment you need. We think it best for your main office to be here in Riyadh, because it will give you a relatively secure operational base. Sam will put the resources of the Agency at your disposal. This mission will be top priority for both the United States and for Saudi Arabia."

Within one week, Stevens had a new apartment and offices in a modern villa on the outskirts of Riyadh. He brought several men with him from the squadron, including Dave Braxton and the Intelligence Officer Jimmy Devlin. General Suleman was on hand to represent the Saudi Government. John Rinks, an old acquaintance, headed the CIA contigent. Rinks was an "Old Mid-East hand" and one of the top dirty-tricks men in the business. His looks were deceiving. One would expect to see the pudgy, middle-aged, bespectacled gentleman on a college campus rather than on the clandestine battlefields of the world. Rinks brought with him three Intel Analysts--all Middle East experts--and several communications and electronics types to operate the sophisticated paraphernalia that was being installed.

The task ahead was not going to be easy. Finding the reactor was going to be like finding the proverbial needle. It could be in any one of a dozen countries--even down in central Africa. After locating it, they would have to find a way to destroy it.

Stevens placed Braxton in charge of organizing and training a "special action squad," whose mission was as yet undefined.

Since supporters of international terrorism were helping Khadafy, Stevens decided to concentrate on the terrorist groups as potential sources of information. This meant using the Agency resources to gather and correlate data with other friendly nations. What he wanted to do was to refine and integrate this intelligence in order to monitor the worldwide terrorist activities, with the objective of gaining information on the Libyan strong man.

Since money was no problem, Stevens thought if he pumped enough cash into the terrorist pipeline he might get some results. Devlin already had contacts in Europe and Northern Ireland, so he departed with a bag of money to cast upon terrorist waters.

Soon they were receiving daily intelligence reports via coded teletype from the CIA and Defense Intelligence Agency (DIA). Through satellites, they began systematically to photograph North Africa and the Middle East. Before long they were identifying new terrorist training camps in Iran, South Yemen, and Libya, but there was no sign of any nuclear reactor. All reports and information coming in were negative with regard to a possible site for building nuclear weapons. Stevens' staff of experts was beginning to doubt the existence of such a facility.

Then one day a lead came from Iran. An anti-Khomeni faction headed by Iranian Army Colonel Abar Ben Dahgn made contact with one of the Saudi Princes in an effort to get Saudi backing to overthrow the Khomeini regime. In a subsequent meeting, one of the Iranians told Prince Mohamad that Colonel Dahgn had information concerning a nuclear reactor.

The Iranian Colonel was persuaded to have a clandestine meeting with the Prince. William Emerson's villa near Athens was chosen for the rendezvous.

Under the guise of a short vacation, Bill Emerson, Alana, Prince Mohamad and his wife and their bodyguards flew to Athens in the Prince's Lear Jet. Since the two families had vacationed together before, it was a good cover for their real intentions.

Two days later, Stevens and Braxton followed aboard the weekly Air Force courier flight to Athens. Since they flew military air, it was easy for them to carry personal sidearms. After Cairo, Stevens wasn't about to venture out of Saudi Arabia unarmed. Emerson's chauffeur picked them up and drove them to the Emerson home. On the way, Stevens felt the nervous anticipation of seeing Alana again. He hadn't seen her since the night of his scuffle with Paul, but she was frequently on his mind. He could still remember the warmth of her body against his. Just the thought of her filled him with a warm desire.

TRIPOLI, LIBYA.

Four hours after Stevens departed Riyadh, Colonel Mustapha Amak was reading a message handed to him by an aide:

GENERAL STEVENS DEPARTED RIYADH ABOARD U.S. AIR FORCE PLANE ENROUTE TO ATHENS. BELIEVE HE WILL BE STAYING AT

Lately it had become apparent that the American General was heading up some sort of counter-terrorist organization whose main target was the leader of Libya. This was their first opportunity to get at him since Cairo. They must not fail this time! Mustapha picked up his phone.

ATHENS.

The Emerson villa was a picturesque, white-concrete edifice of Spanish-Mediterranean architecture, situated on a cliff overlooking the deep blue waters of the Aegean Sea. The red-tiled roof, olive trees, and fences of oleanders were right out of the life and times of Zorba the Greek.

Alana met them at the door. She was wearing jeans and a T-shirt. Her perfect figure took Stevens' breath away. His heart beat faster at her nearness.

"Come in," she smiled, her brown eyes sparkling. "The others are on the patio."

She led them through luxuriously furnished rooms, and out onto an enormous patio.

Prince Mohamad had discarded his traditional robes and was wearing a dark blue business suit. He was drinking a martini. His wife was without veil and looked lovely in a Western style cocktail dress. Her beauty was a close match to Alana's.

The patio jutted over the turquoise waters below. White-topped waves lapped hungrily at the narrow beach. Stevens was instantly captivated by the setting. He walked over to the railing and looked out to sea. He took a deep breath, inhaling the fresh salt air. It was exhilarating.

He felt Alana beside him. Her shoulder touched his. "This is my favorite place in all the world!" she said, almost reverently.

"I can't recall ever seeing a more beautiful sight," he

agreed, looking down at her.

She didn't know whether he was talking about the view or her.

They stood there, side by side, not speaking, both feeling the nearness of the other. The sun set slowly, its redness finally dipping into the sea.

At dinner they feasted on fresh shrimp, then tangy fish soup, and finally sweet Mediterranean lobster. This was washed down with a dry Greek wine and half-glasses of Ouzo. Alana presided over dinner like a concerned Italian mother. She was never still. First she was in the kitchen supervising preparations; then she was checking the table setting; and she watched carefully to ensure that everyone had a full glass.

"I swear, sometimes I think she would rather be keeping house than to be a business executive," remarked her father as she finally settled at the table, a satisfied smile on her face.

She looked boldly at Stevens. "Dad tells me that our special guest won't be here for a couple of days, so I thought I'd show you the sights in Athens tomorrow." Her eyes challenged him.

"That sounds like a good idea to me," he said evenly, returning her bold look. She smiled, and instinctively he knew that she was inviting him into her life. The next move was up to him!

Suddenly he felt guilty, and he felt himself wanting to retreat back into his protective shell. Here was a beautiful woman, obviously interested, and he felt hesitant. Nuyen's memory haunted him. There had been many women since she died, but Stevens knew that Alana would be different. If he went to her, his love for Nuyen might be lost forever.

When he finally went to his room, he was torn with conflict. He knew he couldn't sleep. He was afraid to sleep, because he feared that he would dream of his dead wife. Finally he re-dressed in slacks and shirt and silently opened his door and walked down to the patio. He stood there

187

looking out to sea.

Alana couldn't sleep either. A slight breeze blew in through her open window, and she felt chilled. She got out of bed to close the window. Looking down, she saw Stevens standing there, looking off in the distance. After a while he walked over to the bar and poured a glass full of bourbon, then began pacing back and forth. He reminded her of a caged tiger, and she wondered what troubled him so much that he couldn't sleep.

Alana went back to her bed and picked up the book that Jim Moore had sent her by Braxton. The title was *America's Greatest Heroes*. She opened the book to the chapter titled: "Frank Stevens, U.S. Army."

She read in graphic detail of the two days leading up to the Battle on Hill 555: how Stevens led the enemy away from his wounded men, then returned and hacked a path through the jungle to lead them to the hill; how he stayed behind and fought a delaying action while his men made their slow, agonizing climb up the hill; how he made it to the top, running a gauntlet of enemy fire and being severely wounded in the process; how the tiny group of Americans fought off waves of Communists; and finally, low on ammunition and his men all incapacitated, how he had hidden them in the cave; how he then called artillery and napalm on top of his position; and finally, his magnificent stand atop the boulder.

She closed the book and sat quietly, trying to visualize the horror and glory of that night. She had a sudden urge to join him on the patio--to hold him in her arms and soothe his troubled mind. She was no longer undecided about Frank. She loved him, and she wanted him!

17

Before going downstairs the next morning, Stevens slipped his German-made Heckler and Koch automatic from its light-weight shoulder holster and checked it carefully. He removed the magazine from the butt and re-inserted it. He pulled the slide to the rear, injecting a shell into the chamber; then he flicked the safety on. Two spare magazines were snapped to a special strap that hung from the opposite shoulder. The PT-13 was one of the latest in the line of H&K automatics. With its larger grip and extended magazine, it carried 15 rounds of 9mm ammo. Stevens liked its firepower and balance. In his hands, it was a devastating weapon. He strapped on the holster, put on a sportcoat, and stepped in front of the mirror. Underneath the tan jacket, it would only be noticeable to a trained eye. Even though only a few trusted people knew he was in Athens, he felt a lot more comfortable as he touched the butt of the weapon with his right hand.

Alana was dressed in a cotton print skirt, a sheer blouse, and white sandals. She wore her long hair loose over her shoulders. At first glance she appeared to be in her late teens. As Stevens opened the door for her on the driver's side of the Mercedes, he caught the sweet scent of her perfume.

"I must say that you are no doubt the most beautiful woman in the world," he said, sliding in to the car beside her.

She looked at him and smiled, surprised by his compliment. "Why thank you, Frank, but why these sudden words of flattery?"

"Well, first of all," he answered, "I've wanted to say that since the first day I met you, and second, they are not words of flattery. It's just the truth--a statement of fact."

Their first stop was at the open bazaar. After two hours of looking and bargaining, Stevens had purchased a kotta rug, several brass carvings, and some antique copper pans. Finally they stopped at a small teahouse.

"I think you're the first man I've met that really seems to enjoy shopping," Alana said, taking a sip of her tea.

"I do, but I'm also a compulsive buyer. My home in California is filled with things I've bought during my travels. I guess the decor is multinational, a little bit of everything."

She looked at him across the table. "Where is your home?"

"Well, I bought a little place in Lockwood Valley, California."

"I've lived in California most of my life, but I don't believe I have ever heard of Lockwood Valley."

"It's located about 80 miles south of Monterey, in the foothills of the Santa Lucia mountains. Really a beautiful area, with thousands of oak trees, and good hunting and fishing. However, the thing I like most about the area is the people. Most are farmers or cattlemen, and to me they personify what is really great about our country. It's hard to describe, but I feel at home there. I have lived all over the world, but Lockwood Valley is where I want to settle someday."

"Whenever I want to get away from everything, I head home," he continued. "I relax, go fishing or hunting, or help one of the local ranchers at a round-up or branding."

"You sound like you really love it there," she said.

"Yes. It's my Avalon--my Shangri La," he replied enthusiastically.

"Perhaps some day I'll get to see your home." She eyed him thoughtfully.

"Charlie would like you,"he said matter-of-factly.

"Who's Charlie?" she asked.

"Well, there are actually two Charlies," he returned. "Charlie #1 is a unique person and one of the finest men I know. He is a genuine American cowboy--the last of a dying breed. He has a great zest for living and really knows how to enjoy life. I guess I envy him because I haven't found out yet how to feel contentment. If Charlie likes you, there isn't anything he wouldn't do for you. He's the type that once you meet him, you'll never forget him, especially if you hear him laugh. I think you would like Charlie #2, also--he's my horse!"

Alana was caught by surprise, and she laughed aloud. She realized that this was the longest statement she had ever heard him make.

Later they stopped for a late afternoon lunch at a small outdoor restaurant. "I don't know when I've had more enjoyable day," Stevens said honestly.

"Nor do I," said Alana gaily. "You ought to let your hair down more often, General. People might begin to think you are human." This brought a smile to his face.

"See," she said triumphantly, "that's twice in 24 hours that I've seen you smile." Her eyes twinkled. She continued. "You don't often talk about yourself, do you?"

"Well," he answered, "there really isn't much to say."

"Isn't much to say?" She raised her eyebrows. "Why you've seem more and done more than any man I've ever met. You are America's legendary war hero; you're almost a national institution. You have a lot to say. In fact, I really would like to read a book about your life. Did you know that General Moore told me that you were the greatest soldier he ever met, the greatest fighting man in the U.S. Army?"

He interrupted her: "I think General Moore is prejudiced. He tends to exaggerate things just a little."

Alana could see that he was truly modest, so she changed the subject. "By the way, how's Gaby? I understand you have been seeing a lot of her."

"Yes, quite a bit. She's fine, thank you."

In exasperation she snapped coldly, "Don't you think she is a little young for you?" She was surprised at herself for saying that. Why had she? This was none of her business, nor was it typical of her inborn courtesy.

He spoke softly. "First you call me a national institution, and now I'm an old rake. Alana, I'm not completely over the hill, yet," he said graciously, lightening a tense moment. They laughed.

"I'm sorry, Frank. I had no right to make that remark. If you like Gaby, she must be a very worthy person."

He stared at her, and she was a bit unbalanced by his look. She flushed. "You have eyes that seem to look right through me. I just can't quite figure you out, Frank Stevens. I do know why I made the remark about Gaby. I'm jealous! I'll tell you now that I'm a woman who has not loved for a long time. I must warn you to be careful and not give me any false ideas, or we could be in trouble."

After lunch they started back toward the Emerson home. When they were about two miles from the villa, they noticed a blue light flashing up ahead. Stevens glanced in the rear view mirror. A black Mercedes was moving up fast. As they approached the blinking light, they saw a car overturned in the ditch. An ambulance was blocking the narrow road, and two white-coated attendants were leaning over a form lying beside the road.

Instinct began to gnaw at Stevens' stomach, and the hair on the back of his neck began to tingle. This same sensitivity had saved his life on numerous occasions. Alana was curious about the obvious accident but entirely unaware of possible trouble.

"Look. There's been an accident. Someone's injured," she said, slowing down.

"Stop the car here!" he ordered quietly. "Don't go any closer!"

Alana reacted to the tone of his voice and knew something was wrong. "Why, Frank, what's---?"

"Just do as I say!" he snapped.

She braked sharply. Stevens said slowly and distinctly: "When I start shooting, open your door and jump into the ditch. Then get over that stone fence and keep on rolling down the hill."

"Frank, I don't--"

"Do as I say! Get ready!" Another glance in the mirror told him that the black Mercedes had stopped 20 meters behind. There were two men in the car. Now he was certain this was a trap. The only way he could save Alana was to take them first. He had to stay alive long enough to do that. He didn't think of death--it had been a constant companion for many years. But, he must save Alana. In a flash he realized that he loved her and that he must not let anything happen to her.

He opened the door and stepped out casually. Waving his left arm toward the ambulance, he called: "Can we help?" Almost in the same instant he drew his automatic. Alana screamed as the stillness was broken by two shots Stevens fired. The two attendants were knocked back against the ambulance as his slugs tore into them.

For an instant, Alana froze in shock; it still had not dawned on her what was happening. She had seen Frank pull his gun and shoot down two men in cold blood! But, as he had ordered, she began to move. Opening the door, she jumped out into the ditch. Then all hell broke loose as the sound of automatic weapons ripped through the air. She could see Frank turn to the rear, crouch, and calmly fire, the heavy automatic recoiling with each shot. She couldn't believe this was happening!

Broken glass fell all around as their car was riddled with bullets. She froze, hugging the ground.

Suddenly Frank came flying into the ditch and crushed her to the ground. "I told you to keep going," he roared. Roughly he picked her up and heaved her over the low stone fence. "Roll, roll!" he yelled.

She involuntarily obeyed, the steep hill maintaining her roll. She felt the sting of sharp rocks gouging and cutting. When she quite tumbling, she crawled into a niche between two large rocks. The sound of battle raged above. She felt helpless and afraid. Fear, as she had never before known it, paralyzed her. She clung to the rocks, and over and over she cried: "Frank! Frank!"

The firing stopped as abruptly as it had started. Suddenly her fear vanished, and she was flooded with anxiety about Frank's safety. She picked herself up from the protection of the rocks and called: "Frank, where are you? Are you alright?" There was no answer. With no thought of herself, she began to claw her way frantically back up the steep hill. Her skirt ripped as she crawled over the stone fence.

Three men lay by the ambulance. Darkening pools of blood covered the roadbed. The blue light on the ambulance still was revolving slowly, giving an unreal feel to the battlescene. The two men in the Mercedes were mere lumps: one was lying face down in a pool of blood, the other hanging out of the driver's seat. The front of his face was gone and gray stuff oozed out onto the ground. Alana gagged.

Then she saw him! Stevens was lying half-out of the ditch beside the road. His right arm was extended in front of him, still gripping the automatic pistol. There was blood running from his head. She thought he was dead. She ran to him and gently turned him onto his side. She saw blood seeping from his left leg. Then she realized that his chest was rising and falling--he was alive! She cradled his bleeding head in her lap. Using her dress, she held it against the wound to staunch the flow of blood.

194

A few minutes later, Emerson, the Prince, and his bodyguards were there. From the house they had heard the firing and rushed to the scene.

They found Alana crying and holding Stevens to her breast. "Help him, please!" she pleaded. "Don't let him die!"

Emerson grasped his daughter's shoulder and bent down to examine the stricken soldier. The head wound was just a graze. It looked worse than it actually was. The only other wound was the bullet hole in his left thigh. It had gone clear through. There wasn't much bleeding, so evidently no main arteries were severed. He stood up and urged Alana to release her grip. "I think he's going to be alright, honey."

Several minutes later, as she climbed into her father's car to ride to the hospital with Stevens, she looked at the battle area. Frank had saved her life. She knew that he had been willing to sacrifice his own life for her. Five assassins lay dead, cut down by his bullets! With a sickening feeling, she realized that this was the type of life he had lived for years. She also knew, with some finality, that the would-be assassins never had a chance against General Frank Stevens.

Stevens regained consciousness on the way to the hospital. As Alana leaned over him, his first words were: "Are you alright?"

She covered his mouth with hers, and as the pain and relief took over, he closed his eyes again.

Alana was treated for minor cuts and bruises. She waited with her father for news of Stevens. "Dad, how did Frank know it was an ambush? He just started walking toward them, then drew his gun and started firing. I didn't even know that he was carrying a gun. I thought he had gone crazy. Then, they started firing back."

"Honey, men like Frank develop a sixth sense when it comes to danger," returned her father. "That's why he's still alive after all these years. That's why you're alive! I just thank God he was with you."

The doctor walked out of the emergency room, smiling. Alana stood up and walked toward him. "He's going to be fine," said the doctor, taking her hands in his. "The scalp wound looked much worse than it was. A bullet went clear through the thigh and missed all of the bones and arteries. He only has some muscle damage which might cause him to limp for a while, but he'll be up and around in a couple of days. From looking at the scars on his body, I would have to say that this is one of his lesser escapes from death."

Alana cried--tears of happiness. "Is he awake?" she asked.

"Yes, he's awake, and he asked for a bottle of bourbon!"

Alana turned and looked evenly at her father. "Dad, I love him!"

"I know, honey. I've known for a long time--even before you yourself realized it. And, I'm glad!" He kissed his daughter on the cheek.

Two hours later, Alana walked into Stevens' room. He was sitting up in bed. There was a small bandage on his head, and his wounded thigh was covered by the sheets.

"I brought you some flowers, and this," she said, holding up a bottle of Seagrams. "You do like flowers, don't you?"

He smiled. "I love flowers," he said, as he reached for the Seagrams.

"That's three smiles in four days, General Stevens," she said cheerfully. "I do believe you have a sense of humor after all."

Stevens' smile disappeared. "Alana, I'm sorry this happened. I should have known after Cairo that they would try again. Please forgive me; I never should have placed you in danger."

"Hey! Wait a minute! I'm a grown woman. With the exception of the last part, I thoroughly enjoyed today. How do you know that they weren't trying to kidnap me? Look at it this way--I saw you in action, and I have every confidence in your ability and your reactions!"

"Nevertheless," he began. "I put your life in dan--"

196

She put her fingers on his lips. As she moved her hand away, she leaned over and gently kissed him. "That's for saving my life."

"You could have been killed," he insisted stubbornly, "and all because of me!" There was a trace of a tear at the corner of his eyes.

"It won't work, Frank. I'm not going to lose you because you think that being with you could be dangerous for me. Frank Stevens--you're not going to use that for an excuse!"

Driving back to the villa with her father, she thought back over the ambush. "Blood and Ice" was a fitting description of her gladiator. Now she understood why men that he had served with in combat worshipped him. Now, she too, was a combat veteran. She had heard bullets fired in anger and had seen men die. She had developed more respect for Frank Stevens than she thought she could have for any man except her father. She was more determined than ever to be with him--forever.

Two days later, when he returned to the villa, he walked with a pronounced limp. Alana fussed over him like a doting mother. She fixed a deck chair for him on the patio. She brought him tea and cookies, snacks, magazines, bourbon and books. Stevens was embarrassed with the attention.

At 3 p.m., Alana went out to check on him and found the chair empty. She looked down and saw him limping along the beach.

18

That evening, they were all in a celebrating mood. They started out with Dom Perignon Champagne, cold crab chunks and escargot, then finished with broiled lobster and pasta. After dinner they adjourned to the patio and sipped cognac.

Stevens glanced over at Alana. The fresh sea breeze stirred her long, dark hair. She was wearing a flowered cocktail dress that was cut provocatively low, allowing the magnificent cleavage of her breasts to show. The dress hugged her perfect figure and seemed to caress her with silken fingers when she walked. She had been plying him with drinks the whole evening. Her attempt to loosen him up may not have been noted by Stevens, but the others certainly were aware.

Prince Mohamad held up his glass: "Gentlemen, I would like to propose a toast to our beautiful hostess, Alana." They all drank.

Emerson returned: "To peace and good friendship." This time Alana joined them.

It might have been the drinks, but Stevens surprised them with his simple toast. Without taking his eyes from Alana, he held up his glass to her and said fervently: "To the woman I love," then drained his glass.

Alana started in astonishment. Then she held up her glass, and with tears in her eyes, she said in a husky voice: "To *my* love!" and placed her glass to her lips.

Stevens' throat closed. A flood of emotion engulfed him.

Bill Emerson had been expecting this. It had just been a matter of time and the right circumstances. He also realized that it was time that he and the Prince made a hasty retreat. "Your Excellency," he said smoothly, "I have some papers that I would like to show you." They both rose, and the Prince kissed Alana's hand before following Emerson into the house.

For a while, neither Frank nor Alana spoke. Finally, Stevens said quietly: "I love you!"

Her voice trembled, "And, I love you!"

As he stood up, she came into his arms, and they kissed-- a long, hungering kiss. She held him tightly. Their hearts were beating together. He ran his hands over her bare shoulders, down her back, and across the curves of her buttocks, pressing her closely against him.

"Oh, Frank. I have loved you so much, for so long!"

Reluctantly he released her, and they walked to the railing, his arm around her waist. He murmured: "You are the most beautiful woman in the world."

She turned to him again. As he gazed down into her upturned face, she said: "I will love you forever and ever."

When he took her into his arms, everything and everyone else was forgotten--the battles, the killing, Nuyen. Everything was washed aside by her embrace and the feel of her body against his.

"Frank," she whispered, "I have wanted you, longed for you, since the first day we met." He was engulfed in the most beautiful moment of his life.

Finally he pushed her back, and his hands gently cupped her breasts. She looked up at him, then closed her eyes to feel the thrill of his touch. She ached with desire.

"Beautiful," he murmured, "simply beautiful!" They both

felt overwhelmed by their building passions. Then there was the sound of a phone ringing.

Emerson called out to the patio: "Frank, I'm sorry. It's for you. It may be important."

Reluctantly Stevens dropped his arms. They both laughed at the inopportune interruption. He kissed her quickly. "Remember where we were," he teased. "I don't want to lose my place."

It was General Moore calling from Riyadh. "Frank, I have some bad news. It seems Colonel Abar has been arrested. We received word about an hour ago. I guess your rendez-vous is off."

"Well, Sir. It looks like we go back to the drawingboard," said Stevens. This was, indeed, bad news. It meant that a new contact would have to be found in Iran.

Emerson took the opportunity for a little personal con-niving. "Frank, Prince Mohamad and I must fly back tomor-row, but why don't you stay here a few days and let that leg heal? Alana can stay and be your nurse."

Alana and Frank exchanged glances. They could be alone together! The hands of fate, and devious fathers, work in strange and sometimes wonderful ways. Since the house was guarded, Stevens felt it would be relatively safe for Alana.

On the way to the airport the next afternoon, the Prince turned to Emerson: "It appears that there is a budding romance in the offing."

Emerson smiled. "It has been budding since the first day they met. Right now I would say it is in the blooming stage. What a pair those two will make!" He sat back, grinning. Both men were making plans for Frank Stevens' future.

Stevens was sitting comfortably on the patio. Alana walked out, stood behind his chair and put her arms around him. "I've given the cook the night off, and I'm going to prepare

Chateaubriand for two. How does that sound?"

He reached around and pulled her onto his lap.

"Frank! Your leg!" she squealed.

"My leg is fine," he said, covering her mouth with his.

"By the way," she said smugly, "I have also disconnected the phone."

He laughed out loud.

"See," she said, "you are beginning to smile and to laugh again."

"Do you have any idea of how much I love you?" he asked.

"No, but please tell me!" Her eyes sparkled.

"God, but you have wondrous eyes," he said, kissing each one in turn.

She was wearing a sleeveless blouse and a soft skirt. He caressed her neck and kissed her ears. His hands moved down and lightly ran over her breasts. She wasn't wearing a bra. He undid the top buttons and exposed her breast. "Beautiful," he murmured.

She turned toward him, and raised herself slightly so that he could reach her breasts. He kissed them.

She trembled with pleasure. Then she rose, took him by the hand, and led him upstairs to her bedroom.

As he closed the door, she stood waiting. He began to undress her slowly. First he unbuttoned her blouse and slipped it from her shoulders. Then he unzipped her skirt and let it fall to the floor. She stepped out of it, then she placed her thumbs in the elastic band of her silk bikini and started to push it down.

Her hands fumbled with his shirt buttons. He slipped it off his shoulders and tossed it aside. She ran her hands over his bare chest. He stepped back and pulled off his slacks.

They stood looking at each other's bodies. His eyes drank in her beauty. Her thick lustrous blue-black hair tumbled about her smooth shoulders. "You are even more beautiful than I could have imagined," he breathed.

"I love you," she said, and came into his arms. He picked

201

her up and carried her to the bed.

"Frank! Your leg!"

"To hell with my leg," he said, lowering her onto the bed.

She lay on her back looking up at him. Gone were any feelings of doubt. Now there was only wonder!

He covered her face with kisses. He kissed her throat; then moved down. She made contented sounds and writhed on the bed.

For the first time in her life, she felt sensual and completely willing and expectant.

"Yes! Oh yes, Frank! Ah--"

She tried to catch her breath as she came and came in a pulsating rage of passion that never seemed to end. Her moans turned to cries of pleasure: "My Love! My Love!"

Finally she came back down from the pinnacle. She didn't understand herself. All of this pleasure! It was unreal; and yet, with him, it seemed so natural.

Frank moved up on top of her and looked down into her radiant face. She was sobbing with pleasure, the tears gently rolling across her cheeks. "Oh, Frank my love! Please take me now!" Her hands reached up to guide him.

"I love you," he said.

"Oh--" she cried. She surged up against him. She smelled sweet and fragrant and her lithe body moved with his--they moved as one.

"Frank, I'm coming! Oh God!" She cried out again as the sweet, wonderful, joyous spasms rocked her.

He still wanted more of her. He rolled over on his back and pulled her atop him. She bent down to kiss him, and her long hair made a screen on each side of her passionately radiant face.

He lunged against her. They groaned with pleasure as they climaxed together.

She collapsed across him, spent. She covered his face with kisses and tears. She had surrendered her body to him, and for the first time in her life, she had felt an ecstasy so deep, so total, that she couldn't believe that this shamelessly passionate woman was her. "For me," she said sincerely, "this was really the first time. I at last feel like a woman! For the first time, I really feel like a woman!"

His hands gripped her shoulders, and he pulled her down to him and they kissed a long, tender kiss. Finally she rolled off of him and lay by his side, her head cradled on his shoulder.

"So that's how it's supposed to feel," she murmured, sounding as if she had just discovered a new treasure. She raised up on one elbow and looked at him: "You're the only real man I've ever known; and this is the most wonderful day of my life! I love you, Frank Stevens." With a satisfied sigh she lay back and closed her eyes. Her hand sought and grapsed his.

They lay holding each other for a long, pleasant time. Finally Alana broke the magical silence. "I think we might need more sustenance than love, so I should think about some dinner." She kissed him, got up from the bed and went into the bathroom. She let the warm spray run over her tingling body. She felt like singing!

She emerged from the shower, wrapped in a large towel. She padded over and sat on the bed; leaning over she kissed Stevens. "Thank you so very much, my General!"

He put his arms around her and drew her close. "It is I who thank you, my beautiful lady!"

"Did you really enjoy it too?" she begged.

"My darlin'--it was ecstasy beyond description!" he answered truthfully. "Let's eat later," he suggested.

She obeyed his command with hesitation.

Alana kept her eyes closed, and delighted in his delicious touch. She felt desire rising within her again.

"Oh, Frank, I want you again. Now?"

"Oh, how good you feel," she gasped. Her completion was first, but she continued caressing his back, tensed her muscles and began moving with his rhythm. "Let me make you happy, too!" she whispered. She stole a look at his face and felt a sense of triumph as she sensed his equal pleasure. She felt the spasm boiling up inside of her.

They stayed together, a long time, contentedly: touching, speaking of love, and coming slowly down from the high plateau.

"I suppose I will have to tell Sallie,--" she thought aloud.

"What do you mean, tell Sallie?" he asked, surprised, thinking maybe they were going to compare notes!

"To tell her that she was right. Today I saw them all-- the fireworks, shooting stars, and experienced the loss of control--everything!"

Stevens wasn't sure he understood, but he did know that of all the women he had known before, none could compare with this lovely creature. Her abandoned and intense lovemaking was the sweetest thing he had ever encountered.

They ate on the terrace by lantern light. The Chateaubriand was outstanding. Stevens became conscious of long-dead feelings--love and happiness. He experienced an inward joy. He realized that his life would never be the same again.

After dinner, Alana put a tape on the recorder and they danced. "I have never known such happiness," she said, looking up at him lovingly.

"Nor I, my love. I wish tonight would never end."

"But tonight is just the beginning for us, isn't it? I hope you are going to sleep in my bed tonight, otherwise I couldn't sleep."

"I don't know. Don't you think the neighbors will talk?" he kidded.

"Well, if they don't, I will," she declared. "I want to tell the whole world that I love Frank Stevens!" Then, she walked over to the patio rail and yelled loudly: "I LOVE FRANK STEVENS!"

Stevens joined her at the rail and yelled: "WORLD, I LOVE ALANA AMES!"

She touched him and turned: "Underneath that hard

exterior beats the heart of a warm romatic."

Before getting into bed, Alana took a small penlight from her dresser drawer and placed it under her pillow. Stevens lay down beside her and took her into his arms. As he held her, Alana realized that for the first time in her life she had a sense of being dominated by someone other than her father--another real man. It was a glorious feeling to have a strong man hold you, and love you, and yes--even fight for you. She pushed him away and whispered, "Just a minute." She reached over and turned off the lights to plunge the room into instant darkness.

"Have you become shy?" he asked.

"I never could be shy with you again. Not after today," she answered. Reaching under her pillow, she pulled out the penlight and placed it between her breasts. "I want you to touch me in a certain place," she begged.

"Where?" he asked in a puzzled voice.

She began blinking the penlight: "About 3 feet south of the blinking light."

Stevens laughed out loud. He had heard that command re-told dozens of times but never in a situation like this. "You've been reading my press clippings?"

"Oui, Mon General," she said, drawing him to her.

When he wakened the next morning, her naked body close to him aroused him. He snuggled against her back, placed his arms around her, cupping both breasts. She awakened with a rising passion and crawled on top of him.

"What a beautiful way to wake up," she said. He moved slowly, and she matched his movements until the fire in him drove her to abandon. He held her tightly, matching her ardor. Pressure built. She remained on the brink for what seemed like a deliciously interminable time, but when she felt the moment had come, she let it happen and felt his joy.

19

TRIPOLI, LIBYA.

The hands of Khadafy's Chief of Intelligence, Major Mustapha Amak, trembled as he poured himself a stiff drink of the forbidden Scotch he kept hidden in his lower right-hand desk drawer. His hand-picked, hit-squad had failed, and Brother Colonel was raving mad! Amak had just left Khadafy's office, and he considered himself lucky to get out alive. When the leader found out about the failure, he flew into one of his trantrums; and Amak thought his boss was going to draw his revolver and retire his Intelligence Chief. It would not be the first time that the Libyan leader killed one of his own key officers in a fit of rage. Somehow, through the grace of Allah, Amak survived, but he knew the third time had better be the charm. He took his dagger letter-opener and stabbed the picture of General Stevens, which lay face-up in the center of his desk.

ATHENS, GREECE.

Frank and Alana were like newly-weds, living and loving in the rapture and adventure of their new found love. They lived and loved only for each other, oblivious to the world around them. They kissed and hugged and caressed, and they took great pleasure in making each other happy. They swam and made love on the secluded beach; they hiked and made love on a small knoll near the villa; they bathed together and made love. Each time they found new delight in the other's body.

Poor Dave Braxton! He knew his duty as his General's bodyguard, but he had to use all of the tricks he had ever learned to guard them without infringing on their privacy. However, wherever they went, Stevens' H and K automatic always was within his reach.

Alana often would tease him and say: "Did you bring the gun, dear?"

They couldn't seem to get enough of being together. After making love, they slept nude, holding each other all night. It was the first time in years that Stevens had slept a deep, untroubled sleep. And, for the first time, Alana slept fulfilled and satisfied.

On the morning of their third day of newly discovered love, they were seated at the breakfast table. "I've got it!" said Stevens suddenly, his toast half in his mouth.

"You've got what?"

"I think I know how the attackers found out I was here."

"Tell me," she said, excitedly.

"Well, I think that dear, sweet Gaby may not have been all that she appeared to be, sweetness and innocence."

"What do you mean? Could Gaby have been an agent?" asked Alana, surprised.

"Yes, and I think that she is pretty damned good at her business if she could fool me."

"You should know," chided Alana. "Had you told her that you were coming here?"

"No, but I told her that I would be gone for a few days on business. All she would have to do is have someone watch the airport, and they would know that I hadn't left by commercial flight. Everyone knows that the Air Force has a bi-weekly flight to Athens. It was no secret that your father has a home here and that you all had left for a so-called vacation. It would have been a matter of simple deduction. I'm going to call General Moore, right now, and ask him to run a background check on Gaby. Forgive me, it won't take long."

Before he could initiate the call, the phone rang. A servant said, "Sir, it's for you."

Stevens returned within a few minutes. "That was the Athens police. They have identified two of the assassins. I'm going down to headquarters."

After he left, Dave Braxton came into the kitchen and accepted Alana's offer of coffee. The giant looked up and drawled: "Mrs. Ames, I've never seen the General this relaxed before!"

Alana was both pleased and surprised by his confidential remark. "Dave, you have been with the General for a long time, haven't you?" she asked.

"Yes Ma'am, off and on for over 15 years. We kinda started together."

"Did you know hiw wife?"

"Yes'm. I was in his Special Forces Team in 'Nam when he met her."

"He never talks about her, does he?"

"No Ma'am. He hasn't said her name--at least that I know of--since the night she was killed.

"Dave, I guess you know by now that the General means a lot to me. Will you tell me about his wife?"

He nodded. "Well," he began, "she was a little thing, half French and half Vietnamese, I guess. She was really beautiful and a real lady. Not like some of those--" he faltered. "Uhh, you know what I mean. Anyway, she was older than the General. He was a captain then. We were working with this Vietnamese Colonel who was an Intel-type, and Nuyen was one of his agents. Her parents had been killed by the Vietcong, and I guess she became an agent to avenge them. From what I heard, she was pretty good at her job. She worked with us in an operation where we had to uncover a local Vietcong District Chief. That's where the General met her. Before long, he was seeing her regularly. Soon they became engaged. General Moore was a Colonel then and Commander of the Special Forces in 'Nam. He took care of the red-tape so Cap'n Stevens and Nuyen could get married. She quit the intelligence business, and he got her a visa to go to the States.

"Well, the night she was to leave, our team jumped into North Vietnam. On the way to the airport, the Commies killed her driver and kidnapped her. We didn't know about it 'cause we were in isolation. When we got to North Vietnam we walked into a trap. Everyone was killed but me and the General.

"He was quite a catch for them. There had been a price on his head for a long time. He knew the locations of many of the units operating in North Vietnam and Laos.

"They tortured him for 10 days. By the end of that time, he was more dead than alive, but they couldn't crack him. Finally they brought his wife to the camp. That was when they broke him--by torturing her in front of him. He talked then; told them what they wanted to hear. Most of the information was useless, for when our headquarters lost contact with us, the word went out. Units changed locations, radio frequencies, and codes.

"Then they tied him up in his hut and took his wife into the hut next door. I heard her screams most of the night, but there was nothing I could do. You can imagine what went on in Cap'n Stevens' mind! Finally, toward morning, her screams stopped.

"The following night I was awakened by the Cap'n. He had killed his guard and escaped. He cut me loose and led me to the edge of the camp where we found a truck with the keys in it. Then he told me to stay there and wait. I asked him where he was going, and he said: 'To find my wife.'

"I didn't stay where he told me to--I followed him as he

went from hut to hut, killing the North Vietnamese as we went. He was like an avenging angel of death. He killed them all, but he couldn't find his wife nor her body. Finally he just stood in the middle of the compound and cried. I'll never forget the sight. He was covered with blood--just standing there, holding his knife at his side. He yelled at me to 'get the hell out of there.' As I walked toward him he passed out. It's not a very pretty story, Ma'am."

Alana sat mute. Her heart ached for the man she loved and for the woman he had loved.

"After that," continued Braxton, "The Captain wanted to die. He thought her death was his fault. Also, he felt guilty because he had talked. After we were rescued, he volunteered for all of the dirtiest jobs. He seemed hell-bent on killing every Communist in Vietnam, and he didn't care whether he lived or died.

"I'll tell you, Mrs. Ames, he's the coolest man in a firefight I've ever seen!"

Alana remembered how he had walked into the guns of the assassins--all blood and ice.

"But, he seemed to lead a charmed life," continued Braxton, now eager to talk about his favorite subject. "Instead of getting killed, he just got more medals and promotions. You'll never get this story out of him, Ma'am. He never talks about it, and he never mentions her name."

Alana's voice quivered: "You think a lot of him, don't you?"

"Yes, Ma'am. He's the best there is. They don't make 'em any better. He saved my life, not once, but several times!"

"I think he's the best, too, Dave. Do you think I can make him happy?"

"Well, Mrs. Ames. You're the first woman he has really cared for since his wife died. I know that for a fact. As I've already told you, I've never seen him this happy before."

"Dave, thank you for telling me this. I love him very much. What you have told me helps me to understand him better."

She put her hand atop his massive paw.

When Stevens returned, Alana greeted him with open arms and a special kiss.

"What was that all about?" he asked.

"That, my sweet, was for saving Dave Braxton's life!"

He mumbled something about Braxton having a loose lip, and walked on into the house.

Braxton looked up. "General, what did you find out?"

Stevens poured himself a cup of coffee and sat down at the table. "It looks like Khadafy was behind the ambush. Two of the attackers have been identified as members of the Palestine Liberation Front, which is headed by Abu Nadal and whose base is in Libya; and the other three were Libyans, but they have not been identified." He smiled up at Alana. "And it looks like sweet little Gaby is an agent of Khadafy's too! Well, at least we know who our enemy is. Evidently Brother Colonel does not like what we are doing."

Stevens took a pen and paper and commenced to write.

"What are you writing?" asked Alana.

"I'm sending Gaby a telegram." When he finished, he showed it to Alana:

DEAR GABY: I'M STILL IN GOOD HEALTH. SORRY TO HEAR YOU ARE QUITTING AND LEAVING RIYADH. NICE TO HAVE KNOWN YOU--YOU DO A GOOD JOB. GOOD LUCK.

FRANK

"I'm sure you know how good she is at her job, Frank," Alana said, half-seriously.

"Dear one. All of the women I've made love to pale in comparison to you, and that is a simple true fact."

"When she gets this telegram, won't she be able to get away?"

"Yes, I hope so. It would be a shame to see such a talented young lady have her head chopped off."

Alana reached over and kissed him. "You are a most

unusual man, Frank Stevens. The sooner Gaby gets out of your life, the better."

He looked at her: "Are you jealous of Gaby?"

"You're dead right. I am!" she returned.

"I guess I like that," he said, taking her in his arms.

That night, after making love, Stevens was lying on his stomach, completely relaxed. Alana was on her side, running her hands gently over his scarred back. The room was bathed in moonlight, and a gentle sea-breeze touched the open window.

"You haven't mentioned Paul. Do you realize that?" she asked, breaking the magic silence.

"You know I don't care about him," he mumbled, "only you."

"I've wanted to tell you that I'm divorcing him."

"Good!" he answered. "He's a REMF anyway."

"What's that?" And he told her. "That's ugly."

He rolled up on his side, facing her. "I know, and you're a shameless hussy, but I love you."

She said: "I hope you do. But, if I am a hussy, it's your fault. You bring out the bad, or maybe the best, in me. Both, I guess. I know one thing for sure; I'll never get tired of making love with you. You've given me an insatiable appetite for your brand of loving. There's an old saying that if you scratch a woman, you'll find a rage. At last I know what it means."

He gently pushed her onto her back and began running his hands over her: "You, my love, have given me a rapacious appetite--for you."

Under his touch, her stomach and thighs responded, growing heavy with passion. "And you, beloved, have awakened a sleeping tigress. Please carry on."

Later, Alana lay back exhausted. Her body tingled, and her legs quivered from the love-making. At that moment they were both at total peace with themselves, and with the world.

20

Reluctantly, Frank and Alana left Athens and returned to Riyadh. They both felt born anew. Over the last few days, their priorities had changed, each of them becoming number one in the other's life.

William Emerson met them at the airport. First he noted that Stevens walked with a slightly more pronounced limp. Then he observed the change in both his daughter and the young General. There was a brilliance in her eyes that had never been there before, and Stevens' features had softened and he was quick to smile--a definite change. On the way to his villa, he glanced in the mirror. Alana and Stevens were holding hands in the back seat. A slight smile of satisfaction covered Emerson's face.

They had a light lunch before Stevens departed for his quarters. As he left, Alana went into his arms, and they kissed long and fervently.

"I'll pick you up for dinner tomorrow evening," Stevens called as he walked to his car.

Alana blew him a kiss. She turned to her father with a radiant smile. "Oh Dad, I'm in love!"

He held her close. "Does he make your toes curl?" he asked.

She laughed. "Yes, Dad, he makes my toes curl, and there are shooting stars and fireworks. I've never felt this way before."

"Then it must be love. Your mother always said she knew she loved me, because I made her toes curl. I'm so happy for you both, honey. Frank is a good man."

"Yes, and he's the most man I have ever met besides you," Alana announced emphatically.

Emerson could not remember when he had seen his daughter so happy. Having experienced a great love and a happy marriage himself, he knew the way she felt. He watched her dance up the stairs. Then he turned and went into his study and sat down behind his mahogany desk. The wheels of thought began to turn in his head as he doodled on a notepad. Without realizing it, he began planning the future for Alana and her man.

Stevens worked hard for the next several weeks. He decided that it was time his organization began to act rather than react. He and Alana spent as much time together as they could. Several times she stayed all night at his quarters. Her father made no comment; he understood, and he was pleased with the affair.

Through Egyptian intelligence channels, Stevens was notified that an ex-CIA agent, Edward Sipes, was staying at a hotel in Cairo. Ed Sipes was ex-Special Forces, ex-CIA, and had been tried in absentia by U.S. courts for selling arms to Libya. He had disappeared from a Lebanese hotel earlier in the year, and it was presumed that he had been killed.

Stevens called Braxton into the office. "Dave, take who you need and go to Cairo and bring Sipes here--alive."

Five days later, Sipes was in their hands. Stevens turned him over to Devlin. Thirty-six hours later, a very tired looking Devlin came into Stevens' office with news that Sipes was singing. He handed Stevens a document of facts.

Yes, according to Sipes, Khadafy was trying to build nuclear weapons. Sipes had helped hire the scientists and helped procure the Plutonium from France. He didn't know where the Uranium had come from.

No, he didn't know where the reactor was located. He presumed it was somewhere in southern Libya.

No, he didn't know what Khadafy planned to do with the bombs, but he suspected they were to be used against the Jews.

Yes, Khomeini and South Yemen were involved in a plot with Libya to overthrow the Saudi Arabian monarchy. Fanatical Shiites were being trained in a special terrorist training camp in South Yemen.

"That's the best we could get out of him," announced Devlin. "There are more details on arms sales and terrorist training activities, but they are in a separate report that's being finalized now. What do you want me to do with Sipes?"

"Turn him over to the Agency. They'll know how to handle him," answered Stevens.

★   ★   ★   ★   ★

Since Abar, the Saudis had been supporting anti-government guerrillas in South Yemen--clandestinely. Prince Mohamad proposed that one company of the mercenary squadron move into the Empty Quarter and link up with a South Yemen guerrilla force to attack and destroy the Shiite terrorist training camp. Purdy chose 2d Company, commanded by an ex-Green Beret, to perform the mission.

Ten days later, 2d Company and 100 South Yemen guerrillas stormed out of the Rub al Khali, crossed the border into South Yemen, and razed the terrorist camp. By daylight they were back in hiding in the desolate wastes of the Empty Quarter. The mercenaries were becoming adept at navigating and living in the desert waste. Like avenging Bedouin tribes from ages past, they could move and strike swiftly and disappear back into the sandy wasteland.

Another project undertaken by Stevens' organization, at

the request of the Saudi Government, was the training of a Saudi detachment in counter-terrorist techniques. A special cadre from the merc squadron was selected to instruct the detachment.

U.S. AMBASSADOR'S HOME RIYADH, S.A.

Alana looked stunning in a classic white evening gown. Stevens was wearing a white formal evening jacket, with black tie. The Ambassador's guests were at the buffet. In lieu of alcoholic drinks, fruit juices, Pepsi, tea, and coffee were being served.

Alana stood with her hand resting lightly on Stevens' arm. This was the first time that they had appeared together in public.

"You look mighty handsome tonight, Sir," said Alana in a low tone.

Stevens smiled down at her. Her beauty made all other women at the party seem pale by comparison. They had been invited by Emerson, who told Stevens that the Ambassador wanted to meet the American soldier.

Emerson looked across the room at his daughter. Alana radiated happiness. Anyone could see that she and Frank Stevens obviously were very much in love. What a striking pair they made, he thought. He watched them and thought of his own wife and how much he still missed her. He realized that Alana was a great deal like his wife. Strange, but he never had seen the likeness before. He thought of their future. Of course, someday, Frank would run the Emerson Corporation; but right now, William Emerson had other plans for his future son-in-law.

Ambassador Robert Danker walked up and shook Emerson's hand. The two men had been friends for more years than either cared to remember. Before being appointed Ambassador, Robert Danker had been the Chairman of the Board of AVARCO Oil Co.

"Bill, you old son of a gun! How are you?"

216

"I'm fine, Bob--and you look like the life here is agreeing with you."

"Hell, Bill. I only weigh ten pounds more than I did in 1942!"

"Good! Keep it up! Is this a convenient time to introduce Frank Stevens to you?" he asked and led the Ambassador across the room.

"Well, General Stevens," said Danker, putting forward his hand. "I'm delighted to meet you. I've heard a lot about you. You seem to have made a most favorable impression upon the Saudis."

Stevens shook the proferred hand. "Sir. It is an honor to meet you, Mr. Ambassador. I believe you know Alana Ames?"

"I have known Alana since she was just a gleam in her Daddy's eye," exclaimed the Ambassador, leaning over to kiss her cheek. He whispered in her ear: "Is that a gleam I see in your eye?"

Alana blushed. "Yes, it is, Uncle Robert," she answered. "You see, my General has made other converts here besides the Saudis."

"I'm so glad," he said, truthfully. He saw the happiness in her eyes. He turned toward Stevens.

"General Stevens, the Crown Prince is most impressed by you. He thinks that you would make a good diplomat, as well as being an outstanding soldier."

"I'm surprised by that," returned Stevens. "I have always felt that soldiers should steer clear of politics and diplomacy."

They continued to discuss the Middle East situation. In between conversational segments, Stevens met various members of the Diplomatic Corps.

As they were leaving, Alana whispered to her father: "Don't wait up for me. I think I will be out late tonight."

When they got into their car, Alana nuzzled Frank's neck. "I don't want to part with you. Can we go to your place for a while?"

217

He kissed her on the lips and replied: "Your wish is my command, fair lady."

Alana looked forward to being alone with him. She couldn't think of him without feeling the need for him. Sitting beside him, she tried to visualize a future without him, and couldn't. Their lives had become as one.

Once home, in his bedroom, they stripped each other slowly. He took her in his arms and kissed her gently. He could feel the warm fullness of her naked body against his. In her arms he felt a joy that he had never experienced before. He lifted her gently in his arms and carried her to his bed.

He kissed her, and her breathing quickened. His hands ran slowly over the curves of her body, causing her to moan softly with the joy of her rising emotions.

"I feel like a finely-tuned musical instrument, and you are the greatest musician in the world," she murmured, her tongue playing with his ear. "I feel like saying, come play with me, and I'll help you make beautiful music."

When their passion had overwhelmed them, she straddled him in her favorite position. His touch was electric! Her joy and sexual satisfaction was overwhelming. "Oh, my darling! You give me so much happiness!" she gasped, as her body spasmed against his. "It just gets better and better!"

At dawn, exhausted but happy, they fell asleep, snuggled close to each other, smiles on their faces.

Stevens had returned to the world of the living!

21

Stevens was confident that if there was a Libyan nuclear reactor in the Middle East, or in North Africa, that sooner or later they would locate it. When they did, he would need a strike force ready to go. He decided to prepare for that eventuality.

He selected 50 former U.S. Special Forces and British Special Air Service veterans and moved with them to Al Hasa in the Eastern Province. They began training in special assault techniques, including HALO (High-Altitude, Low-Opening) parachute techniques. In less than two weeks, his force conducted 10 jumps from over 12,000 feet. It had been three years since Stevens had made a jump. However, with some 465 military jumps to his credit, the technique came back to him quickly. Besides, there really isn't much to learn about making a parachute jump. It is mostly a matter of taking that first step into space.

He had just returned to his office one day when he received an urgent phone call from an excited William Emerson.

"Frank, Alana flew to Rome alone, and I'm worried!"

"I tried to call her last night," returned Stevens, "but there wasn't an answer, so I figured she was with you."

"No. Yesterday I went to Jedda on business, and when

I returned, she was gone. She left a note saying that the U.S. Embassy in Rome had called and told her Paul had been in an auto accident. Here, let me read you the note:

'Dad, I received a call from the Embassy in Rome. Paul has been badly hurt in an automobile accident, and he's asking for me. Tell Frank that I love him, and I know he will understand that I have to go.' "

Stevens felt the short hairs on his neck tingle. Not from jealousy--he could understand Alana going to the aid of her ex-husband--however, he instinctively felt that something was terribly wrong.

"Hello, Frank. Are you still there?"

"Yes, Sir. I'm thinking."

"The minute I read her note, I called the Embassy in Rome, and they said they knew nothing about any Paul Ames, nor about a call to Alana!"

"My God!" Fear grabbed at Stevens' gut. "I'll be in Riyadh in two hours," he said, slamming down the phone.

When Stevens and Braxton arrived at Emerson's, Mary and Jim Moore were there, along with Tom Purdy. Emerson showed the strain he was under. "Frank, I received a call about an hour ago from someone who identified himself as a member of the Italian Red Brigade. He said they had Alana, and they will exchange her for you. He said he'd call back later and give instructions, but only to you."

Stevens sat down and put his head in his hands. "God! It's happening all over again," he moaned.

Mary Moore walked over and put her hand on his shoulder. She didn't say anything, for nothing she could say would help in this terrible situation. She was worried about Alana and her heart ached for him, and she felt cold fear. This poor man--not his second love, too!

Suddenly the phone rang, sounding unusually loud in the quiet house. Stevens picked up the receiver: "Stevens here."

A male voice, with a slight foreign accent, said: "General

Stevens, we have Mrs. Ames."

Stevens felt a sick fear gripping him. He tried to remain calm. "Is she alright?"

"Yes, she is fine. Do you want to speak to her?"

Then he heard her voice: "Frank? Is that you?"

"Yes, honey. Are you alright?"

"Yes. I've been treated fine--" She was cut off.

"General, if you follow my instructions, no harm will come to Mrs. Ames. If you don't, we'll send her back to you one piece at a time."

"I'll do whatever you ask. Just don't hurt her," he pleaded, feeling panic-stricken as he had once before.

"O.K. Listen! Fly to Rome. Check into the Savoy Hotel. A room has been reserved in your name. We will contact you there, day after tomorrow, at 1800 hours."

"What do you want in exchange for Mrs. Ames?" asked Stevens.

"Why, General. I thought you knew. We want you."

"All right. I'll turn myself over to you in exchange for Mrs. Ames, but only when I am assured she is well and safe. I warn you, no harm had better come to her!"

"It's you we want. She's only a pawn, but you're in no position to bargain nor threaten us, General."

Stevens walked over and put his hand on Emerson's shoulder. "I heard Alana's voice. She sounded O.K. It sounds as if they are just holding her hostage in exchange for me. Don't worry, Bill. We'll get Alana back safe."

Stevens went into the study, closing the door behind him. He had to be alone. His mind was in a turmoil. The world was closing in on him. Tears rolled down his cheeks, and he shook with silent sobs.

Mary Moore opened the door, started in, and when she saw Stevens, she stepped back and reclosed the door softly.

Emerson paced the floor. General Moore sat silently, staring at his untouched drink. Mary sat down beside her husband and took his hand. "Jim, he's reliving a nightmare.

221

I don't know how he can stand this without cracking up. Do you think we should call a doctor and ask him to give Frank a shot to calm his nerves?"

Dave Braxton overheard her and stood up: "No doctor!" he said emphatically. He walked over the liquor cabinet and took out a bottle of bourbon and two glasses. He went to the study, entered, and closed the door behind him.

Stevens was pacing back and forth across the room. Braxton poured a glass half full of bourbon and handed it to Stevens. "I know what you're going through, Sir, but there's no help for it. What you gotta do, General, is to make a plan."

Stevens didn't answer. He drained the glass. Fortified by the stinging liquor, Stevens' head began to clear. He pushed the black thoughts from his mind and began to pace again. "Thanks, Dave, I'll be all right now. Just leave me alone for a while."

Braxton left, leaving the bottle behind. As he went back into the living room, the others looked up at him, expectantly. "The General is having a rough time, but he'll be all right. He's making a plan now. The kidnappers don't know it, but they are living on borrowed time." They all accepted the news and sat nervously waiting. Emerson was sick at heart, and worried to death, but he knew Stevens would find some way to save his daughter.

At that moment, Stevens strode from the study. "Dave, call the staff. Have them come here immediately." An hour later, Stevens outlined his plan to his staff.

★ ★ ★ ★ ★

When Alana had arrived at the Rome airport, a young man identifying himself as an Embassy Staff Officer had helped her claim her luggage and guided her to an awaiting car. At the end of the parking lot, another man jumped in and stuck a pistol in her face: "Just be calm, Mrs. Ames, and you won't get hurt."

She began to scream. A hard hand slapped her face, snapping her head back. She reached up. Blood trickled from a cut on her cheek, caused by the abductor's ring. Her eye throbbed from the force of the blow. Suddenly she realized how stupid she had been to come to Rome alone. She knew immediately why she had been kidnapped. She was Frank Stevens' only weakness, and since they couldn't get him any other way, they were going to use her.

"Is Paul even here?" she asked. "Or was that only a ruse?"

"No. He's here. We're going to take you to him now," said a harsh voice.

They drove into the country and stopped at a small farmhouse. The two men quickly shuttled her inside. Paul came to meet them.

"Paul! How could you do this?" she asked, with new hatred in her eyes.

He smiled sheepishly. His face was red and puffy from alcohol, and he was unshaven. "I'm sorry, Alana, but I had no choice. Don't worry, I have their word that no harm will come to you. All they want is Stevens."

Alana couldn't believe her ears! She felt nothing but loathing and disgust for her ex-husband. His weakness was a curse. "Well, you can't get him through me," she screamed. "I'll kill myself first," she sobbed.

The abductors tied her in a chair, firmly but not too uncomfortably. They left one hand and arm free. They brought her some bread, cheese, and wine and set it on the table beside her. Paul took his bottle of bourbon and left the room. She ignored the food but asked the female gang member if she could use the bathroom. Afterward, she was re-tied more securely to the chair.

She slumped against her bonds, feeling a dreadful fear for Frank. She knew he would try to free her and that he would willingly sacrifice his life for her. He had always blamed himself for his wife's death, and now he was placed in the same impossible situation again. She didn't fear for herself, for she knew that Frank would find some way to help her, but a dark fear for him flooded her mind. She cried at the unfairness.

ROME.

Stevens paced the floor of his hotel room. Bill Emerson sat silently watching the brooding soldier. A dark mask clouded Stevens' face as he continued his pacing. Occasionally he glanced at his watch. Stevens had been pacing all day. He had not slept, eaten, nor sat still for 24 hours. Emerson could imagine how the pain of the past ran through his mind.

Stevens stopped, and looked at Emerson. "Bill, I'm so sorry. Alana wouldn't be in this danger except for me."

"Don't blame yourself, Frank. Alana loves you. You have given her more happiness in a few short months than she has ever known in her whole life."

Stevens' mind was filled with thoughts of Alana: her big brown eyes, her long black hair, her laugh, her smell, the feel of her body. It haunted him. Now her life was in danger because of her love for him. Nuyen had died because of her love for him. It simply couldn't happen twice. He must save Alana. Those filthy-- They would pay for daring to touch her; he vowed they would pay. When Alana was safe, they would pay!

The sound of the phone was like a thunderclap. He dashed to the desk and grabbed it: "This is Frank Stevens."

"Yes, General Stevens. Listen carefully to your instructions. If you do exacty as I say, Mr. and Mrs. Ames will not be harmed. Drive to the village of Sano. It is located 20 kilometers south of Rome on Highway #77. The Monastery of Caen is located just south of Sano--you can't miss it. The Alvian River runs nearby. A footbridge crosses this river to the cemetery. At 2200 hours, be at the eastern end of the footbridge. Got it?"

Stevens' tape recorder had the message. "Let me speak to Mrs. Ames."

"Frank!" Her voice sounded clear and lucid.

"Yes, darling. Are you alright? Have they hurt you?"

"I'm O.K. Only, don't listen to them," she screamed. "Don't turn yourself over to them--they'll kill you," she pleaded. "I--"

A voice interrupted: "General, follow your instructions and she will be set free. You're the one we want." Click.

Stevens turned to Braxton and ordered, "Get the staff in here--now!"

At 2200 hours, Frank Stevens stood alone under the lamp-post at the eastern end of the Caen footbridge. The bridge had three lights, one at each end and one in the center. The areas on either side of the bridge were shrouded in total darkness. Stevens' heart skipped a beat as he saw Alana appear in the light at the far end of the bridge.

The dead silence of the quiet night was broken when a voice, distorted because of a battery-powered megaphone, announced: "GENERAL STEVENS. PLEASE REMOVE ALL OF YOUR CLOTHES."

Stevens stripped down to his shorts, shoes, and socks. "EVERYTHING OFF!"

He obeyed. He stood there, totally naked. A slight breeze, and tension, made his teeth want to chatter. He cupped his hands and yelled: "Where is Paul Ames?"

"DON'T WORRY ABOUT MR. AMES. HE WILL STAY WITH US BY CHOICE. NOW, GENERAL, WALK SLOWLY TO THE CENTER OF THE BRIDGE. MRS. AMES, CROSS THE BRIDGE. DO NOT MAKE A SUDDEN MOVE OR WE'LL GUN YOU BOTH DOWN!"

"The one called 'Sal'--the one talking on the megaphone." Looking up at him she wondered who this man was, with his face as ashen as death. Gentleness had been replaced by a killer look. She knew she had signed Sal's death warrant.

Standing there, they were both vulnerable. The terrorists would not hesitate to shoot them both. Her grasped her shoulders with both hands and pushed her back. "Everything will be alright. Go! Your father's waiting for you on the other side."

"HURRY OR WE'LL SHOOT YOU BOTH. NOW!"

Stevens turned and started toward the voice. "I'm coming, Sal," he called, his voice deadly.

Reluctantly, Alana stumbled toward safety. Her father rushed out and half-dragged her into his arms in the darkness. She didn't know how he was going to do it--but she knew her captors were about to die! She had seen the look in Frank's eyes.

Her father swept her behind a parked car. She saw armed figures crouching in the shadow. He handed her a pair of goggles: "Here, put these on."

She saw Stevens walk slowly, deliberately, toward the far side. She didn't know that overhead, at 25,000 feet, a C-130 aircraft was closing its doors. The passengers had exited several seconds before and were free-falling toward the bridge at 190 miles per hour.

With the black-lensed goggles, Alana entered a new world. The car she was standing behind gave off a bright blue-white luminous glow. She looked in wonder! Five cars, glowing brightly, were parked in a Vee formation pointed toward the bridge. Across the bridge, Frank's naked body glowed with the same eerie luminous light--as did her hands and blouse, the places where she had touched him.

Overhead, and closing fast with the ground, Dave Braxton held his arms out wide, tracking toward the glowing arrow. He glanced at the luminous altimeter taped on top of his reserve chute. Ahead of the arrow, he could see two luminous dots: one would be Stevens' clothes--the other, his boss.

The C-130 had taken off with its cargo of specialists at the same time Stevens had left the hotel. The pilot had begun his run on the homing device in Stevens' car at the same instant Stevens shut the car door. The parachutes of the rescue force opened automatically at 500 feet, and with the special toggle-lines attached to their feet, the jumpers began steering towrd the luminous figure. They unfastened their silencer-fitted Scorpion submachine guns and prepared for action. They were using the same kind of parachutes used by the Army's Golden Knights Parachute Team. The Para-Glides resembled an inverted mattress. With them, an expert could hit a three-foot target from 20,000 feet.

Alana held her breath as the drama unfolded. As he closed with the terrorists, she could see Frank, his naked body glowing like a monster emerging from the swamp. Then several dark figures came out of the night sky, looking like gigantic bats, swooping down on their prey. She knew instinctively that one of the bats was a 290-pound black angel of death named Braxton.

There was a splash as one of the jumpers missed the far bank and landed in the river. Then sounds like muffled BB-guns broke the night silence. The ghostly figure of Frank Stevens became a blur as he attacked her abductors. There were screams from the other side now--screams of men dying in fear and pain. Several loud blasts cracked across the brdge as the terrorists tried to fight back. Alana held her breath, and her hands dug into her father's arms. He held her close.

Men were rushing across the bridge from this side. Stevens' men, dressed in black, were hidden in the darkness by their camouflage. It was all over in a few minutes.

One man walked back, retrieved Stevens' clothes and raced to the far side of the bridge.

Then she saw Frank coming toward her. She ran out to meet him.

"It's all over, Alana."

She hesitated: "And Paul--?"

"Paul is dead. They are all dead. There was no other way."

She nodded and buried her head against his shoulder.

He forced her head back. "Your father will take you home."

"But I want to be with you, now," she pleaded.

"It's no good, Alana. You have almost been killed twice because of me," his voice faltered. She saw tears in his eyes. "I never want to put you in danger again!"

What he was saying began to sink in. "Frank, I love you. I want to be with you, whatever."

"And I love you, too--more than anything else in the world," he said, pushing her away. "But, I want you to live--!"

He turned and disappeared into the darkness. She started after him, but her father grasped her and held her back. He, too, had heard their exchange. "Let him go, honey. I know you've been through a lot, and Frank has died a thousand deaths. He needs some time to think this thing out."

"But Dad," she sobbed, "I don't want to live without him. He is my life!"

Emerson put his arms around his daugher and held her close. "It will work out, honey--just give him time."

TRIPOLI, LIBYA.

Major Mustapha Amak calmly folded the deciphered message from the Libyan Embassy in Rome and placed it on the desk in front of him. General Stevens had done it again. Amak knew the price of failure. He reached down and opened the lower right-hand desk drawer and removed his closest friend, the bottle of forbidden Scotch; and he poured a glass full to the rim. He drained it in one gulp. He removed his automatic pistol from the holster at his hip and pulled the slide to the rear. There was an audible click as he released the slide, and it shot forward seating a round into the chamber. He calmly placed the barrel in his open mouth. He closed his eyes and pulled the trigger!

22

TRIPOLI, LIBYA.

Dressed in white robes and a pale blue turban, Colonel Moammar al Khadafy sat cross-legged on the richly carpeted floor of his black Bedouin tent. Three female bodyguards, wearing blue berets and armed with AK-47 Kalishnikov assault rifles, lounged in the far corner. Outside the tent, five members of his real bodyguard, tough, well-trained, East German Security Men, were more alert. A plain green flag, Khadafy's personal banner, the same as that of Mohamed the great Prophet, waved in the strong desert breeze.

The Libyan leader was looking at a cartoon of himself in the Arab newspaper, *Okaz*, published in Jeddah, Saudi Arabia. It showed the Libyan strong man walking on his hands while the rest of the Arab world walked upright. Brother Colonel was not amused.

As was his custom, whenever things were not going well or when the burdens of office became too heavy, Khadafy would retreat back into the solitude of the desert, back to his roots, back to his Bedouin heritage where he could meditate and pray. He loved the desert and he knew the desert loved him. There is an old saying that says, "You can take the Arab out of the desert, but you can't take the desert out of the Arab."

Khadafy was an angry and disappointed man. He was angry at the other Arab nations and disappointed at the turn of events that had put him on the fringes of the Arab world. He had asked the other Arab nations to send an army of 10 divisions and 500 airplanes to fight the Jews. He had even offered himself as the leader of the Pan-Arab force--after all, it was Allah's will! Not one other Arab nation responded. Even Syria pulled back rather than open a second front as he recommended. He told the other Arab leaders regularly that a sixth obligation must be added to Islam: "The Jihad or Holy War."

In August, he had been scheduled to be the Chairman of the Organization of African Unity, but most of the African leaders did not show up at the conference. The humiliation was something he would never forget nor forgive.

He had vowed to build a one million man army, but even with his People's Militia, the Cubans, and the female platoons, he was still 200,000 short. And now, for the first time since taking power, there was a money problem developing. America's economic and political pressure on Europe was beginning to be felt. Oil revenues had dropped 20 percent in the last six months.

The last straw was poor Mustapha's failure, for the second time, to eliminate the American General Stevens. At least Mustapha was man enough to do the honorable thing. Stevens was heading an organization devoted to fighting terrorism and Libya. This made him a dangerous enemy and a threat to Khadafy's plans.

Brother Colonel knew that Allah often worked his will in strange ways. He firmly believed that he had been chosen by Allah to unite the Arab peoples. Had not the other prophets before him--Abraham, Moses, Jesus, and the last, Mohammed--suffered setbacks and tribulations before they achieved victory? "Inshallaha!" (It is God's will.)

His plans were unchanged. He would have his nuclear

bombs, and with them he would destroy Israel. He would have his Jihad. He would march at the head of an Arab Army through the rubble of Jerusalem. The decadent monarchy of Saudi Arabia would be destroyed and replaced by a Revolutionary Islamic Council. There would be a total Arab oil embargo against the United States. He would bring the capitalistic American giant to its knees.

Finally, the Arab people would recognize Moammar Khadafy as a true Prophet--the savior of the Arab world. His destiny to lead the Arabs to greatness was foreordained by Allah. Inshallaha!

RIHADH.

Frank Stevens returned to Riyadh and went to work with a vengence. He tirelessly split himself between his office and the Special Assault Force. He drove his men almost to the point of exhaustion.

He tried to force thoughts of Alana from his mind. He was on a terrorist hit-list whose strings apparently were being pulled by Khadafy himself. He knew that as long as he was working on his current project, neither he nor anyone close to him was safe. His love for Alana was so strong that he couldn't bear to have anything happen to her. The only way to keep her safe was to stay away from her. However, no mater how hard he tried, she was ever on his mind.

His first break in locating Khadafy's nuclear reactor came from an unexpected source. Three weeks after returning from Rome, Stevens received a call from the CIA Station Director at the U.S. Embassy: "Frank, our Embassy in Morocco called, and a woman named Gaby Deveroux walked in off of the street and asked for political asylum. She says that she works for you and must talk to you."

It could be another of her deceptions, thought Stevens; however, she just might have some useful information. "Yes, she's one of my agents," he lied. "Tell your people to keep her in protective custody. I'll send a couple of men to pick her up."

Twenty-four hours later, a very scared Gaby was seated in his office. She waited nervously in her chair, not quite knowing what to expect from this man she had wooed and betrayed. She hoped that she had him figured right. She knew there was no going back to the people she had worked for. Stevens was her only hope for survival. Her voice trembled: "Frank, I'm sorry. I am truly sorry. Please don't hate me!"

He stared at her in silence for ten seconds. "No, Gaby. I couldn't hate you. As a matter of fact, you are very good at your job. You had me fooled!"

"I was the fool, Frank. First, for ever getting involved in this business and then for falling in love with you. That wasn't part of the plan. You see, I've never met anyone like you. Knowing you, and learning to love you, I came to realize that you weren't the enemy. Can you believe that?" Her big eyes widened, and she nervously twisted her handkerchief.

He offered her a cigarette and lighted it for her. He hesitated, trying to find the right words. "Yes, Gaby. I believe you, and as I said, I couldn't hate you."

"I received your telegram," she stammered. "Thanks for giving me a chance to save my life. I don't know why you did it, but I am grateful."

He grinned. "I just didn't want to see you get your pretty head chopped off." His voice turned serious: "Now, what's this business of claiming that you work for me?"

"You were the only person I could think of to turn to. When I decided to leave the Party, there was no turning back. They are after me now." She hesitated, obviously terrified. "I couldn't work for them anymore. I realize, now, how wrong--how misinformed I was!"

He interrupted her. "Gaby, who are 'they'? Who were you working for?"

"Colonel Mustapha Amak, the Chief of Libyan Intelligence, was my direct superior."

233

"Gaby! How on earth did you ever get mixed up with Khadafy's crowd?"

She put out her cigarette and reached for another. Stevens lighted it, and she inhaled deeply. "My family raised me to hate Jews. When I was going to the University of Paris, I joined the Anti-Zionist League. It was through the League that I met Mustapha." She paused, trying to find the right words.

Reluctantly, and haltingly, she continued: "I-- Well, I became his mistress. He told me about all of the wonderful things that he was going to do to destroy Israel, once and for all. After graduation, I went to Libya for training, but I just wasn't cut out to be a soldier. I don't thing I ever could kill anyone. So, Mustapha brought me in to work as a translator. Then, last year, he sent me to Riyadh."

"When I arrived, you were assigned to report on me?" he asked evenly.

"Yes, but I was just supposed to watch you and get information on your work. I didn't want to endanger you!" There were tears in her eyes now. "When you left for Athens, I almost didn't tell Mustapha, but I guess that I was hurt, knowing that you were there with Alana. After I sent the message, I wanted to kill myself. I knew that you didn't love me, but I felt that you cared for me a lot." She was crying, and her shoulders shook.

She was silent for a while. Finally she sniffed and dried her eyes with her handkerchief. "When I returned to Tripoli, everything was changed. Mustapha got drunk and started bragging about the atomic bombs. I was horrified! I couldn't believe what I was hearing! Then he killed himself!"

Stevens' pulse began to pound. He tried to control his excitement. He leaned forward in his chair: "Gaby, what's this about atomic bombs?"

"They plan to use them on Israel. They want to start a Holy War. Mustapha said that Khadafy soon would be the leader of the whole Arab world. He--"

234

Stevens broke in impatiently: "Did he say how soon this would happen?"

"Not exactly," she answered quickly, "but just as soon as the bombs are ready."

Stevens paused, almost afraid to ask the next question--afraid of what the answer might be. "Gaby. This is important. Did he say where they were making these bombs?"

"Yes. In Chad. He said that northeast of Hadra, there was an old cement factory where the bombs were being assembled."

CHAD! So that's where the reactor is located, he thought, barely able to conceal his excitement. His immediate urge was to grab this young girl who had betrayed him and cover her with kisses.

Gaby interrupted his exuberant thoughts: "Frank. What's to become of me?"

"Gaby, let me ask you: do you want political asylum? And are you willing to give us more information?"

"Frank, the answer to both questions is yes. I've grown up a lot in the last few months, thanks to you. I see things differently than I did before. I'll help you in any way I can."

"O.K. Good! Officially then, we'll tell everyone in my government that you have been working for me all along. Now I want you to talk to Mr. Devlin, our Intelligence Director. Don't worry. He won't hurt you, but he'll be able to ask you the right questions. Just give him the most complete answers that you can. Then we will fly you to the United States, change your identify, give you money and a new life."

"But what will I do in America?" she asked.

"You can do whatever you want to do. If you still want to teach French, the government will set you up at a University. If you want to stay in the intelligence business, I'm sure that can be arranged. It will be entirely up to you. You will get a large financial reward--I'll see to that. It will be enough so that you'll never have to worry about money again."

"Why are you doing this for me, Frank, after everything

I have done to you?"

"Gaby, the information you have given me will save thousands of lives and maybe even avert a major war. The least I can do for you is to try to assure your security and your future."

"What about us, Frank? Will I see you again?"

"No Gaby. For your own safety, you must never contact me again. I won't know who you become nor where you will go. It's for your own good. I want you to be safe."

With tears in her eyes, she kissed him goodby. Stevens called for Devlin, who escorted Gaby from his office.

"Treat her well, Dev," ordered Stevens. "She's one of us now."

★ ★ ★ ★ ★

Within two hours spy satellites that can take photos up to a one-eighth inch resolution, that can pick up an ant on the ground, were sending them photographs of the cement factory in Chad. The pictures showed a complex of large concrete buildings on a strip of barren desert, screened by security fences and a contingent of security forces.

Gaby's other information was almost as valuable as the location of the nuclear reactor. She identified the traitorous Egyptian general working with Khadafy and gave them names of Libyan agents in Saudi Arabia and Iraq. She furnished locations of contacts in Germany and Italy.

Stevens dwelled on the irony of it all. Gaby had betrayed him, and yet, because of a feeling for her he had warned her and given her a chance to escape. His unintentional gamble had paid off with high odds. Now, thanks to her, he had a chance to stop the Libyan strong man. Stevens was just a little more than grateful for the fact that he could keep a stiff prick longer than the average man.

As the photos of the nuclear reactor site rolled in, a large mosiac was being prepared. Photo copies were dispatched to Washington, and three hours after the first photo was taken, the Director of the Central Intelligence Agency was showing pictures of Khadafy's reactor to the President of the United States. Two hours later, the President was meeting with the Joint Chiefs of Staff and the National Security Council.

Stevens and his staff went into a marathon planning session. Contingency plans were checked and double-checked. New plans were prepared and updated. Finally, after 48 hours, Stevens accepted a final plan for conducting an assault on Khadafy's reactor site. Teletypes were singing back and forth between Stevens' office and Washington. Then the machine clicked out:

B.G. STEVENS, FRANK, 508-34-3544, IS ORDERED TO ACTIVE DUTY EFFECTIVE UPON RECEIPT OF THIS MSG. GEN STEVENS IS DIRECTED TO PROCEED BY FASTEST MEANS POSSIBLE TO WASH D.C. AND REPORT TO DIR CIA.

> BY ORDER OF THE PRESIDENT
> OF THE UNITED STATES

237

23

WASHINGTON, D.C.

Stevens was the lone passenger aboard the Air Force DC-9 from Riyadh to Andrews Air Force Base. There he was met by Samuel Bates, Deputy Director of the CIA, and they boarded a Marine helicopter for the short hop to Langley.

The global headquarters of the U.S. Central Intelligence Agency is located in a pleasant, relatively serene, wooded suburb of Washington, D.C. From here, the vast tentacles of the world's largest and most sophisticated intelligence network reaches out to all corners of the globe. An agent in the jungles of Angola or the mountains of Peru can bounce messages from a satellite miles above the earth, and these messages can be received and decoded within nine seconds at Langley. Five minutes later, the information can be in the Director's hands. The Director is always within reach of a phone direct to the President. Ten minutes after sending a message, an agent can receive instructions that could change the fate of nations.

Most of the actual brain work--the planning, scheming, conceiving, and deciding--is not done by the cloak and dagger troops in the field. Instead, it is accomplished in the gray stone layrinth that is the CIA Headquarters. Here one finds a plethora of certified geniuses, PhD's, sophisticated computer equipment, and intricate communications systems. One also can find an equal number of ulcers, nervous breakdowns, and heart attacks. The drive and stress are greater than that found in Wall Street, General Motors, and Chrysler Corporation combined.

There are two categories of CIA personnel: the "blacks" and the "whites." The blacks are those engaged in covert operations--the cloak and dagger types. The white are the overt, or open, employees, most of whom work at Langley. Altogether, the CIA has about 200,000 people on their payroll overseas and some 20,000 in the United States. The annual budget of this mega-intelligence organization is in excess of two billion dollars.

Stevens was not a newcomer to the ways of the Agency. He had worked for the CIA before, in Vietnam and in Chile. Before he took command of Fort Irwin, he had spent the previous two years on special duty, working for Jim Moore, when the General was Deputy Director of Covert Operations.

Bates ushered Stevens through the intricate security system and into the main conference room. In a meeting that lasted six hours, Stevens briefed the Director and his staff on his plan to destroy Khadafy's atomic bomb factory.

The next morning at 0900 hours, Stevens and the CIA Director walked into the oval office at the White House. The President was dressed casually in a light blue, Western-style shirt and Wrangler jeans.

Even after six years in the awesome position of responsibility, the President looked 40 rather than his 70+ years. He rose from behind his desk and met Stevens in the center of the room with a firm handshake. "General Stevens, I'm glad, finally, to meet you."

Stevens remained at attention and said stiffly: "Mr. President, it is an honor to meet you, Sir."

The President placed his arm around the soldier's shoulder and guided him over to a wall covered with personal photographs and memorabilia. "Come here. I want to show you something." He pointed to a grouping of five pictures in a large frame. There was Sergeant Alvin York, America's most decorated soldier in World War I; General Chesty Puller, the famous Marine hero of Nicaragua, World War II and Korea; General George S. Patton, old "Blood and Guts" himself; Audie Murphy, America's most decorated soldier during World War II; and finally, to complete the ensemble, in the lower right-hand corner was a photograph of Frank Stevens when he was a Lt. Colonel. "See, this is my own personal gallery of America's greatest heroes. I've been a fan of yours for years, General," said the President, proudly.

Stevens felt insignificant beside these other great heroes. He really never considered himself in the same class.

"I'm deeply honored, Mr. President," he stammered, beginning to feel a little embarrassed.

The President took the frame from the wall and removed the photograph of Stevens. "Would you do me the honor of signing it for me?"

How could one refuse the President? "Yes, Sir. It would be my pleasure!"

At that moment, somewhat overwhelmed by the President's friendliness and obvious sincerity, he couldn't think of anything earth-shaking to write! He simply wrote: "With best wishes and deepest respect. Frank Stevens."

"Thank you, General," said the President, replacing the photograph in the frame. "That now makes my personal gallery of heroes complete with signatures." He placed it back on the wall hanger and stepped back to see if it was straight. After a minor adjustment, he walked over and sat behind his desk. "Please, sit down." He motioned to the two chairs in front of his desk.

A white-coated orderly entered the office and served them coffee. He departed immediately.

"Now, General, tell me about your plan to destroy

Khadafy's nuclear reactor." The President sat down his coffee cup and leaned back in his chair.

Stevens took the satellite photos and maps from his briefcase and spread them out on the President's desk: "Mr. President, I have a force of 50 men, trained and ready. The majority of them are Americans, but there are a few Brits."

The President interrupted: "Using British forces may be a bit of a problem, but I don't think so. When Mrs. Thatcher is informed of the specifics, I am sure she will go along."

Stevens continued. "My force has an average age of 39 years, but they are combat experienced, and they are trained to a fine edge. They are the best anyone could find anywhere. They understand the mission and are dedicated to success."

The President interrupted him again. "The age factor doesn't bother me at all. I would opt for experience every time. Some people may feel that I'm too old for my job, but I feel 20 years younger than I am, with 20 years more experience."

"You look 20 years younger, Mr. President," Stevens said honestly, causing the President to beam.

"Sir, I would like to beef-up my force with a 50-man section of the Delta Force from Fort Bragg, and I would like to have a company from the Air Force Air Commando Group at Eglin to provide helicopter support." Stevens paused, waiting for a reaction from the President.

The Delta Force at Bragg is America's highly trained counter-terrorist unit. They are all volunteers, and must be Airborne, Ranger, and Special Forces qualified--no easy accomplishment. The Air Commando Group from Eglin is trained as experts in deep helicopter penetration activities such as the raid conducted on Sontay Prison Camp in North Vietnam. This group of skilled pilots fly the new Blackhawk helicopter troop carrier and an enhanced version of the Cobra gunship which provides fire support.

The Chief Executive remained silent for several minutes,

then he nodded his head for the General to continue.

Stevens explained: "The night before the attack, a small team will infiltrate by parachute into the area and reconnoiter the objective. I will be with this team. We will be carrying a new computer device called the PPLD, or Parachute Precision Landing Device. This little gadget will control the parachute assault phase of the attack. It can put 50 men, jumping from 25,000 feet, into an area the size of a ballpark.

"The helicopter force of 50 will infiltrate Chad from Egypt. Using Nap of the Earth Flying, to avoid radar detection, they will arrive at the target at the same time the paratroopers land. The helicopters will land here, on this roading leading into the complex." He pointed to the road in the photograph. "Most of the jumpers will land in this soccer field, behind the reactor." Again he pointed to the blown-up photograph. "Other teams will land at other preselected sites within the compound."

"Going in, several of the helicopters will be carrying fuel pads. They will stop about here--" He pointed to a spot on the map about halfway to the objective, "and drop off the fuel pads and a small security force. We will refuel here, on our way back. These empty choppers will be used to evacuate the paratroopers after the mission." He paused to see if the President had any questions.

The President nodded his head for Stevens to continue.

"The Pathfinder Team will set up the PPLD for the jumpers and mark the landing zone for the helicopters. We hope to be able to secure these two gates and guardposts just prior to the arrival of the attacking force. If not, we will have to go in with hot gunships and assault the gates. If we have to do this, our casualties may be higher. The keys for success of this operation are simplicity and surprise.

"Sir, we also will need four nuclear experts to go in with us. They will be essential to identify the nuclear components and to ensure that demolitions are correctly planned."

The President listened intently as Stevens discussed other

aspects of the operations. Stevens had his undivided attention. Occasionally the President would stop him and ask a question.

When he had finished, the Nation's Chief Executive stood up and walked slowly around his office in silence. Then, in a calm, determined voice he said: "If Khadafy is successful in making a nuclear bomb, and fool enough to use it, the very least that could happen would be the death of thousands of innocent people. It could start World War III. There is no choice, General. He must be stopped.

"For some time, Kahdafy has been trying to be the first Arab leader to possess nuclear weapons. He tried, unsuccessfully, in 1969 to buy atomic bombs from Red China. He tried to get the French to build them a nuclear reactor under the guise of constructing a desalinization plant. He even tried to buy a reactor from an American firm.

"When first I learned that the reactor might be in Chad, my first impulse was to turn the information over to Israel. We know what the Jews would do. They might even use their own nuclear weapons. If Israel moved against Libya, particularly now, after the Lebanon crisis, it would set fire to the entire Middle East. Therefore, we eliminated that alternative.

"The National Security Council and the Joint Chiefs of Staff studied several other alternatives. A bombing raid was eliminated because it could not be 100 percent certain of destroying all of the nuclear components at the site. Infiltrating agents to sabotage the project is too risky. Too many things could go wrong.

"We considered sending the 'Blue Light Force,' but since the Iranian fiasco, there are still some questions as to results.

"We came to a unanimous conclusion that our best course of action was to listen to your plan. First of all, you are our most successful commander in this type of operation. Secondly, you have a force that is already trained and one that has been battle tested in recent months. Finally, and most important as far as I am concerned, you are a proven winner! You either possess uncanny ability or exceptional luck--or maybe both. I'm inclined to go with a winner."

The President walked over, placed his right hand on Stevens' shoulder: "Frank," he said quietly, "can you do it?"

Stevens felt no qualm. His voice was firm. "Yes, Sir. We can do it!"

"O.K. The job is yours," the President said emphatically. "Your official position will be 'Special Assistant to the President,' with the rank of Major General. This operation will be officially sanctioned. Once you have destroyed the nuclear reactor, I will announced to the world that you were acting on behalf of the United States and its President."

He turned to the CIA Director. "General Stevens is to have your complete cooperation. This mission is top priority! Frank, I'll notify the Joint Chiefs that you are to have a free hand, but I would like for you to brief them this afternoon."

Stevens was impressed with the decisiveness of the President. He remained silent, digesting the President's orders. He was back on active duty--a Major General! He was in charge of the entire operation. If the mission were successfully completed, the President would announce it to the world. A realization of the awesome responsibility was forming in his mind.

The President then said: "How about some lunch?"

Stevens looked at his watch. He had been with the President for over three hours. However, a "how about" from the Commander in Chief is the same as an order.

An orderly brought salads and small finger sandwiches. "We'll eat right here," said the President, reaching for a tuna and rye. "It's more private."

The CIA Director rose and said: "Mr. President, General, if you will excuse me, I have pressing matters." Stevens rose and shook his hand. "General, good luck! Anything you need, we're ready." He left, and Stevens sat down.

The President took a sip of white wine: "My favorite.

Durney Johannasberg Reisling from California," he explained.

Stevens smiled and nodded. He was a devotee of Bill Durney's wines also, but he made no comment.

"Say, has Bill Emerson ever told you that I used to date his wife before they were married?" asked the President, munching on his sandwich.

Stevens looked surprised. "No, Sir."

"Yes, I had quite a crush on her. Beautiful woman. Alana reminds me of her. We were just getting serious when Bill came on the scene and charmed her away from me. I turned out to be an usher at their wedding! Bill and I have been close friends since a long time back. Now I hear that you and Alana have been seeing a lot of each other. I can understand that, for she is a beautiful girl, just like her mother."

The President then asked about Alana's rescue from the terrorists, and Stevens briefly told him the story.

When they finished eating, the President sat back and looked evenly at Stevens. "General, are you a Republican or a Democrat?"

"I'm registered as a Republican," Stevens answered respectfully, "but I don't vote a straight ticket. I vote for the person.

"Um! Well, I can't fault you for that," said the President with a wry smile. "I've known a couple of good Democrats in my time."

The President reached for the jar of jellybeans on his desk. "Dessert?" he said, pouring several into Stevens cupped hands. "Have you ever considered going into politics, General?"

"No, Mr. President. I've always thought that soldiers were not suited for politics."

"Well, I disagree with you there, General. Who else has earned the right to speak out more than a man who has fought for his country?"

They discussed general topics for a while longer. The

President asked him his views on the Middle East, Saudi Arabia, Lebanon, and world politics in general. At one point, he asked Stevens what he thought of Menachem Begin, the former Israeli leader.

"In my opinion he is a terrorist, Mr. President," answered Stevens frankly, "and I don't trust him. He's always been a terrorist, so he thinks like one. It's not within him to change."

The President raised his eyebrows. There was a slight smile on his face, but he didn't agree nor disagree with Stevens.

Then they both stood, and the President escorted him to the door. He grasped Stevens' hand. "Frank, already you have served your country faithfully and well. You have undergone mental and physical suffering. If there were any other way, I would not ask you to lead this attack."

Stevens interrupted the President. "Sir, I wouldn't have it any other way. This is something that I can do, and that I must do."

"Well, then--go get 'em General, and God be with you."

Stevens stepped back and saluted his Commander in Chief. After Stevens departed, the President walked back to his desk and picked up Red Phone #3, calling his CIA Director: "Fred, what's the casualty estimate on the Chad operation?"

"Between 60 and 80 percent, Mr. President."

"I think this is the best way to go, don't you?"

"Mr. President. This is the only way."

★ ★ ★ ★ ★

Later, at Andrews AFB, as Stevens started to board the special jet that was to take him back to Riyadh, a black limousine drew up and stopped. An overcoated young man came running over and handed Stevens a small bag. "From the President, Sir. For the road," he smiled.

Stevens looked at the small plastic bag with the initials

"RR" on the outside. He smiled and reached inside for a jellybean as he walked up the steps and into the waiting plane.

247

24

Stevens tried to sleep on the flight back, but it was impossible. The most important assignment of his life lay ahead of him. The consequences of failure were overwhelming: possible loss of lives; embarrassment to the United States; a loss of American influence in the world, and especially in the Middle East; and the terrible spectre of nuclear warfare possibly becoming reality with its apocalyptic destruction an ever-present danger with someone like Khadafy having his finger on the button.

Before leaving Washington, he had made arrangements for the Delta Force and Air Commando Squadron to join him in Saudi Arabia. The rotor blades on the helicopters would be removed, and they would be transported by giant C-5A Galaxys.

When his force was assembled in Arabia, they would move *en toto* to the Empty Quarter where they could train away from the prying eyes of the rest of the world. This was the cool season in the barren desert, so the climate would very nearly match that of Northeastern Chad.

His thoughts turned to the woman he loved. Until he met Alana, the lonely satisfaction of being a soldier had suited him, but that was no longer true. He loved her, he wanted her, and he needed her. He realized now that love between a man and a woman was the one thing that made this barbaric world tolerable.

RIYADH.

"Alana, if I were you, I'd just pack my suitcase and move in with him, lock, stock and barrel!" Mary Moore said, with an enigmatic grin.

"Mary! I'm not even sure he wants me. He hasn't called for a month,' Alana replied in exasperation.

"Now, you know better than that," said Mary, "And you know why he's evading you. He's afraid of putting you in danger--again. Honey, you must remember he blames Nuyen's death on himself, and now you have faced death, twice, because of him. Don't you realize what it would do to him if something happened to you?"

"But Mary, why doesn't he understand I would rather be in danger with him than safe without him?" said Alana, impatiently. "I'm almost a prisoner now. There are always at least two guards with me everywhere I go. I can hardly take a shower alone without making them feel they are shirking their duty."

Mary grinned. "Honey, please be patient. Frank's been through some terribly tough times. Also, do not forget that he has some vitally important things on his mind right now. As I said, if you can't be patient, then just move in with him. I'll bet he wouldn't throw you out!"

The advice and sage words didn't placate Alana; her pride was hurt. Frank's seeming indifference hurt her deeply. She needed him; she believed he needed her. She just couldn't understand his logic. Maybe, she thought, he loved his violent world and macho way of life more than he loved her.

An entourage consisting of General Moore, Bill Emerson, Tom Purdy, Percy Winters, and Dave Braxton met Stevens at the airport. They drove to Emerson's office where Stevens briefed them on his trip to Washington. When they were finished, Emerson insisted on driving Frank to his quarters.

As they started driving, both men were quiet, but Stevens sensed there was something on the contractor's mind. Finally Emerson broke the silence: "Frank, I don't like to interfere in other people's lives, but I can't stand by and see the two people I care for the most be so damn unhappy. Alana is miserable without you, and I feel certain that you love her. I can understand your wanting to protect her, but she's a full-grown woman now; and she wants to be with you regardless of the danger. For what it's worth, I think you are making a mistake trying to protect her in this way."

Stevens answered with some difficulty: "Bill, you know I love her, and I'm miserable without her. But, she is alive, and she's better off away from me until this operation is over. Then I hope to quit," he said, surprising even himself. "Then I'll get on my hands and knees and beg her to marry me!"

"Frank, why don't you see her and explain that to her? I think if you would just make some kind of commitment, it would help her. Right now her pride is suffering, and she doubts her own judgment--which causes anger and frustration."

Stevens looked at Emerson. The older man saw something in Frank's eyes that he had never seen before--fear!"

"Sir," Stevens began, speaking hesitantly. "This operation we're undertaking is extremely risky, but of world-wide importance. We must face up to a possible 80 percent casualty result. Now honestly--just what do you think my chances are of coming out of it alive? I don't want her to know the risks of the mission, and I don't want to promise her anything that I can't guarantee. But after this, if I come back, --"

Emerson interrupted him. "Frank, don't be either stupid or melodramatic. You have the skill and the reason of right

250

behind you, and you are the best qualified soldier in the world to complete this operation successfully. You'll be back!"

Once in his quarters, Stevens rethought his conversation with Emerson. He had an overwhelming desire to see Alana before he left Riyadh again. He went to bed, but he couldn't sleep. Her picture on his bedside table smiled at him and beckoned him. He got out of bed and dressed.

Alana met him at the door in her robe and slippers. Her eyes were blinking awake. She glanced at her watch and said cooly: "Isn't it a little late? Or early?"

"Yes, Alana. You're right, of course; but I've missed you, and I couldn't sleep, and I wanted to talk to you. I know I should have called first."

"You haven't called in a month, and now in the middle of the night you decide you want to walk to me?" Her eyes were angry.

"Yes. May I come in?"

She opened the door and preceded him into the living room. "Care for a drink?" she asked.

"Yes, please," he answered quietly.

She mixed a bourbon and water, then joined him on the couch. "Now," she said casually. "Why did you suddenly decide you wanted to see me?"

Alana wanted to hurt him, almost as much as she wanted to hold him. As far as she was concerned, there was no excuse for his avoiding her.

"Alana," he said quietly, "I just wanted to talk to you."

"Well," she said angrily, "why have you waited so long?" There was pain in her brown eyes, and her lips were trembling. "Why didn't you come when I needed you? Rome was a pretty traumatic experience for me, even Paul's death. I needed you then, Frank, but you never bothered!"

He looked at her in amazement, surprised at her outburst. "Alana! You were almost killed because of me. I didn't want to put you in any more danger!"

251

"That's what I keep hearing," she blurted out, "from Dad, from Mary and Jim, from everyone. 'He's just thinking of you,' they say. Well, I just can't believe it! I think you are more in love with your adventurous life than you are with me."

"Alana, you should know better than that. I love you more than anything, or anyone!"

"O.K. Prove it," she shot back. "Quit your job--now!" she said biting her lower lip. Tears streamed down her cheeks.

Stevens was stunned; maybe he had made a mistake-- in fact, several of them. He had misjudged this woman. Her will and pride were as strong as his. Right now she wanted to hurt him, but it was mostly his own fault. He reached out to her: "I do love you!"

"Don't touch me," she said shrilly, her voice trembling with hurt and anger. "Don't come near me. Go back to your violent world--go on and get yourself killed!"

Stevens stood up and looked down at her. She saw the hurt in his eyes. Without another word, he turned and walked out of the door.

His abrupt departure surprised her. She hadn't expected that. In his eyes there was more than hurt, there was fear. What have I done, she thought? She jumped up and ran to the door, calling after him, but he was gone. She buried her face in her hands and sobbed.

The following afternoon, Bill Emerson returned from his office to find a visibly distraught daughter sitting alone at the kitchen table. He joined her. "I had a talk with Frank last night, honey."

Alana looked up. Her father could tell that she had been crying. "So did I, Dad, and I'm afraid I blew it!"

"Why?" he asked. "What happened?"

"Frank came by about 2 a.m., and I said some really nasty things that I didn't mean. I wasn't nice to him," said Alana sadly.

"Dammit," swore her father. "I don't know what I can do with the two of you. You're both a couple of stubborn idiots. What did Frank want to talk to you about?"

"Well, I guess I really didn't give him a chance to say," she admitted. "Oh, Dad! I don't want to lose him, and I don't know what to do. I love him so much!"

"--and he loves you, too, honey."

"Well! He has a helluva way of showing it," she said.

"Alana. You know damn well he has only been thinking of your safety and that you have been acting like a spoiled child!"

Alana digested his criticism and felt chastised. "Yes, Dad. You are right. Last night I hurt him deeply--I could tell by his eyes. Now, he might never give me a second chance!"

"He'll be back," her father said positively.

"Well--. He'd better," she said softly, "or his child will be born a bastard!"

Alana's confession hung leadenly in the air. Emerson finally looked up, questioningly: "You--. Are you pregnant?"

Alana nodded. "Yes, Dad. After all of these years, you could become a grandfather."

"So that's why you've been so damn difficult to live with lately," he said. A wide smile began to spread over his face. He reached across the table and grasped her hand. "Pregnant? Pregnant! That is absolutely wonderful!"

Alana felt so relieved, and for the first time, she could feel elated. She had been bursting to tell someone, but she really didn't know what her father would think. "Dad? You aren't ashamed, or disappointed in me? You aren't mad?"

He squeezed her hand tenderly: "Hell, no, honey! I am overjoyed. Mother and I always planned on a grandchild, but that was up to you. Your baby could not have a finer father--but have you told Frank?"

"No. I can't tell him until I feel certain that he wants me," she said stubbornly.

"Why you ignorant child! We should go tell him, this very

253

minute!"

"Why? Why?" Then she read the answer in his face. "Dad, he's leaving soon, isn't he?"

He nodded. "Let's hurry."

She leaped up and ran up the stairs, her mind made up and filled with exaltation. She skipped back with a small suitcase and said: "Dad, please understand? I want to stay with him now, and forever. The rest of my things don't matter for the moment. I think you know.

Fifteen minutes later, when they arrived at Stevens' quarters, they found the door locked. Alana pulled her key from her purse and unlocked the door. The rooms were empty! In the bedroom, her photograph was missing from the nightstand. In its place was an empty plastic bag with the initials "RR." Alana recognized its significance. She had received several such bags of jellybeans in the past.

She opened the drawer of the bedside table. Her silk scarf was missing. She remembered the night she had given it to him. After having made love, she reached for her scarf lying nearby. She had pressed it in his hand. "Oh, Frank! This may be fantasy and a sort of fairy tale, but I remember reading that a maiden should offer her banner to her warrior as he goes into battle."

He had pressed it to his lips, pulled open the drawer, and placed it tenderly inside. "If ever I go off to battle, I shall take your token. Please be here, waiting for me, when I return." The scarf was gone.

The only thing in the drawer was a blue felt box. Alana opened it. Inside was a bronze five-pointed star, surrounded by a laurel wreath in green enamel, suspended from a bronze bar bearing the inscription "Valor," and surmounted by an eagle. In the center of the star was the head of Minerva, encircled by the inscription "U.S.A." A light blue ribbon woven with 13 white stars held the Medal of Honor, to be worn in suspension around the neck. Alana reclosed the box, softly, and reflectively.

She returned to her father. "Frank has located the nuclear reactor, and he has gone to destroy it?"

Emerson held his daughter close to his breast. "Yes, honey."

Alana released him and sunk to the couch. "Dad, I'll wait for him here."

★ ★ ★ ★ ★

THE EMPTY QUARTER

Wearing camouflaged fatigues and the two stars of a Major General, Frank Stevens explained the forthcoming operation to his assembled forces. As he had been authorized to do, he then swore the American contingent into the U.S. Army. Next, Percy Winters, bearing the Queen's Commission, did the same for the British participants. Until the end of the mission, they all would be active duty members of their respective armies. The British Prime Minister had entered the venture as a full partner after having been apprised of all of the facts.

For the next three weeks, the American-British Strike Force rehearsed as a team. Stevens honed them to a razor's edge sharpness until he was confident that they were as ready as they ever would be. Air Force C-5A Galaxys flew in the 12 Blackhawk helicopters, the six Cobra Gunships and their crews, to an abandoned World War II airstrip in Western Egypt.

Via C-130 Hercules, Stevens flew to Egypt with the paratroopers.

D-DAY MINUS ONE SOMEWHERE IN EGYPT.

The Hercules sat on the empty runway. The maintenance crew was making last minute checks in preparation for the flight.

General Moore sat watching Stevens pack. He was wearing

255

desert camouflage fatigues. His Randall fighting knife and his old homemade survival kit were taped to one strap of his Ranger harness. Stevens' H and K automatic was in a shoulder holster under his left arm. Taped to his leg, just above his left boot, was a .25 caliber Berreta automatic. In his right boot was a razor-sharp throwing knife. A piano-wire garrote was coiled around his left wrist. His basic weapon, a new Scorpion submachine gun, was fitted with a noise suppressor. The modern-day gladiator applied black camouflage to his face.

Stevens then sat down at the table and looked across at his friend and mentor. He spoke in a calm, determined voice. "Jim, in all of the battles I've entered, this is the first time that I've felt that I might not come back. If anything happens to me, give this to Alana." He handed Moore an envelope.

Moore took it, silently, and placed it in his briefcase. He knew only too well the danger that lay ahead for the young General. He had never heard Frank speak this way. He was aware that when a man had a premonition of his own death, too often it turned out that some special sense had issued the warning. He walked with Stevens to the waiting aircraft, and at the steps he grasped his hand. Moore looked seriously at his protege: "Frank, don't cut corners. Some people think you can catch bullets in your teeth, but you and I know better. Be careful!"

Stevens put his hand on Moore's shoulder and nodded. Then he turned and disappeared into the black belly of the airplane.

Three minutes later, there was only a distant hum in the dark sky. Operation Desert Strike had begun!

25

The airplane flew on a regular commercial route from Cairo to Luanda, Angola, at an altitude of 26,000 feet. At 2340 hours, it deviated a mere three degrees to the south in order to drop its human cargo on the Landing Zone, a dry lake bed five miles east of Khadafy's nuclear complex.

After takeoff, the men put black nylon jumpsuits on over their uniforms, over which they strapped parachute harnesses. Each man was wearing a special helmet with a visor and oxygen mask. In full gear, they looked like celestial argonauts.

A crew member walked over, held up his hand, and shouted: "Five minutes, General!" Then he too put on an oxygen mask.

The back end of the Hercules slowly began to yawn open. The jumpers shuffled awkwardly to the rear of the ramp and waited. The red light turned green, and they walked off into the dark void and began their fall to earth, four minutes away.

Stevens stretched his arms and legs out wide and arched his back to stabilize his free fall. Below, the scrubby desert wasteland looked like a giant black carpet stretching to the stars. Wind whistled through his helmet sounding like a wailing Nebraska blizzard.

The parachute opened automatically, with a pop, at 500 feet. The canopy leaped out of the backpack and filled with air, bringing the General to what seemed like an abrupt stop.

He routinely looked up and checked his canopy. He reached high on his risers and bent his knees slightly, preparing for impact. His feet touched the ground lightly, and he made a perfect standing landing.

He climbed out of his harness and peeled off his jumpsuit. He switched on his sending device and sat down to wait until his team homed in on him. Thirty minutes later, they had buried their parachutes and jump gear and were headed toward the cement factory--hoping they had been dropped on target.

Satellites had been sending them continuous photos for over a month. By studying them, they were able to tell what time the factory workers got up, where they slept, and where the security force was billeted. Vitally important to Stevens' plan was the habit of the motorized patrol. When leaving the compound, they made a wide circle on a dirt road about 2,000 meters out and returned in one hour. They remained there for 30 minutes before repeating the sweep. The routine of this patrol was to be their primary ticket of admission into the factory complex.

The compound was surrounded by a 12-foot, heavy-gauge, wire mesh fence which formed the inner perimeter. Another hundred meters out, there was a second fence--this one electrified. A single dirt road entered the complex from the east and passed through two gates, each one guarded by a cement blockhouse with two or three guards. With the exception of the high fences and blockhouses, the complex appeared to be what it was supposed to be--a cement factory. According to the photos, no one wore military uniforms. Everyone dressed in the robe and ghutra of the desert Bedouin. However, once the KH-11 satellites zeroed in on the complex, with cameras that could photograph a tennis ball rolling across the ground's surface, it didn't take an expert to see that there was more going on there than the mere making of cement. After studying the thousands of time-phased photos, the experts concluded that the security force totalled around 100 men.

From a position near the outer road circling the complex, Stevens' team lay and watched several sweeps of the motorized patrols. They wanted to make sure that their pattern had not changed. Finally, as the gray light of dawn filled the sky, Stevens was satisfied that they could go in as planned. He moved the team back to a hidden lager position where they burrowed deep into a brushy thicket to wait for daylight. Stevens tried to get some sleep, but he was too keyed-up. He removed Alana's scarf from his tunic. It still carried her scent. When this is over, he thought, and if I survive, I'm going to take her to Lockwood Valley and stay for a long, long time. No more battles, no more killing. He was ready to holster his guns.

A gnawing apprehension enveloped him--that old feeling that he would not survive this venture. In the past, before a battle he always had been single-minded, thinking only of the job at hand. This time it was different! He was day-dreaming of Alana and experiencing cold fear for the first time.

The day passed silently for his team. Braxton sat near him, also unable to sleep. He moved closer to his commander. It was obvious to Stevens that his Top Sergeant wanted to talk. He looked over at Braxton and spoke quietly. "Yeah, Dave. What's up?"

Braxton leaned closer, speaking low so the others could not hear. "General, what would you think if I told you I was in love with a white woman?"

Stevens thought for a moment. "Well, Dave. What would you think if I was stuck on a black woman?"

I would think it was none of my business," answered Braxton quickly.

259

"That's how I feel about you, Dave. My only concern is whether or not she makes you happy."

"She does, Sir. Maxine's quite a woman."

"Then I get to meet her when we get back--right?"

"Yes, Sir. I want you to meet her." Braxton leaned back and shut his eyes, relieved to get that off his mind.

Percy Winters, his empty sleeve pinned to his side, chain-smoked and nibbled on candy bars to relieve the tension. Stevens had had second thoughts about bringing Winters along as the ground control officer. A one-armed man had a decided disadvantage in a firefight. But, Winters was persistent. He probably was the only one-armed man in the world that had mastered the free-fall parachute jump. He and one other raider would remain in the thicket at the edge of the clearing and would set up the PPLD for the airborne force and use radio and strobe lights to guide in the helicopters to land on the dirt road leading to the compound. Probably the cleared space on each side of the dirt road was heavily mined, so the choppers would have to land on the road itself.

Stevens carried a small GE transmitter and receiver for communications with Percy. He wore an attached earplug so Winters could keep him informed about the progress of the assault elements.

Just after dark, they moved over to the dirt road circling the factory complex, and again waited. The motorized patrols remained on schedule. One passed their location at 2015 hours. Stevens glanced at his watch. The helicopter assault force should be in the air and heading toward the Chad border. Another patrol passed by them at 2145 hours. The C-130 Hercules with its 50 raiders should be taking off from the Cairo airport. At 2315 hours, another motorized patrol passed. The next one should arrive at 0045 hours.

Their first task was to capture these two gun jeeps without alerting the main garrison. By now the heli-borne force should have made their one stop, dropping off heavy rubber pads filled with fuel and a small security force. On the way back, the helicopters would have to stop and refuel to reach friendly territory.

Dressed in robes and ghutra, Dave Braxton lay face down in the middle of the dirt road. At 0045 hours the two jeeps approached right on schedule. The lead jeep stopped about 20 meters from Braxton, and one guard started to dismount. The quiet of the night was suddenly broken by the muffled coughing of silenced weapons as Stevens' team gunned down the six guards. The battle was fixed! There would be no stopping now.

They stripped the guards and put on their robes and headdresses, then dragged the bodies back into the brush. It was 0100 hours. The attack force would arrive in one hour. Had they been unsuccessful in commandeering the jeeps, the alternate plan was to have the gunships attack with suppressing fire as the helicopters landed.

They headed toward the target. At the edge of the clearing, Percy Winters and his assistant climbed out of the jeep. He gave Stevens a thumbs-up, then set about getting the PPLD and radio working.

As they approached the first gate, Stevens looked at his watch: 0145. They were cutting it pretty thin. Percy should have broken radio silence by now. His earphone came to life with Percy's unmistakable Cockney accent: "I've made contact with both elements. We are on schedule!"

WASHINGTON, D.C.
NATIONAL COMMAND CENTER.

The President, the Director of the CIA, and the Joint Chiefs of Staff sat in a semicircle, watching the young radio operator as he poised to receive the first news from the AWACS aircraft (Airborne Warning and Control System). The AWACS in Egypt flew parallel to the Libyan border to perform several functions: they were the radio link between Stevens' force, the U.S. Sixth Fleet, and the National Command Center; they also could warn the assault force of approaching Libyan aircraft; and they could monitor most of Libya's radio frequencies and jam them if necessary.

In the Mediterranean, the U.S. Sixth Fleet was steaming toward Libya. The British Aircraft Carrier HMS HERMES and her fleet of destroyers had sailed earlier from Gibraltar and were on the way to join the U.S. Fleet. Aboard the baby-flattop, OKINAWA, a Marine Battalion Landing Team stood by their helicopters, ready to go to the assistance of Stevens' force, if necessary.

In the morning, Khadafy would wake up with the U.S. Sixth Fleet and a British Task Force in the Gulf of Sidra. If he decided to come out and play, the Admiral of the U.S. Fleet had his orders.

The President nervously tapped the tabletop with his fingertips. He could have had instant communications with Stevens and his attacking force via AWACS and satellite but had decided against it. The Iranian fiasco had been caused partially by too much interference from high levels. The President absent-mindedly popped a jellybean into his mouth and looked at the bank of clocks on the wall showing the time in various parts of the world. His eyes settled on the new addition labeled CHAD. They should have heard something by now, he thought, worriedly.

Just then the radio operator bent over his pad and began writing. The young man was so skilled he could decode almost as fast as the transmission came in. He put down his pencil and turned to face the awesome assemblage of rank and power: "Sir, Desert Strike (Stevens' call sign) has broken radio silence and made contact with the two assault forces. The operation is a GO!"

There was a stirring in the room. They all knew that for better or for worse, the die had been cast. There was no turning back. The President's heart skipped a beat. Still no one in the room had spoken except the radio operator. The President turned and faced the group: "Gentlemen, all we can do now is pray, and that is exactly what I'm going to do." He bowed his head.

26

Braxton drove the commandeered jeep, while Stevens rode beside him. An ex-Green Beret Sergeant by the name of Haverson manned the jeep's machine gun. The second jeep-load of raiders followed in a cloud of dust. As they approached the first gate, a guard stepped out and swung it open. Covering his face with his ghutra, Stevens waved as they passed through. Braxton tramped down on the gas pedal, and they sped toward the inner gate, leaving behind a cloud of friendly dust. The second jeep rolled to a stop in the swirling haze, and the raiders piled out to deal with the guards.

The lead jeep was nearing the second gate when they first heard the sound of approaching helicopters. Stevens glanced over his shoulder. Amid the dust, he could see his men fighting hand-to-hand with the guards. Ahead, a suspicious guard hurriedly tried to close the gate. Stevens raised his Scorpion and pressed the trigger, spitting 9mm death! As the silenced bullets tore into his chest, the guard uttered a death-scream and flew backward into the dirt.

As Braxton maueuvered the jeep through the gate, a burst of automatic fire splattered against the engine cover. The jeep swerved left, and smashed against a cement blockhouse, throwing Stevens out into the dirt. His weapon flew out of his hands. As he started to get up, a figure leaped at him from the right. Stevens instinctively knocked the man's AK-47 aside with his left hand, and in a single motion, he drew his Randall knife and plunged the blade upward, stabbing his assailant just beneath the rib-cage. He tore the knife out as the guard stumbled backward. The warm, sticky blood spurted out over his arm. The smell of blood and feces stung his nostrils.

Lights were going on throughout the complex. Sirens began a shrill wail. Looking across the compound, Stevens could see paratroopers landing in the soccer-field near the reactor building. They looked like a flock of ducks settling upon a farm pond. Stevens thought it just a bit ironic that the young men of Delta Force flew to battle in choppers, while "old men--the mercenaries--jumped from a plane flying at 25,000 feet.

Fifty meters to their front, the door of the barracks suddenly opened, and armed men began pouring out. Stevens and Braxton stood side-by-side in a combat crouch, firing short, even bursts, while Haverson opened up from the jeep. In the dust in front of the barracks, their combined firepower piled up bodies in a mound. Yet, for some unknown reason the Libyans kept coming out of the door, directly into the hail of lead. By the time the building was emptied, the pile of bodies was several-men deep. Blood was absorbed quickly in the thick dust.

The lead helicopter touched down near the outer gate. The rest landed in-trail, behind it, on the road. The Delta Force dismounted quickly and rushed up the road toward Stevens' location. Heavy automatic fire from a building to their left forced Stevens and his squad to the ground. Tongues of flame reached for them; bullets ricochetted and whined over their heads. Haverson was stitched acoss his chest and flung backward from the jeep. His legs twitched for some seconds, blood gushed from his mouth, and then he was still.

Stevens snatched his radio from his pocket and called the helicopter gunship commander: "Cobra Leader, this is Desert Strike. Over."

"Desert Strike, this is Cobra Lead. I hear you loud and clear. Over."

"Desert Strike Six. Am located by the jeep at inner gate. Do you have my location? Over."

"Roger, Six. I have you in sight. Over."

"This is Strike Six. Building 100 meters, 200 degrees from my location. Take it out. Over."

"Wilco, Strike Six. I'm rolling in hot. Keep your head down."

The Cobra swooped in low over their position and fired a salvo of rockets. The wooden building disintegrated in a blast of smoke and flame.

As the Delta Force came up to his position, Stevens stood up and turned to meet them. Braxton's voice was loud with warning: "Behind you, General!"

Stevens spun and fired from the hip at a shadowy figure rushing toward him. The top of the man's head exploded in a cloud of bone and matter, and his torso continued on past the General and crumpled against the jeep. Lying in the dust, his feet continued the running motion, then he kicked himself still. One of the young Delta Force troopers stopped to look at the dead Libyan. It was probably the first man he had ever seen killed in combat. He froze and looked as if he were going to vomit. Stevens grabbed him firmly by the shoulders and pushed him to the right.

"Keep moving, trooper. You have a job to do."

The soldier moved off toward his comrades.

The Delta Force split into two sections: one going left, the other right, and they began their sweep. The noise of battle reverberated in his ears as Stevens leaned back against the jeep. Automatic fire built up into a maddening clatter, interrupted by grenade explosions, as his two forces worked toward each other. Stevens' radio crackled.

"Desert Strike, this is Angel Six. Over." It was the commander of his airborne force.

"This is Strike Six. Go ahead."

"The reactor and generator power plant are secured. Over."

"This is Strike Six. Good work. Consolidate your position. Be on lookout for Delta Force sweeping toward your position. Over."

"Roger that. Just informed we got the radio station, too. Believe they got a message off. Over."

The heavy din of firing was beginning to subside as his men began mopping up. The factory workers had no stomach for a fight, and they surrendered in droves. A few pockets of soldiers still hung on, desperately.

Finally the firing stopped. The smell of fear, gun powder, and battle hung heavily in the air. Near the outer gate, the Delta Force doctor was cutting, sewing, compressing, and bandaging wounded raiders who either walked in or were carried to the makeshift aid station.

The team of nuclear scientists inspected the reactor, taking pictures and instructing demolition squads where and how to place explosives. Prisoners were herded together in the soccer field, where Devlin located six Europeans among them, disguised as laborers. No doubt they were either scientists or technicians employed by the Libyans. They would be taken along when the raiding force pulled out.

Winters waited for Stevens at the outer gate. "General, we have ten men KIA, and 17 wounded."

Stevens felt a lump in his throat. Victory was always costly. "How about Haverson?" he asked.

"Dead, Sir. He took it in the chest."

Phillip Haverson had been a good soldier: Twenty years in the United States Army, three tours in Vietnam, retired as a Master Sergeant. However, when he retired, he found that decent jobs were unavailable, so he returned to what he knew best--soldiering. Tonight he had become America's first soldier to die in a ground battle since the Vietnam War--a dubious distinction and one that the old soldier would have gladly finessed. However, he had volunteered for this mission, and he had known about the risks of his profession.

Finally the complex was rigged for demolition. "O.K., Percy," relayed Stevens. "Let's load up and get the hell out of here."

The prisoners were moved beyond the second perimeter fence, and the raiders began loading in the helicopters. Winters came running back to Stevens' location: "Sir," he yelled, "Cobra Lead has spotted armored vehicles coming from the north."

"Shit!" cursed Stevens. He thought for a second, then made a difficult decision, one which was fiendish but one that might save the lives of his men. "Percy," he asked, "how many prisoners are out there?"

"About 150, Sir."

"O.K. Turn them loose and drive them north," he ordered. "Hurry them along, even if you have to shoot behind them."

Winters understood. He flipped a salute and began shouting orders. The prisoners began to move, apprehensively at first. When they realized they were being freed, they began running north, unaware of the approaching armor force. A few shots in the dirt behind them hurried them along.

As the last raiders withdrew through the gate, Stevens nodded to Braxton. The Sergeant Major twisted the crank on the hand-powered generator. The resulting chain of explosions shook the ground like an earthquake and turned the night into a fiery inferno. Brother Colonel's dreams of becoming a world nuclear power went up in smoke and fire.

Stevens pulled out his GE and spoke into the mouthpiece: "O.K., Percy, Send 'Home Run'!"

In the lead helicopter, Winters already was lifting off. He rogered Stevens' order, then picked up the radio on the AWACS frequency: "Fire Fox, this is Desert Strike. We have a Home Run. Over."

"Desert Strike, this is Fire Fox. Roger. Understand Home Run. Over."

"Fire Fox, this is Desert Strike. That is correct. Going on listening silence now. Out." Home Run was the code word for mission completed!

Now there was firing in the north as the approaching enemy began to fire at the freed prisoners. The raiders were loading and taking off as rapidly as possible. Stevens and Braxton walked toward their chopper. The Cobras that had hovered overhead like mother hens went into action and closed on the approaching enemy armor.

WASHINGTON, D.C.

The radio operator listened carefully as the message came in. Unable to conceal his excitement, he spun his chair around: "Mr. President," he announced, "We have a Home Run!"

The President was silent. He bowed his head and said a prayer of thanks. Operation Desert Strike was a success!

CHAD. 0450 HOURS.

Attacking like a swarm of mad hornets, the Cobras began scoring direct hits with their hellfire missiles. New fires lighted up the desert as enemy tanks began brewing-up, one by one. The Libyan soldiers dismounted from their armored personnel carriers, and the Cobra's mini-guns sounded like zippers as thousands of white-hot rounds zipped out, churning the sand red with blood.

A hot fist smashed into Stevens' left leg and slammed him to the ground. He tumbled back to the ground. He reached down and felt his leg. There was a gaping hole in his thigh! His first thought was, "Oh shit! Not the same leg, again!" Thick, sticky blood poured out. Through his mind flashed the truth of his premonition.

Dave Braxton turned and saw his commander struggling. He ran back and picked him up, cradling him in his huge arms as if he were a child. He ran toward the helicopter as bullets kicked up dust around them.

Enemy bullets ripped into Stevens' helicopter. Then the crack of a high velocity tank-shell ripped through the night. The helicopter exploded in a blinding fireball!

27

The sun was just beginning to redden the eastern sky as Jim Moore waited at the abandoned airstrip. The raiders had maintained listening silence since leaving the objective so as not to give away their route to unfriendly radio listening stations. They were to land at this desolate spot, have a meal, and board two C-140's. Then they would fly to Riyadh for transfer to a 747 for a nonstop flight to the States. A medical station was set up near the runway to care for critically wounded. Serious cases would be flown to a U.S. military hospital in Athens.

The helicopters and their crews would fly to Cairo where they would load aboard a C-5A Galaxy and fly directly to their base in Florida.

Moore was carrying an unopened bottle of Jack Daniels. He craned his neck and looked anxiously to the west. Then he heard it! The familiar, unmistakable Whop Whop of rotor blades slapping at the crisp desert air.

Having stretched the limit of their fuel, the helicopters flew straight in and landed. Moore counted the birds. One was missing! Well, that was a lot better than had been predicted, he thought. He looked for Stevens' helicopter, the C&C #429. Then he realized that it was the missing bird.

Oh well, Frank's on another aircraft, he said to himself, but fearing his logic.

Percy Winters stepped out of the lead helicopter and walked swiftly toward Moore. His empty sleeve flapped in the winds caused by the whirling rotor blades. He stopped in front of the gray-haired American and reached for the bottle of Jack Daniels. There was no victory elation in his eyes--only tears. He tipped the bottle to the west and slugged.

Moore's stomach tightened. Fearing the answer, he reluctantly asked, "Where's Frank?"

The British officer looked up, pain contorting his weathered, camouflage-streaked face. "He's still there," he said, pointing to the west. "His helicopter exploded in midair. No chance of survivors!"

General Moore suddenly felt very old, very weary, and very insignificant as the impact of the loss hit him. "There's no doubt? What about Braxton? They were together?"

"Yes. They were together," returned Winters.

Moore shook Winters' hand, turned, and walked away slowly. His shoulders shook with silent sobs.

RIYADH, SAUDI ARABIA. 0600 HOURS.

Alana, her father, and Mary Moore sat in the Emerson library and listened to the shortwave radio. The President of the United States of America was making a special televised broadcast to the world:

A FEW HOURS AGO, A COMBINED FORCE OF AMERICAN AND BRITISH COMMANDOS, LED BY U.S. ARMY MAJOR GENERAL FRANK STEVENS, ATTACKED AND DESTROYED A TERRORIST NUCLEAR REACTOR SITE IN NORTHERN CHAD. FIRST REPORTS INDICATE THE RAID WAS COMPLETELY SUCCESSFUL, AND THE COMMANDOS HAVE RETURNED TO A FRIENDLY NATION. WE HAVE NO FURTHER

INFORMATION, FOR THE STRIKE FORCE IS ON RADIO SILENCE UNTIL THEY ARRIVE AT THEIR ULTIMATE DESTINATION.

Emerson looked at his daughter and smiled. "Well, honey, he did it!"

She looked back at him, tears of joy in her eyes: "Of course, he did it. There was never a doubt."

The broadcast continued. The President explained the circumstances and intelligence that culminated with his decision to authorize the raid. He purposely avoided using Khadafy's name; instead, he placed the blame on international terrorists and called for a unified effort to stop terrorism. Then he elaborated on General Stevens, outlining his career and explaining why the young General was selected to lead the raid. He ended his report by saying: "The entire world can be thankful that in times of extreme crisis, the right man appears at the forefront."

Pride flooded Alana. She felt like laughing and singing. She was deluged with mixed emotions: relief, elation, love. "Oh, Dad! I'm so proud of him," she sobbed.

"Honey, we all are. He is truly a rare man." Then his eyes twinkled. "By the way, I heard a rumor--just a rumor, mind you, that a couple of unscheduled American planes may come into the airport this afternoon. How would you like to be there with me?"

She rushed into his arms and kissed him. "What shall I wear?" she squealed, excitedly.

He looked at her for a few seconds, then his face brightened: "Why don't you wear a maternity dress? That ought to get his attention!"

The world reaction to the raid was more favorable than the President and his advisors had expected. The Western nations were generally full of praise; the Arabs breathed a big sigh of relief and remained silent; the Russians were secretly glad. Publicly, the Russians denounced the raid as an "act of American aggression." Castro was furious! The Ayatollah Khomeini called it an act of war! The government of Chad said they didn't know about any terrorist nuclear plant. Khadafy was strangely silent. His hands had been caught in the cookie jar. The fact that the U.S. Sixth Fleet was standing off his shores was a direct challenge which told him to "put up" or "shut up." He chose to say nothing. "In-ashallah!"

Security was tight at the military airport near Riyadh, but a select few waited for the return of the raiders. A chartered Pan American 747 waited on the loading ramp, ready to fly the Commandos to London, and then on to the United States. Tom Purdy was there with the American and British members of the mercenary squadron which hadn't participated in the raid.

Alana was standing with her father, Purdy, and Mary Moore. As had been agreed, there were no Saudi officials present. At 1700 hours, they heard the distant drone of airplane engines. Minutes later, the two C-130's could be seen approaching from the south. Alana had a lump in her throat, and her heart beat wildly with anticipation. She scarcely could control her emotions.

Instead of landing, the two planes flew low over the field in close-trail. Slowly they wiggled their wings as they passed over. There was a stir among the British mercenaries. One of them said: "It looks like a fly-by." The planes made a wide turn and approached the field, flying evenly at 500 feet.

Tom Purdy spoke, almost to himself, as he realized the significance: "Oh my God! No!" His face turned ashen white.

As the aircraft approached, the British came to attention and saluted. Alana looked anxiously at Purdy. "What is it, Tom? What's going on?" A single, empty parachute came out of the lead aircraft and began to flutter to the ground.

Tears streaked Purdy's face: "God dammit--they got him!"

Emerson grabbed Purdy's arm: "Tom! Tell me! What's happening?"

"Sir, it's a custom," began Purdy, his voice trembling. "In the British SAS, if their commander is killed on a mission, they fly over the airfield and drop an empty parachute--a salute to their fallen leader. It means that Frank is gone; that's what it means!"

As the empty parachue floated to the ground, the two aircraft broke formation and began their landing pattern.

Alana's happy heart turned to ice. She watched with mounting concern and anguish. A terrifying fear gripped her stomach. "No-o!" she screamed. "No! It's not true!" She tried to run toward the empty parachute, but her father's strong arms restrained her. She strained and trembled as the big transports landed, repeating over and over again: "He's alive! I know he's alive!"

The C-130's rolled to a stop, and the large back doors yawned open. As the raiders began to deplane, Alana broke free from her father and ran out to the planes. The raiders were silent as they field by. Alana watched for Frank's face to appear. Bill Emerson caught up to her and put his arms around her shoulders; Stevens had warned him this might happen. Every few seconds, Alana would call out: "Frank?" as if she expected him to answer and appear.

Percy Winters and Jim Moore joined them. The pain of loss was etched on their faces. Moore embraced his sobbing wife, then came over and put his hands on Alana's shoulders. "Alana, it was quick. His helicopter exploded in midair."

"No!" she yelled back. "He's not dead. I know it!"

The unloading was finished. There was nothing more to do but leave. They walked slowly away from the aircraft, passing ten rubber body-bags. Eight were covered with American flags, two with the British Union Jack.

"We interrupt this program to bring you a special message from the President of the United States."

IT IS MY SAD DUTY TO ANNOUNCE THAT THE BRAVE SOLDIER WHO LED THE DARING RAID INTO CHAD HAS BEEN LOST. AS MAJOR GENERAL FRANK STEVENS' HELICOPTER WAS LIFTING OFF AFTER THE VICTORIOUS COMPLETION OF DESTROYING THE NUCLEAR REACTOR IN CHAD, THE AIRCRAFT WAS HIT BY ENEMY FIRE AND WAS DESTROYED. A SEARCH WAS MADE BY SUPPORTING GUNSHIPS, BUT NO SURVIVORS WERE FOUND.

BESIDES GENERAL STEVENS, A TOTAL OF 14 AMERICANS AND TWO BRITISH SOLDIERS LOST THEIR LIVES ON THE OPERATION. WE MOURN THE LOSS OF EACH MAN WHO SO GALLANTLY GAVE HIS LIFE IN THE SERVICE OF HIS COUNTRY.

I HAVE ASKED CONGRESS TO AUTHORIZE THE SECOND AWARD OF THE CONGRESSIONAL MEDAL OF HONOR TO GENERAL STEVENS. HE FOUGHT MANY BATTLES AND WON MANY VICTORIES. THIS LAST VICTORY WAS NOT ONLY FOR OUR COUNTRY BUT FOR ALL MANKIND. AMERICA HAS LOST HER GREATEST SOLDIER: THE WORLD HAS LOST A GREAT MAN: I HAVE LOST A FRIEND. EACH OF US BENEFITED BY HIS EXISTENCE. LET US REMEMBER, FOREVER.

Emerson reached over and switched off the radio. Alana sat quietly, staring at nothing. General Moore pulled out the letter that Stevens had given him and handed it to Alana. "Frank asked me to give you this."

She opened the envelope. In it was a note and the
to his home in Lockwood Valley, made out to her. The n
read: "My Darling, You gave me a lifetime of happines,
Yours Forever, Frank." She carefully replaced the contents
in the envelope, then walked over and placed the papers on
the desk. She covered her face with her hands and murmured
over and over: "But he's not dead. I know he's not dead!"

A few miles away, at King Faisal Hospital, Maxine Davenport had been given a strong sedative. She, too, had lost her
loved one.

28

CHAD.

Alana was correct. General Frank Stevens was still alive, but prospects of his continued survival were not good.

When the command helicopter exploded, Braxton was still 30 yards away, carrying the wounded General. The blast knocked them down, scorching their faces and hands.

When Cobra Lead saw Stevens' helicopter raise up, and then explode, he believed the General was on board. He broke radio silence and notified Percy Winters. The British officer's first impulse was to turn the whole strike force around and go to the aid of his commander. However, after Cobra Lead convinced him that no one could have survived the explosive fireball, he reluctantly continued the withdrawal as Stevens had planned it. Having been halted by the onslaught of the Cobra attack, the Libyans now were moving into the battle area.

Braxton reached down and slung his unconscious commander over his shoulder and headed toward the brush. As he moved, he could feel the General's blood pouring down the front of his fatigue shirt. He had to stop the flow or Stevens would soon bleed to death. Once inside the protection of the brush, he tenderly laid him down and examined the wound. He tore open the wet, trouser leg and placed a field bandage snugly over the wound. Using his scarf, he cinched it tightly above the bandage as a tourniquet. Then he picked up Stevens again and stumbled along eastward.

He moved on past dawn, not stopping until the burning heat of the sun forced him to find shelter in the shade of a tamarack tree. He reexamined Stevens' wound. The compress had stopped the bleeding. That was good! His leg was broken, and muscles had been torn. It was a nasty wound that needed immediate attention. He cleaned it as best he could and sprinkled sulpha powder on it.

Stevens groaned and his eyes fluttered open. "Where are we?" he asked. His lean face was taut with pain.

"General, I'd say, we are about 10 kilometers east of the objective."

"Dave, help me up. Let's see if I can walk."

"Sir, your leg is broken! You can't walk!"

Determined, Stevens grasped Braxton's arm and tried to pull himself up. The pain was too great, and he fell back to the ground, drenched with sweat.

Braxton pulled a morphine syrette from his aid kit and jabbed it into Stevens' thigh, just above the wound.

"Dave, you have to leave me. I want you to leave me here and head east."

"No way, General! You know better than to even suggest that. We'll get out, and we'll get out together. Hell, we did this once before, remember?"

Stevens did remember, and he knew Dave Braxton would never leave him as long as he was alive. He lay back and passed back into the soft cushion of black unconsciousness.

Braxton took stock of their situation. They had less than a canteen of water and there was no water for 200 miles. He had his M-16 A2 rifle and Stevens' pistol; one first aid kit with a half-packet of sulpha, one morphine syrette, and 12 tetracycline tablets. Also there was Stevens' old survival kit still taped to his shoulder harness. It probably hadn't been opened for 10 years. The General only wore it as a matter of habit. Braxton cut it from the harness and sliced off the tape. Inside was a small signal mirror, fish hooks and line, several vitamin tablets, razor blade, wire to make snares, water purification tablets, and two bouillon cubes. They were good items for the jungle, but not much use in the desert. The plastic Swedish Army compass that the General wore around his neck was another story. They needed that.

He felt Stevens' head. It was hot with fever! Taking a handful of tetracycline tablets, he placed them in Stevens' mouth and forced them down with water. Then he picked him up again and continued moving to the east, making pitifully slow progress. They were fortunate in one respect. This was winter, where the temperature climbed to the 90's during the day and dropped to the 40's at night. If it were summer, they would have been dead in several hours. Braxton tried to pace himself--walk 50 minutes, rest for 10--but by the end of the second day, he was at the end of his physical limit. The hot sun broiled them during the day, and the cold desert froze them at night. Finally the stalwart sergeant could go no further, and they stopped on a sandstone ledge.

Braxton was awakened by a hand on his shoulder. He opened his eyes to find Stevens fully conscious, his eyes clear: "Dave, listen! Do you hear anything?" There was the unmistakable sound of sheep bleating in the distance.

"Yes, Sir!" answered Braxton. "I'll check it out."

He returned an hour later, carrying a goatskin water bag and leading a burro. Hanging from the wooden saddle was a dead sheep. He handed the water bag to the General, who gulped thirstily. "I met a shepherd and borrowed a few things."

"Did you kill him?" Stevens asked, looking up.

"No, Sir! I probably should have, but what's the use. Who's he going to tell out here?"

Stevens looked up at his comrade: "I'm glad, Dave. We have killed enough for one lifetime."

The Sergeant found enough scrub wood to build a fire, and they feasted on mutton. Braxton felt his strength returning. He loaded Stevens aboard the burro and they headed eastward, trying to put as much distance between them and the shepherd as possible.

They travelled all that night and the next day. By evening they were again without water. Braxton had been giving a portion of his share to Stevens. The pace was beginning to tell on the black giant. He no longer removed his boots when they stopped, for he knew his feet were so swollen he would never get them back on. Blood seeped through their torn canvas tops. His body was covered with cuts and scratches. These abrasions were festering, and tell-tale red streaks indicating infection radiated from several of them. Still he plodded on, leading the burro and its human burden toward the east. They had no way of knowing how far they had travelled. They did know that without water it would just be a matter of time before they dehydrated, and then it would be finished.

Braxton began to feel dizzy as dehydration and infection battled within his body. They could no longer talk to each other, for their lips had cracked and their tongues had swollen in their parched mouths. Without sulpha and tetracycline, Stevens' infection began to return. His wound oozed a white puss, and the desert flies swarmed around him. He realized that they were both rotting. Finally Braxton sank to the ground and lay still.

Stevens rolled from the burro, landing on his good side. He crawled over to Braxton. The Sergeant had a raging fever, his face was ashen, and his pulse was rapid and erratic. Leaning on his good leg, and somehow finding a hidden reservoir of strength, he dragged, pushed, and lifted the giant Sergeant up onto the patient burro. Stevens couldn't believe the stamina of the little animal. Sadly he realized that before too long he would have to cut the burro's throat to get liquid.

Stevens tied his left hand to the wooden saddle, then using

Braxton's rifle as a cane, he began slowly and painfully to hobble on eastward. Each step was agonizing. The unchanging horizon swam before his eyes. Only the steady clop, clop of the burro's hoofs punctuated the quiet of the empty desert. Day passed to night. Stevens continued his slow, deliberate movement east, his body numbed to the pain. Sometime in the pre-morning light, he passed out. The burro continued on a few steps, dragging the unconscious General, then stopped and stood patiently. As the sun rose, death hovered over them, but it did not descend.

The silence awakened Stevens. He was hanging underneath the burro. In his semiconsciousness, he dreamed he heard voices. He tried to pull himself up, but there was no strength left in him. The thought of voices persisted. He canted his head and listened again, then tried to focus his eyes in the direction of the sound. There, a few yards away, were four fierce-looking horsemen staring down at him. Then he noted the three hash-mark scars on their faces. Beberini! He tried to talk, but his swollen tongue couldn't function. Coarse hands untied him, laid him back on the sand, and he felt the delicious trickle of water entering his parched throat. "Beberini!" he whispered hoarsely. "Colonel Abdullah Sabeh! Colonel Sabeh!" He sank back into the darkness.

★ ★ ★ ★ ★

RIYADH.

William Emerson was worried sick about his daughter. She resolutely refused to consider that Stevens was dead. She moved to his quarters and insisted: "He's alive, and I'm going to wait for him here."

A memorial service for the dead raiders was to be held in Washington, D.C., in four days. The President expected the Emersons to attend. In addition, Alana was scheduled to attend an awards ceremony and accept Frank's second Medal of Honor. The English Prime Minister would be there to present the dead American General her country's highest award, the Victoria Cross.

The news agencies discovered the story of Alana's kidnapping and Stevens' daring rescue. They were making a to-do about the gallant soldier and his beautiful fiancee. Alana steadfastly refused to talk to any reporters.

Emerson tapped the desk with a pencil. Somehow he had to find a way to make Alana face the tragic truth. Suddenly his office door burst open, and there was Jim Moore, his face shining with happiness. "Bill, Frank's alive!"

Emerson jumped up: "Good God! Are you sure?"

"I'm sure. I just got word that he and Braxton both are alive, and in the military hospital in Athens! They walked out; and they there were picked up by friendly tribesmen in Sudan, but they're both in pretty bad shape. I'm flying there immediately, and I want you and Alana to come with me."

Emerson embraced his friend with joy, then slapped him on the back: "Well, hell! Let's go get Alana!"

Alana was sitting quietly at the kitchen table when Moore and her father arrived. Without knocking, her father opened the door and ran to her. He put his hands on her shoulders as she stood up to face him, questioningly.

"You are more steadfast than the rest of us put together," he said. She could tell his news by his eyes. Tears spilled from her eyes.

"I told you," she sobbed happily. "I told you he was alive!"

William Emerson took his daughter in his arms and patted her back like he would a small child. "Yes, Honey. I know you told us all along."

Alana pulled away and looked at General Moore. "What about Dave?" she asked, brushing away the tears.

"Dave Braxton made it, too! They walked out together," answered Moore.

"How is Frank? Tell me, quickly," she begged.

Moore's face became serious. "The main thing, Alana,

is that he is alive, and he has a great chance for a complete recovery. Right now he is in pretty bad shape. He has been shot in the leg, he is suffering from infection, dehydration, malnutrition, and total exhaustion; but he was conscious enough to send you a message. Just three words--'I need you.' "

"Those are the three most important words in the world to me. How soon can I go to him?"

"I'll have a plane ready to leave two hours from now," answered Moore. "Frank asked me to bring one other person, a Maxine Davenport."

Alana looked puzzled. "Who's Maxine Davenport?"

"Apparently she is Dave Braxton's private nurse," smiled Moore.

29

ATHENS, GREECE.

A nurse wheeled Braxton into Stevens' room. His bandaged feet were cushioned on pillows, and in his hands he carefully balanced two tall glasses of good U.S. bourbon. The nurse stationed the wheelchair by the bed, locked the wheels, and departed.

"Well, General, we lucked out again; however, I don't think either of us could win any beauty contests."

Stevens raised his head from the pillow and smiled weakly at his friend. Slowly, and with a great deal of pain, he reached over and accepted the glass Braxton offered. "Inshallah!" he said, swallowing a mouthful. The fiery liquid burned his parched lips and swollen tongue, bringing tears to his eyes. But it was good! "You're right, Dave; we were damned lucky that someone found us. But one of these days, our number is bound to come up. The doctors tell me that both of us will be up and about, good as new, very soon. Thank God we were together. Neither of us would have made it alone!"

There was a rap on the door, and the nurse reentered. "Sergeant, cocktail hour is over. I must take you back to your room. Both of you gentlemen have visitors, and I am sure you will want to pretty-up and have privacy. Chug-a-lug, now."

"Are the visitors female?" asked Stevens.

"Yes, Sir," answered the nurse.

"Dave, it has to be Alana and Maxine," said Stevens. "Give us half an hour, and then I want to meet that girl of yours."

Braxton saluted, with a wide grin, as the nurse wheeled him from the room. Stevens propped himself higher in the bed, brushed his hand over his hair, and watched the door eagerly.

Alana didn't knock; she just rushed in and sped to his bed-side. "Oh Frank! I knew you were alive. I knew you would never leave me, just when we had found each other." She placed her hands tenderly on each side of his face. "My beloved, are you in pain? Thank you for sending me the message. I need you, too, for the rest of my life!" She delicately touched her lips to his.

"Alana, my darling, I didn't think I would make it this time. I didn't dare hope that I would ever see your beautiful face again, or think of a future, or ask you to marry me."

"Of course, the answer is yes, Yes, YES!" She covered Stevens' burned and cracked face with kisses. Her tears of happiness fell onto his bare chest. Finally, she pulled away and looked at him. His haggard appearance, deep-set eyes, and the numerous cuts and bruises spoke for what he had been through. Then she saw his left leg encased in the heavy cast. "Not the same leg, again?" She moaned, shaking her head sadly.

Stevens nodded: "Yup! The same leg; but it is still salvageable--I won't be a cripple." Then he held her at a distance, the sparkle in his eyes turning serious: "Is your father here? I want to do this properly and ask him for his daughter's hand in marriage."

"Of course, beloved. Let me bring him in now," she beamed.

★ ★ ★ ★ ★

WASHINGTON, D.C.

The special dinner hosted by the President of the United States was attended by a host of notables. In the two months since the world had learned of the Chad raid, many lives had changed. General James Moore had stepped down from his job in Riyadh, and now was Vice President of Emerson Corporation, working at the main office in Los Angeles. Percy Winters remained on active duty in the British Army and had been promoted to Brigadier General. For his action in Chad, he had been awarded Britain's highest medal for heroism, the Victoria Cross. His wife was attending the dinner with him. She had informed him on the flight over that she was with child again. Tom Purdy and his wife were there, and he was now Program General Manager of Emerson's Saudi Modernization Program. Jimmy Brolin (Devlin) was present. He now headed an international anti-terrorist intelligence organization with offices in Riyadh and Rome.

Retired Command Sergeant Major David Braxton and his wife Maxine were there. Maxine wasn't yet pregnant, but it wasn't for lack of trying. Braxton still worked for his long-time friend, General Stevens. He, too, had been awarded his Nation's highest award, the Congressional Medal of Honor, for his herosim in Chad.

After dinner, the President rose and walked to the rostrum. The respectful guests stood and applauded. "Ladies and gentlemen, please be seated." He waited until there was silence. "I would like to take this occasion to make a special announcement. Tonight I am pleased to name the next Ambassador to the Kingdom of Saudi Arabia. I would like to introduce him and his lovely wife at this time. He is a man you all know and admire. A man for whom I have great respect and whom I call a trusted friend. He is the most decorated soldier in the history of our Nation. A man who has won two Medals of Honor, and the only American to have been awarded Britain's highest award for heroism. He is a man who recently has won perhaps his most cherished award--the heart of the woman he loves.

"I only plan to loan this great soldier to the State Department, because if the need ever exists, and I pray that it never happens, he would be the man I would want to lead our sons and daughters into combat."

The President paused, glanced down the head table, and nodded: "General and Mrs. Stevens--"

Stevens was wearing the blue dress-mess formal uniform of a Major General. The blue ribbon with white stars, holding the Congressional Medal of Honor, was around his neck. The beautiful black-haired lady who joined him wore a white satin gown that was noticeably snug at the waist. Stevens put his left hand under her chin, tilting her face upward, and kissed her. Her face was brilliant with love, pride and happiness. The General hooked his cane to the back of his chair, and taking his wife's arm to steady himself, he slowly limped to the speaker's platform.